# ANDREW SZEPESSY

Andrew Szepessy was born to Hungarian refugees in Brighton in 1940 and was raised in London. After reading English at Oxford and studying at the Budapest Academy of Drama and Film, he held positions at the BBC and London Film School. Szepessy went on to work as a scriptwriter, director and editor for the Norwegian Film Institute and to establish the Film Studies programme at the University of Bergen. He later settled in Hungary, where he continued to write until his death in 2018.

ANDREW SZEPESSY

# Epitaphs for Underdogs

VINTAGE

Most of the following incidents – in one form or another – took place in the Hungarian People's Republic during the mid 1960s.

The rest – in one form or another – are waiting to happen, or re-occur, somewhere on planet Earth.

# Contents

# PART ONE

# First Sights

# 1

# Slowly, I'll Forget the Colour of Your Silken Hair ...

It was one of those nights of high summer when the air feels like velvet and every shadow blooms. Blackness blossoms into indigo and violet and mauve. And the darkness is as warm and soft as the happiest of childhood memories.

No leaf stirs. Eddies of laughter drift down dreaming avenues. Heady scents – acacia, jasmine, new-mown hay and flowering lime – waft in at every window. Flesh and blood cannot resist such nights and the spirit knows no bounds.

The exquisite temptations of that perfect night were, however, felt most keenly not by some carefree promenader sauntering fancy free but by a random selection of unextraordinary men lodged in a dusty, sun-baked country town somewhere between Budapest and languorous Lake Balaton. The comparison was odious, of course, for the imaginations of these unexceptional men had been liberated by restriction and their memories had been tempered by regret.

Each man was as far from his nearest fellow as stone walls would allow. One hard-boiled, shaven-skulled youngster had even flattened himself like a gecko against the bars of a small window about fifteen feet above the floor. Each man lingered deep in his own thoughts, listening to the night.

Somewhere outside, gusts of merriment sparked in and out of earshot like fireflies flirting in the dark. At any moment, it seemed certain, one voice or another must burst into meaning. But not even the bald gecko ever caught a syllable clearly.

After a while, the laughter died away. Still we listened hard for a long time. Long after it was clear to everyone that the laughter was not coming back.

Silence hung in the soft air, heavy with unspoken thoughts. The faces each of us saw were different, of course, as were the voices we heard in our heads. Different streets ran through our minds – different houses, different hands – totally dissimilar bedroom walls and cups of morning coffee quite unlike each other. The pain in our hearts, though, was much the same for each and every one of us.

Abruptly, our reveries were scattered. An accordion. It was near enough to be loud and clear, but too far away to be inside. It had no idea how many regrets it carried off on the currents of its jolly chords. Since it did not know, it could not care. Nevertheless, it was most welcome. Faces grinned, eyes lit up; even the skinhead gecko on the wall cracked a smile.

From some neighbouring cell, a gruff bellow of delight greeted the invisible accordion-player. Men opened up like flowers. Shoulders eased, brows cleared and everyone strolled about in all directions, as debonair and devil-may-care as if we were going somewhere.

Whatever the time was, it was certainly long past Lights Out. Yet there was still no sign of the duty guard. Not surprisingly, no one missed him. We swapped inconsequential banter with as much casual bonhomie as if we were exchanging evening greetings on some boulevard in Montmartre or Nice. The warm velvet filtering in through the iron bars brought us something irresistibly intoxicating and subversive on its balmy breath.

'Have you heard the one about the Party Secretary from Csepel?' chirped a distinguished head, fashionably grey about the temples.

'The one suing for divorce?' came the pat riposte.

'Oh, you've heard it before, have you?'

'Not more than five hundred times!'

'Ripe for retelling, then!' cried another voice.

'Let's hear it again,' shouted a fourth, 'unless anyone's got anything better to do tonight!'

'"What I demand," announces the Party Secretary, "is that this court grants me a divorce at once!" "On what grounds?" asks the Judge quite politely. "On any grounds she could lay her fat back on!" wails the Secretary. "A-dul-te-ry," notes the Judge. "FLAGRANT adultery!" bellows the important Comrade. "With the same co-respondent?" asks the Judge. "No, no!" shrieks the outraged Official. "At least five different co-respondents!" "One at a time or all at once?" enquires the Judge, keeping a straight face by stickling for detail. "Aaaaargh!" wails the plaintiff. "Ahem," coughs the Judge, doing his best to adopt a diplomatic tone. "I see. Well, when did these, er, co-respondences take place?" "On our summer holiday!" "Oh, yes? Did you go somewhere nice?" "Only Lake Balaton." "LAKE BALATON!" thunders the Judge. 'One more squeak out of you, my ma— uh – Comrade, and I'll have you inside for Contempt of Cour— er – for Abusing the – ah – Property of the – ahem – People! The Law may be an ass, but Lake Balaton is still Lake Balaton! Have you no shame? No pride? No sense of history? Why, Lake Balaton has been the erotic centre of the entire Carpathian region since before the Romans. What goes on there has never constituted grounds for divorce and, as long as there's any sense left in this Cou— er – People's Republic, it never will. Five co-respondents, indeed! A ma— Comrade in your position, ought to be proud his wife has the good of the People so much at heart! Case dismissed!"'

Our voices rose with our spirits until they reached a level that was undeniably contrary to regulations. No one gave a hoot. From where we were sitting, none of us could see what more we had to lose anyway. Meanwhile, our warders carried on being conspicuously absent.

As a rule, they would already have been down on us like a ton of bricks. It was odds-on, then, that the magic of that night had charmed away every member of staff capable of fabricating any sort of excuse at all. There could hardly have been enough dimwits remaining behind to keep routine procedures going, let alone to cope with emergencies.

Whatever the explanation, it was well through many a magnum of vintage summer velvet before a representative of officialdom finally put in an appearance. The sloppy

6

uniform and sour face told us at once exactly how the Comrade Warder felt about being on duty at this moment.

The sight perked us all up no end. Poetic justice in the flesh and with a vengeance! It was as clear as crystal that no one in the entire prison was more unhappy to be here than the skeleton crew of warders sentenced to spend this night of nights upholding Law and Order in the People's Republic – and of those, none could have been less happy than this particular screw.

Our eyes met his. None of us could resist a grin. Authority leaked out of his uniform like air from a harpooned balloon. Shrinking visibly under the warmth of our smiles, he made no comment about the general disorder, ignored the insolence with which everyone omitted to present themselves for inspection and was deaf as a post to the numerous conversations that were not even pausing for breath. Not a word escaped his lips about the absurdly obvious fact that no one was ready for bed, nor – the inescapable presence of our bodies apart – complying with any prison regulation whatsoever.

Perhaps the wonderful air had softened his heart? Or perhaps it hadn't quite softened his brain enough for him to try dragging us all off to solitary confinement without enough manpower on hand to back him up. Anyway, our Sloppy Uniform managed not so much as a single murmur. Instead, he turned and made an awkward gesture out into the corridor beyond our line of sight. At this, a figure stepped suddenly into view. Grabbing its sleeve, our screw bundled the figure into the cell, fumbled off the light and fled.

7

What the official presence of the warder had utterly failed to do, the new man's unexpected arrival achieved instantly. We fell silent to a man. It was not so much the fellow himself. It was the fact of him appearing among us at all. We were all struck by the same thought – if ever there was a night when a man should not have been under arrest, surely this was it!

As far as we were concerned, fair enough! After all, we were all in here already. But this man? Why, just a few brief moments ago this man was surely taking his ease, ambling down some moonlit lane lined with oleanders, filling his nostrils with the heady scent of acacia blossom and listening to the soaring solos of love-struck nightingales supported by massed choirs of courting frogs. On a night such as none of us might live to see again!

He stared calmly back at us without expression. Then, as we were all too astonished to introduce ourselves, he walked over to the far wall, leaned against its harsh brick and retreated into his own thoughts. This brought us to our senses and we all trooped across to greet him.

He was a tall, raw-boned character, deeply tanned, with grizzled hair and some wicked-looking scars. He was getting to look tougher by the minute and I, for one, began to suspect that our sympathy might be misplaced. The spell of the evening soon reasserted itself, however, and we drew him into conversation.

The man's situation was even more poignant than we had imagined. Not only had he been brought in no more than an hour ago, but he'd only been out two weeks. His original sentence had been four years. After three, he'd earned a year's remission for Good Conduct. While trying to catch up with disorganised family matters, he had neglected such administrative niceties as reporting to his local police every day. Added to which, he had not found a job. Ex-Cons – especially those out on remission – were required by law to find employment within eight days of release. Failure to do this, for whatever reason, incurred an automatic conviction on the charge of being a Public Menace, guilty of Deliberately Shirking Employment. This was not a minor offence in the People's Republic.

What with one thing and another, then, our newcomer had just got his year back. We all shook our heads and thought it was a shame. What a pity he hadn't slipped through the net for just one more night! The man sighed and shrugged his shoulders.

'Couldn't even find my wife,' he growled, 'so how can I complain about losing a piddling year?'

We idled over to the middle of the cell and arranged ourselves around the well-worn wooden table on equally well-worn wooden stools. Generations of prison hands had scrubbed both as smooth as bone.

The younger element declined to join us. The bald gecko was still glued to his window on the wall. A shaggy youth whose brother was a detective and a second skinhead lay sprawled on the floor in one corner. Our last teenager was a prematurely wizened little manikin suspected of being a planted Grass. This lad had given up altogether and had hidden himself away under his bunk.

Our high spirits fell by stages into a deep melancholy. The night was still as gentle and as fragrant as before. Only the heady excitement had worn off. We still cared not a fig about warders or regulations and it was still impossible to go to bed. But now we were no longer drunk with expectation. Every breath of that elixir of night racked us with sorrow and regret.

I had never believed it was possible for intangible and subjective emotions to cause such concrete physical pain. But it was so. We ached to find some sort of release while, at the same time, we all knew only too well that the one particular form of release we truly craved was precisely the very one we could not have. It was no good gazing at the purple velvet flowing in through the window. There was no way for our dull flesh to float back out through those iron bars.

We had already paraded all our most comforting proverbs and platitudes and marshalled the last of our most reassuring catchphrases, clichés and circular reasonings. The encouragement we had found in the discomfited screw was exhausted. Nothing remained of the excitement of breaking regulations. The night air was no longer a draught arousing desire, but a drug that would not let us rest. There was nothing left but the silence of despair.

We sat like that for longer than anyone cared to guess, with only occasional echoes from outside for company. Time crushed us harder and harder in its granite fist and each moment inched by more slowly than the last. Our very thoughts stood still.

Suddenly, the night split open. Terrible and lost, like the cry of a seabird, a sound speared up through the soles of my feet and then soared out through the back of my neck, wheeling and turning this way and that with razor-sharp tenderness to settle at last into an ancient melody filled with a deep sadness we all recognised at once.

Hair bristling and palms damp, I raised my eyes from the scrubbed wood of the table and stared round the cell. Utterly unself-conscious, his craggy features soft with emotion, the new man was singing his heart out. We all knew why he sang. It was not for pleasure – neither for his nor for ours. It was because there was too much inside him and it had to get out. There was no other way for him to get through the night.

He was no longer doing time inside stone walls inside a forgotten, backwater township, inside a minor People's Republic, inside the confines of the closed territory of the Soviet Empire in the wrong quarter of planet Earth. He was far away and long ago. And he took us with him.

None of us could take our eyes off him. To us he was Orpheus, King David, Ossian the Bard and Gandalf the Grey all rolled into one. When his last notes died away, there was a long silence. The air seemed fresher and easier to breathe. Then another voice started up from the other end of the table. It was Géza, our gipsy. His face was wet with tears. The song was something dark and intricate. Some long-forgotten memory unearthed by this moment. He had a voice like an old stick and was tone deaf. But now he could no more have sung a bum note than the summer night could have become an Arctic blizzard.

As he finished, we found ourselves looking each other in the face again. Another man took up the load:

*A graveyard is the River Tisza*
*When she blossoms into millions*

11

> *Of butterflies, upon her waters playing –*
> *For not a single pretty flapwing –*
> *Outlives the passing day …*

Then another man:

> *Proud parapets of Kraszna Horka,*
> *Hidden by the veil of night,*
> *Bold Rákoczi's great days of honour*
> *Are gone for ever from our sight …*

And then another:

> *These tiny pearls upon this snow-white page –*
> *How many lies they tell.*
> *But all I ask, my lass –*
> *Is that you write them …*

And yet another:

> *In a green forest,*
> *On the bank of a brook –*
> *There lived once an old gipsy man …*

And another yet:

> *Slowly, I'll forget the colour of your silken hair …*

Better places, better days. Songs made who knows when by men for ever nameless. Words and melodies welling up from countless years of anguish and despair. Fragments of air and memory. Yet what else could help us now?

The mood swelled and grew into an overpowering tide. Nothing could stop us. We hardly heard the screw when he finally came banging on the door. No one noticed when he gave up. None of our youngsters joined in.

This was because they simply didn't know any of these songs. The Communist Regime had classified them as degenerate excrescences of Capitalist Culture and had banned them from all public or private performance or dissemination – largely on the grounds that they kept alive 'irredentist' memories of lost lands and lost relatives and fostered unhealthy and subversive feelings, such as a juvenile longing for some vague, bourgeois concept of Freedom.

Party Anthems and Paeans of Praise to the Fraternal Soviet Union had, however, proved to be inadequate substitutes for the songs that should have been the rightful heritage of a whole generation and the youth of the People's Republic had felt this loss keenly. They were desperate for something to fill the void. Nothing the Party offered did this. Thus was the generation earmarked to carry the red flag of Marxism-Leninism into the rosiest of futures inadvertently turned into diehard fans of decadent, capitalist, Western pop music. It was, perhaps, just a matter of luck that this period should coincide more or less exactly with the rise on the other side of the Iron Curtain of Rock and Roll, Elvis Presley, the Beatles, the Rolling Stones and a veritable plethora of such degenerate excrescences.

Whatever interpretation history will eventually put on all this, on that night of high summer, the People's youth did not sing, but wept uncontrollably in the corner, up at the window and under the bed. Eventually, the detective's brother could stand no more and came pounding on the table, cursing and swearing and begging us to stop. We all knew how he felt, but we could as soon have stopped singing as we could have melted through the walls.

I can't say how long it went on, but by the time we finally fell silent it was well past dawn.

We looked at each other in the morning light, empty and at ease in our skins at last. The detective's brother seemed to have fainted. The bald gecko dropped from the window, buried his head in his arms and burrowed into a corner. There was no sound from under the bed.

Turning his gaze in my direction, the newcomer slapped his thigh and flashed his teeth in a wolfish grin.

'It's just hit me!' he chuckled.

'What?'

'My wife!'

'Your wife?'

'I know where she is!'

'Where?'

'Down at the lake!'

'How can you be so sure?'

'Stands to reason. Where else could she be?'

'Search me.'

'Nowhere else! I'd stake my life on it! Woman's like a wild mare when the fit takes her. Moon-blood flows through that girl's veins. Nights like this don't come back. Old age will pare every man jack of us down to the bone before we get another! My wife's not the woman to waste a night like this, and no one knows that better than me! Tell you what, though, I can't say as I blame her! If I'm being honest, all I can say is this: if I wasn't man enough to find her myself tonight then whatever rutting buck she's riding now should thank his flaming stars for his luck. That lake – a woman like that – a night like this – he should just thank his lucky stars!'

His eyes twinkled and his craggy face was wreathed in a smile of rich good humour unsullied by any hint of malice. He shook his heavy head and chuckled to himself. Then he was off again, deep and low:

> *Slowly – I'll forget –*
> *the colour –*
> *of your silken hair ...*

# 2

# A New Hungarian Stomach

The gipsy in our cell was short and stocky, with friendly eyes and a cheerful grin. On suitable occasions he could also unveil a frown grave enough for a head of state on any coin or a postage stamp. In fact, he was a miner. His hair was neatly trimmed, his moustache decently restrained and his temperament placid. He played no musical instrument and he definitely couldn't sing. All in all, if one overlooked his present company, he could have been considered a credit to official government policy towards ethnic minorities.

This policy could be summed up in one word: 'integration'. Here, the declared aim was the integration of itinerant gipsies into the twentieth century. Less moving from place to place and more moving with the times.

In the eyes of the prevailing authorities, the problem had become big enough to warrant a Ministry of its own. Nothing less would do. Such an organ was, therefore, duly erected. Among the more dazzling propositions flowing from this fountain of light was the idea that, as long as they were wandering, Gipsies were Gipsies. But as soon as any of them showed no further signs of movement, they could be officially declared 'New Hungarians'. To show the way and, at the same time, escape any hint of discrimination, racial or otherwise, the Ministry adopted this title itself.

Géza was a fairly old 'New Hungarian', as he had now stayed put underground for the best part of fourteen years. He seemed to cope with prison conditions tolerably well. Possibly his previous experience of confined conditions, gained as a New Hungarian miner, was now standing him in good stead. Furthermore, he seemed to incur the displeasure of our guards only marginally more often than the rest of us. This, we all thought, was a sure sign of successful integration into the twentieth century.

He was, however, still given at odd moments to intoning outlandish phrases that he seemed to believe were snatches of song. When questioned about this he would answer that if the Beatles could sing, 'Yeah, yeah, yeah' all the time, he could jolly well sing "Szánom, bánom, dínom, dánom' every now and then.

Géza had an abysmal ear for music, which was lucky for him, as it pretty much guaranteed that no one would ever be able to pick any identifiable melody out of the combinations of noises he made. While his performances did not make for easy listening, they certainly saved Géza from falling foul of standing regulations against traditional tunes that might in any way recall the reactionary past.

Officially, the 'Good Old Days' were, of course, still very bad news. Especially, as so much of what was celebrated in song and story had happened in places that were – according to arrangements imposed by the victors of both World Wars and enthusiastically endorsed by all communist regimes including the Hungarian one – no longer Hungary. The trifling details that two out of three 'inland' Hungarians still had relatives in all these places or that these relatives were in every salient respect quite indistinguishable from any other Hungarians bothered the official mind not a jot. By extension from such Party discoveries of 'Non-Persons', such details were 'Non-Facts'. It followed quite naturally, then, that what such mental procrastination might be doing to individual and national psyches was also a 'Non-Question'. Since there was no such thing as 'Old Hungarians', the Ministry of New Hungarians, logically enough, did not concern itself with their 'Non-Problems'.

Géza did not give much thought to what might happen to him after his trial or to how he would cope with his sentence. His adjustment to the twentieth century was not yet complete enough for him to understand that his chances of acquittal were precisely nil. This lack of forethought certainly saved him from the all too modern affliction of worrying oneself silly about things one can do nothing about.

Géza's immunity from anxiety, however, could not be blamed on any lack of imagination on his part. Indeed, he was drawn to the products of imagination like a moth to a flame and was always the most eager of audiences if anyone recited a poem or told a story.

Moreover, the questions he would pose, sometimes weeks after the event, revealed an intellect that, if not exactly swift, was tenacious beyond belief and often disconcertingly direct.

The main purveyor of new poems and the only source of stories, information and gossip about the forbidden West was me. So Géza kept a watchful eye open in my direction. He took to anticipating the conclusion of a new poem even before I was myself aware that the line I was composing was my last. Even now I'm not entirely certain whether the sight of him slinking into the corner of my eye and quietly making himself comfortable on the best available floorboard did not exercise a withering influence on my literary imagination. The fact is, I may well have been finishing poems purely and simply because once I noticed Géza settling down for a good earful, words began to fail me.

Whatever the ins and outs of this, there was no doubt that Géza had an endless appetite for verses and an insatiable curiosity about the other side of the Iron Curtain. He seized every opportunity to pump me about the West and he turned every word I said over and over in his mind. In short, we struck up a sort of friendship. In time, I even came to worry about him.

My misgivings about Géza grew as the time for his trial approached. Not that anyone really knew when their case was coming up, of course. Disturbing a defendant's peace of mind with petty details was obviously considered such bad form that the Authorities were careful not to let slip any clues as to the dates and times of hearings. Géza had, however, been in prison the best part of eighteen months by then and the general opinion was that no matter how much finer the mills of Socialist Law might grind than those of the Capitalist variety, Géza's trial could not be very far away.

I became uneasy about what might happen to him when he left the security of our cell and found himself in sterner surroundings. So I resolved to awaken him as gently as possible to what he might expect from the next years of his life. Since the number of years facing him inside was not going to be negligible, I thought we'd better leave contemplation of their probable total until last. First things first, I concluded. So we started with food.

Géza was a hearty eater and always polished off anything to hand forthwith. Each of us got a daily allowance of something like an eighth of one of the big cartwheels of dark bread common in Hungary at that time. Naturally, these were leftovers from surrounding shops and by the time they got to us their texture tended towards the tooth-defying.

However, they lasted much better than more refined varieties of bread and repaid the tenacious chewer by remaining surprisingly tasty for surprising lengths of time. My jaw muscles got stronger by leaps and bounds, but even so, I could never eat the stuff in the quantities considered normal by my cell-mates. My social conditioning would get the better of my genes and I'd saw my portions into English slices instead of tearing them into Magyar chunks. The net result of this was that, at the end of the day, I always had plenty left over.

In this way, I soon became something of a Bread Baron. Whenever anyone needed extra bread, I generally had some in stock. Needless to say, no one asked for more bread more often than Géza. After a while, he came to take it for granted that his daily allowance should be supplemented by my reserves.

Socialist Law was a new broom sweeping clean. No cobwebs from the Capitalist past including established precedent or hallowed custom were to be tolerated. So sensible limits were set on what any Defence Counsel could do for a client. These limits stopped well short of any such nonsense as defending defendants against anything with which they might be charged. My particular Counsel was a good sort who had previously been a Military Tribunal Judge. After several years of receiving typewritten sentences relating to defendants of whom he had never even heard (many of whom, he discovered at some point, had not even been arrested at the time their sentences arrived on his desk), he had contrived to resign his post without simultaneously resigning his liberty. He achieved this singular feat by performing such a convincing imitation of mental and physical collapse that his malfunctioning was officially classified not as a Criminal Refusal to do his Socialist Duty but simply as an innocent nervous breakdown brought on in no way by Un-Socialist overwork.

Under cover of this diversion, he had arranged his escape to the lowly, but reasonably safe, sanctuary of Defence Counsel. His duties were now purely ornamental and his pay entirely basic. But the wear and tear on his soul was negligible compared with what he had had to stomach every day as a judge. Nevertheless, he still felt guilty about the way things were and had taken to using what little position he had to be of as much practical help as possible. In my case, he forwarded consignments of food, cigarettes and other goodies sent me by various well-wishers.

The rhapsodic convolutions of Magyar history have rendered Hungarians as a whole exceptionally well educated in the needs of those excused from participation in everyday life. My supply system was, therefore, organised with all the ingenuity to be expected from a thorough grounding in pre-war Capitalist Law and over a decade and a half of practising post-war Socialist Law.

A spicy sausage called 'Kolbász' and fine, dry Hungarian winter salami were often included in my deliveries. Both of these were excellent choices, since they combine flavour with nutrition in a compact form that is as convenient for hiding as for eating and lasts indefinitely. Added to which, they proved no less sliceable than bread. My reserve stocks of these commodities soon reached very respectable proportions.

From time to time, we were also issued with a substance known as 'Hitler Salami'. Far from being the overwhelming wurst its title implies, this was a mild and tasteless kind of solid jam. It was supposed to be made from compressed vegetable marrow, dyed appropriate shades of apricot, raspberry or blackcurrant. The colour, I need hardly add, made no discernible difference to the taste. Predictably enough, the advanced technology of Western slicing was as successful with this commodity as with salami and bread.

When my stocks began really piling up, I'd start keeping a finger on the pulse of the cell. As soon as spirits sank below zero on the cheerfulness scale for two days running I'd throw a party. I always made a point of inviting every resident personally. Someone would always look very solemn and doubt whether he could really spare the time but, in the end, everyone always turned up. The idea was to eat everything we had at one sitting.

It always came as a pleasant surprise to see quite how much the general atmosphere improved by the time we polished everything off. Needless to say, no one polished off more, with more gusto, than Géza.

22

It was with all this in mind that one day, when he came to collect his usual supplement, I took him to one side and embarked upon his education by the time-honoured method of Socrates.

'Géza,' I said, 'when they dish out our daily bread, do I get any more than you?'

'What a question!' he answered. 'How could you? You're always last in line.'

So far so good, I thought and pressed on. 'Yet at the end of the day, who has bread left over – you or me?'

'Ah,' Géza shrugged, 'that also is not much of a question. Everyone knows the amount you eat is enough to break any woman's heart. Comes of growing up among foreigners, I suppose.'

'Do I ever ask you for bread?'

'Wouldn't do you much good if you did!' he chuckled.

'Yet when you come and ask me, do I ever turn you down?'

'Never!' he snorted with fierce disdain, as if the mere suggestion was an insult, which he would make it his personal business to avenge.

'So,' I said, confident we were getting somewhere, 'you and I start off each day with more or less the same amount of bread. Yet, without stinting myself, I always have plenty left over. But you are always looking for more to eat. Whenever you come to me for bread, I always have some to give you. Now, tell me, Géza, how can that be?'

Géza frowned his gravest and looked shrewd. He pursed his lips and wrinkled his forehead and started muttering under his breath as if there was a lot more to my question than met the eye. I smiled at him encouragingly. His frown became graver still and he hummed sagely through his nose. I smiled more encouragement. Géza mulled the matter over and then over again. Several times, he seemed on the point of answering, but each time he reeled in his reply for reinspection.

At last, he looked up and said, 'Well, this is the way I see it. You are an educated man. A poet. A traveller. You've seen the world. Your head is full of many things. You always have so much to think about and remember. But me – well, just look at me! All I've seen is the inside of a mineshaft. What can I have inside my head? All I've got is my stomach. What can I do if I don't eat?'

I looked at him for a long moment, trying to imagine what Socrates would have said. Géza beamed at me encouragingly. I mulled as hard as I could, but Socrates ignored me. Géza beamed even more encouragement. Socrates evaporated. Géza twitched his luxuriant eyebrows at me. Obviously, the least he was expecting was illumination, preferably in verse of Homeric grandeur, spiced up with rhymes ingenious and apt enough to have been devised by cunning Odysseus himself.

I handed him his bread and threw in half a Kolbász for good measure. Tomorrow would just have to take care of itself.

# 3

# Inside, Outside, Inside Out

We tramped absent-mindedly round and round and round again. My attention wandered. After a few furlongs, it settled on a gentle old fellow with white hair. Our eyes met. His face lit up in a smile that was little short of seraphic.

It doesn't take a lot of concentration to keep walking round and round in circles. Better still, of all geometric configurations, a circular path is the one that lets more pairs of eyes keep more pairs of eyes in good eye contact more easily and more continuously than any other.

So it was easy enough to keep a close watch on the old man for the rest of morning exercise.

He just couldn't keep a smile off his face. I sniffed news and started working my way up the line as we bunched up to file back inside. He was still twinkling when I slotted in behind him. So I didn't beat about the bush.

'Getting out?'

'That's right.'

'When?'

'Today.'

'Good for you!'

'Thanks.'

'What'd they say?'

'Nothing.'

'Nothing?'

'Just: guilty.'

'Sentence?'

'Just what I've already done.'

'Oh, very neat!'

A hulking screw barked at the man behind me to shut his face.

'What time?'

'After paperwork.'

'Before lunch?'

'Maybe.'

'Witness?'

'No sign.'

'Still?'

'Someone said he's defected.'

'True?'

'Who knows?'

'Hey, you there! Button your lip! What the hell d'you think this is, a bloody holiday camp?'

The warder wasn't really cutting anything short as we'd come to the parting of our ways anyway. The old boy shuffled off down the corridor towards his cell and I came to attention beside the iron door of mine. As soon as it slammed shut behind us, everyone gathered round to hear the news.

The old boy was called Mihály and he had been accused of stealing a coat. According to his charge sheet, the coat was valued at sixty forints. In any currency and even at the artificially inflated rate of exchange officially imposed at that time, sixty Hungarian forints was not very much. There was no suggestion that the coat had belonged to the State. So the alleged crime was just a simple theft that involved neither the Criminal Ingratitude of Abusing the Benefits of the Socialist State nor the even higher treason of Exploitation of the People's Property by a Class Enemy for Personal Gain.

Had either of the latter been the case, then this would have been a much more serious business altogether. Mihály would then have offended not against Private Property but against Political Principle.

As it was, all anyone was talking about, no matter which way you looked at it, was the possible purloining of an item of Private Property – not a concept that carried much weight in the People's Republic. The heart of this matter, then, was a sixty-forint coat.

Despite the draconian shadows – both Hapsburg and Soviet – that still loomed over Hungarian law, this could hardly have been worth six months at most, even if Mihály had been a habitual criminal with a bourgeois background.

According to his charge sheet, this was his first offence. He was over seventy. He had never been anything but a simple labourer and he had already been inside for well over a year.

Part of the problem might well have been that the case was not quite as simple as it seemed. It was not a straight-forward, open-and-shut affair. Mihály had not been caught red-handed. He had not, indeed, been caught at all. He had not even been apprehended by some ever-vigilant officer of the law while attempting to fence, barter, offer as a bribe, sell or otherwise gain personal profit from his purported crime.

By his own account – and the recorded testimony of several people who, apparently, knew him – he had been given the coat on extended loan, as the winter was very cold and he had no coat of his own. The person who had given it to him was a distant relative with whom he was barely acquainted. This acquaintance had told him he was welcome to keep the garment until the weather turned or he managed to get something better. So it came as quite a surprise, Mihály said, to find himself under arrest.

At the police station, it transpired that a complaint had been laid against him. This alleged that he had stolen the coat. Mihály maintained that he had tried to explain matters, but had got no further than saying the garment was in his room before the law had charged off to do its duty. Meanwhile, the old fellow had been deposited behind bars – presumably for safe keeping.

As the day had been an exceptionally mild one, Mihály was not actually wearing the object of his crime at the time of his arrest. When the law returned with the evidence in custody, Mihály identified the coat and attempted once more to offer an explanation. However, it was now decided, naturally enough, that any explanation should be of an official nature and should, therefore, wait until the Official Hearing. In anticipation of this, Mihály was returned to his cell – presumably for safe keeping once more.

This apparently simple theft, then, proceeded to develop various complications.

The complainant, plaintiff or whoever it was who was doing their patriotic duty to Socialist Society by informing on Mihály – that is, the one and only witness for the Prosecution – disappeared and the police proved utterly unable to unearth the slightest clue as to the whereabouts of this personage without whom it would, understandably enough, be very difficult to go to trial.

Furthermore, any testimony that might have been offered by the owner of the stolen property – the relative who had actually lent the coat – was, of course, inadmissible, since under Socialist Law even though the offended item was the property of a person rather than of the People, the Prosecution was nevertheless being brought by the State – and not by an individual. It followed, therefore, that, while the Prosecution – and the Party – had the right to have their say, contributions from private individuals were excluded unless specifically invited by either of the former. Needless to say, such invitations were so infrequent as to be unknown.

So days passed into weeks, weeks became months and still the police appeared to be no nearer to finding the missing link. At the same time and by the same token, Mihály got no nearer to finding his way out of prison.

Incidentally, none of these matters had any connection whatsoever with the fact that, if ever there was a man who was by nature truly innocent, it was Mihály. Indeed, it dawned on even the most guilty of us after a while that whether he really did steal the coat or whether he did not had no real bearing on his innocence. All in all, he was probably the most harmless, genial and unselfish character any of us had ever met.

He was something above medium height, slim, exceedingly well proportioned and in the pink of condition. His complexion was flawlessly clear and of that warm shade of apricot that is most often the result of a lifetime in the open air. He had dancing blue eyes and a magnificent mane of white hair that fitted his beautifully shaped head so well that it always looked becoming, no matter how dirty or dishevelled or badly cut it got. Outside, this must have been a real blow under the belt for many a young buck out to impress a likely lass with his fashionable locks. In here, we all got a kick out of seeing how Mihály's natural mane outmanoeuvred even the most demonic of prison barbers.

No matter how savagely they assaulted his hair, Mihály's head always looked a picture. If, with random brutality, they chopped chunks out here and there, he just ended up as the epitome of avant-garde coiffeur. If they scalped him, he just came out as the model of close-cropped manliness. If they ignored him, he became the acme of bushy bohemian charm. His imperviousness to institutional hair-cutting gave every man jack of us many a good chuckle.

His voice was a musical and astonishingly youthful baritone. Unfortunately, the pleasure of being astonished by it was an infrequent one. For, although Mihály listened much, he spoke very little. His silence, however, was not the wordless despair of some hard man sinking under a heavy sentence. He simply loved listening to other people talk. Indeed, the appreciation that twinkled in his eyes as he listened to something that he considered really interesting or even, simply, well put, was more encouraging than most applause. The truth of the matter was that it just hardly ever occurred to Mihály that he might have anything that was actually worth saying.

He would never ignore a direct question. His inherent good manners were, naturally, far too good for that. But he never began a conversation, never intruded his own opinions and absolutely never volunteered information about himself unasked. He didn't smoke, positively thrived on drinking nothing stronger than bromide-laced water, ate very little, even by the abstemious standards of an unrepentant Western slicer, and seemed quite unbowed by his situation.

Had there been just a jot more justice in the world then than there is now, eligible widows, spinsters and unattached ladies of every hue, humour, shape, size and age might have been queuing up to enjoy the consolation of his company during their sunset years. If prison barbers could not cut down his graciousness, how might he have blossomed under the hand of some appreciative woman? If hostile and repulsive warders did not manage to dim the twinkle in his eye, what warmth might he not have radiated given a little matronly encouragement? And, as Mihály was by nature no more demanding than a budgerigar, all this was potentially available to even the poorest of widows and spinsters.

As usual, however, injustice prevailed, so the unattached ladies of the People's Republic of Hungary had to resign themselves to yet another year of lonely sunsets – with no prospect of remission anywhere in sight.

Meanwhile, as time went by, Mihály became something of a mascot to every man in our prison. Even rogue males with chilling crimes and rock-hard evidence against them cheered up when they saw him. They seemed to feel that if even a lamb like this harmless, old white-hair was in here then all could not be completely lost. It could still, in the end, somehow be that they too might yet retain – or even gain – some shred of innocence.

Although he was not in our cell, we were all keen supporters and followed his case with interest. My news was eagerly seized upon and we turned it this way and that, like hens pecking at a morsel too big to swallow but too tasty to leave. We still hadn't managed to digest it, when the door grated open and I was barked out. My guard parked me beside one of the downstairs offices and disappeared inside.

I had hardly settled down to enjoy the unexpected treat of new surroundings and no supervision, when Mihály got slotted in beside me. His mane nodded its usual greeting but his eyes seemed to lack their usual twinkle.

I studied him closely. The civilian clothes he now wore were so old and shabby that he seemed a threadbare shadow of his former self. There was something here that didn't quite add up. I worried at it for a few moments and then gave up and shelved it in the back of my mind.

'Something wrong?' I whispered. Mihály just shrugged and sighed and looked uncharacteristically morose.

'I know you've lost a year and a good bit for no good reason, but any minute now you'll be free.'

Mihály merely nodded and looked gloomier still.

'Cheer up! There's hardly a man among us wouldn't change places with you today.'

At that, some of the old sparkle came back into his eyes. 'And there's hardly a man among you I wouldn't change places with!'

'Eh! What do you mean by that?'

'Well, when they get out they've still got something. Most of them. But me – I've got nothing. Never married. Oh, there was a lass when I was young. But the new borders split us up. Me on one side. Her on the other. I waited. She waited. I got old. She died. Both waited for nothing. No family left now. Can't hardly remember my village. Best not to even mention hers. Worked outside all my life. Quarry. Not many people, but lots of stone. I used to like stone. Solid. Dependable. Always stayed where you put it. Always there when you came back. No job now. They say I'm too old. No money. Nothing to do. Got a little room in a new block, but if I go out, I don't know anybody any more. If I stay in, all I've got is four walls. Very modern. Very white. Not a mark on them. Each one just like the next. Never know if I'm facing north, south, east or west. But in here, every wall's different. And they're old. Older than me. I like walls older than me. A wall should be older than a man. Stands to reason. A good wall can live for ever. That's nice. Means things can go on and on. And then in here there's people. Lots of people. All sorts. And they all like to talk to each other. Why, you hear something interesting almost every day.'

This was the longest speech I had ever heard him make. I began mulling over whether there might be some special significance to this. Then I suddenly realised what had been bothering me.

'Stripes!' I said. 'You used to wear stripes. But they're only for convicts. You only got convicted yesterday. So how come you were in pyjamas before you were sentenced?'

Mihály turned his gaze from the ground and gave me a shy smile. 'Oh, that,' he murmured. 'Well, as you can see, my clothes are not new and I wasn't sure how long they'd last. So I asked if they could lend me something. Had to give them back now, of course. But it was nice while it lasted. Very decent of them, don't you think?'

I brought the cell up to date. No one could make up their minds as to whether they were glad Mihály was free at last or not. A bit slowly, perhaps, but Justice had certainly been done. Everyone agreed on that. But was it fair? After what they had just heard and, in view of what we all knew of life out there, no one was sure any longer. None of us could decide whether we ought to wish him 'Many Happy Returns' or hope it would all be over soon.

One thing was certain, though. As the days passed, we all missed the old man, with his twinkling silences and his snow-white hair and his apricot complexion. And most of us were pretty sure he missed us. Beyond that, all anyone could say was that if there was any justice anywhere in the Universe, then some comfortable widow, spinster or unattached matron somewhere would surely come across Mihály, at last.

Failing that (and we all knew that justice was not something you could ever count on) then surely the old fellow would find his way back inside again before it got too cold? After all, had not those officially appointed to ensure the welfare of everyone – outside as well as in – already taught him the true value of an old coat?

# 4

# Blue Gipsies

I had always assumed that Gipsies were much like the majority of Hungarians. Then one day the door to our cell flew open and a body fell in. Picking itself up and dusting itself down, the body straightened up and smoothed itself out to form a tall, well-built gipsy of striking appearance.

His hair and eyes were of a startling colour, so dark as to have passed beyond blackness and right through into blue. The most smouldering blue imaginable; so blue, in fact, that they seemed to glow as if they were incandescent. Like the sheen on the head of a mallard drake.

This was nonsense, of course, and I knew it then as well as I know it now. Human beings do not have incandescent eyes or hair or anything else for that matter. Nevertheless, I had many a long day to observe the lad in peace and quiet and, to this very moment, I would not like to swear on oath that neither his hair nor his eyes ever emitted a glow.

His hands were big enough to fascinate women, but delicately formed with long, elastic fingers. Long-limbed and broad-shouldered, his movements were astonishingly light and supple. In the first flush of manhood, he could scarcely have been more than twenty, and his name was Elek.

Our cell had got becalmed. Oceans of monotony stretched endlessly away on all sides. Even after every possible allowance had been made for our position in time, space and the social hierarchy, the dullness was stupendous. Our elders and betters did their best to maintain morale. They sang and joked, told stories and anecdotes, organised mental chess tournaments, discussed the international situation, tried to fathom out the inscrutable West and applied for audiences with the prison pooh-bahs.

More and more frequently, however, they were forced to play their ace: the all but infallible ploy of discussing a man's case with him in unflinching detail and in a light that was, at one and the same time, both irrefutably objective and unfalteringly optimistic. But day followed day, seemingly intent on crushing all our efforts by sheer weight of numbers.

Time generally hung heavy on our hands. But we had always tried to work on the principle that a cheerful cell was, if not exactly a happy cell, at least, a lot less *un*happy than a miserable one. To us a cheerful cell was, also, in some way – no matter how small – a sort of victory in itself. We felt we were still exercising some measure of freedom. We still had a choice: to *be* cheerful or *not* to be cheerful.

If we gave up our option and just let things take their natural course, then not only would we be *more* miserable and have *less* to help us pass the time, but we would also lose our capacity for choosing at all. It would simply cease to exist.

Our choice was, perhaps, pretty limited as choices go. But then very small things will do when there is nothing else. So we kept at it as best we could. Our bonhomie, however, was ringing more and more hollow with each passing day and everyone could clearly see the moment approaching when it would no longer ring at all.

Our main source of concern was Elek. After only a few weeks inside, he was sinking fast. He spent all day gazing listlessly into the air, could never hear a joke through to the punchline and seemed utterly uninterested in his case. None of us could remember ever having seen him smile.

Furthermore, he appeared to have nothing in common with our resident gipsy, Géza. After the first few days, they rarely spoke to each other in their own tongue. Indeed, they hardly spoke to each other at all.

There were several other blue gipsies dispersed in various cells throughout the jail. All of them had come in at about the same time for some offence whose exact nature we had not yet managed to ferret out.

Thinking that he might benefit from contact with a member of his own tribe, we manoeuvred him along the exercise line until he was next to one of his fellows. Nothing happened. It seemed that they had not even noticed each other.

The session came to an end. 'At-ten-SHUN! At – ease, about turn.'

Elek, of course, got the last bit wrong. He lurched left while everybody else turned right. Not a good move for getting on well with the screw on duty. But it did bring the two gipsies face to face. They could not help seeing each other now. They stood staring and then the other one let out a sigh, 'Elek!'

'Csávó!' cried Elek. They were trembling with emotion and their eyes swam with tears. Before we could do anything, the duty screw – a big, burly, bone-crusher – was upon them. He cuffed Elek round to face the right way as if he were correcting an unruly mule and then, just for good measure, fetched the other a solid backhander across the bridge of his nose. A snout shot. Known to work wonders with frisky bullocks. As the blood oozed into the gipsy's mouth, the screw glared at both of them with undisguised contempt. Then they shuffled forward with the rest of the file, their heads hanging even lower than before.

After that, Elek got worse than ever. He hardly ate, rarely moved and never uttered a word. Once, when the spokesman for our cell, a charming swindler in his late forties called Pista, struck up an old, sad song of long ago, Elek turned his face to the wall and stayed like that until Lights Out. He was still in the same position when the sun lit up the cell again.

Another time, one of the screws came in and started raining abuse and curses down on his head. There didn't seem to be any great significance in the act. In all probability, something had simply upset the man and he was just relieving his feelings on the first suitable object that came his way.

For a while, Elek stood there motionless. The tirade cascaded over him.

Then, either stung by some chance phrase or simply because the torrent had become too much for him, Elek straightened up to his full height and raised his fist in the air.

His eyes were blazing and he seemed to fill the room. It was astonishing to see what a big fellow he really was and his incandescent, blue-black eyes and iridescent hair must have looked impressive even to a uniform, because the screw shut up at once.

We all thought the worst was about to happen. Then it did. Only it was even worse. Elek let out a heart-rending groan and brought his fist crashing down upon his forehead. His own forehead. He'd repeated the blow several times before we managed to overpower him and drag him over to his bed.

The screw took advantage of the confusion to sneak out and lock the door.

When we managed to calm Elek down, he looked at us with such defeat and such misery in his eyes that none of us had the nerve to tell him that things weren't as bad as they seemed or that they were bound to get better soon. Shortly afterwards, he was moved out of our cell and some days later we heard that he was dead.

Naturally, I suspected the worst. In those days, life on the other side of the Iron Curtain was cheap. Much cheaper than anyone brought up in the sheltered West could really grasp. The machinery of authority was geared to liquidating even big wheels if they got in the way of top dogs or Moscow. Small cogs didn't rate a second thought. As for any loose screws lying about outside the machinery altogether, why there was nothing to say that such lowly items had ever existed at all.

I was indignant. Not only because of my suspicions, but also because the rest of the cell didn't seem to share them.

Indeed, they seemed to me to be unforgivably unmoved by the whole affair. Before I'd met Elek, it had never occurred to me that hair could be blue. Nor that anyone could actually die of a broken heart. My colleagues, however, had lived all their lives in these parts, so these things came as no surprise to them.

Pista, ever the diplomat, took me to one side a little later and confided that he understood my misgivings only too well and had, indeed, feared the worst himself – almost from the very start.

'But you must try to stop worrying about them,' he continued. 'There's nothing anyone can do to help them. They're defenceless.'

One by one, the others disappeared from morning exercise leaving no more trace than stars at dawn. Eventually, there were no more blue gipsies.

My indignation was still undimmed when we found out what they were in for. Apparently, a young schoolmistress, reportedly in her early twenties, voluptuous and headstrong, had joined them for an open-air barbecue on a fine, mid-summer night. There had been plenty to drink and the young blood in their veins had sung its song. One thing, it was alleged, had led to another until, in the end, no fewer than eleven gipsies were charged with having had carnal knowledge of their educated and attractive guest.

Another four were left out of this charge, but included in the indictment of having roasted her whole on a spit. It was not clear whether she was presumed to have been still alive at the time. Two more were alleged to have been present at the scene of the crime and stood accused of aiding, abetting and participating with the others in eating human flesh. These two had not been included in the charge of murder. Nevertheless, all seventeen had been facing the rope.

I found all this very hard to swallow. To my mind, the whole thing was way beyond the bounds of possibility. However, sources that were usually reliable did report that the remains of the body, which, though not complete, had still been in one piece, had been recovered; that a positive identification had been made by several tried and trusted methods, including checking the body's teeth against dental records, and that semen tests had matched all the accused exactly.

According to the same sources, none of the accused had denied the charges.

Not that any of them had confessed either. Apparently, not a single one of them had uttered a word during the whole process of their arrest and arraignment. This was regarded as corroborating the evidence. I regarded it as corroborating my suspicions.

On the other hand, I had to admit, it did seem an awful lot of trouble for the Authorities to go to just to get rid of a handful of gipsies. All over the Soviet Empire (and in many other places, if truth be told) much bigger business of this kind had always been – and still was – transacted without anyone bothering to erect a façade of legality anything like this intricate or exotic.

My cell-mates took the whole thing as a matter of course. No one had any serious explanation for what had really happened, but nobody suggested that they had done what they had done just because they were hungry or because they were fond of the flavour of female human flesh. On the other hand, no one thought it was remorse that had broken Elek's spirit.

There was one thing, however, about which everyone was quite clear. If the charge was true, then our bonny boys had got off lightly! They had, after all, died of what might be considered more or less natural causes, when even hanging would have been far too good for them!

After they were gone, no one spent much time on their case. Some things, it was unanimously agreed, were impossible to understand and did not bear thinking about. Better to keep your mind on something else. Anything else. Better to just drift with the tide and let the distance between you and the unthinkable just build and build, day by day.

In the circumstances, there wasn't much else we could do anyway. Even I had to see that. So the days slipped by and soon enough nobody even mentioned Elek's name.

Even so, from time to time, at odd moments after Lights Out, above the bunk that used to be his or over by the door, it seemed to me I could see something shimmering in the dark. Something inexplicably incandescent – and impossibly blue.

# 5

# Beyond Any Reasonable Doubt

With all due respect and taking into account all the pressures Imre must have been under, there was not much doubt about his guilt. Imre was a lorry driver and his terms of employment clearly stated that he was responsible for making sure that his vehicle was mechanically sound at all times and punctually serviced at the stipulated intervals.

The lorry was the property of the People and had been entrusted into his personal care. According to the evidence and by his own admission, he had betrayed that trust. It was, therefore, beyond any reasonable doubt that he was guilty as charged of Negligent Misuse of the People's Property.

To a Western ear and in English, the phrase sounds laughable. It was always a clumsy formulation and it is already an archaism well on the way to oblivion. Nevertheless, it doesn't sound quite so comical even today if you translate it into other contexts. A slag heap in Wales, let us say, or a coal mine in the Appalachians. Not to mention an oil rig in the North Sea or a nuclear power plant almost anywhere.

In a small and impoverished country, officially committed to changing the course of History without enough lorries to go round, the idea of looking after what little property the People had was no laughing matter. Not just for saving lorries, mind you, but also for saving people. 'Humanity', one might even say – and not just any old humanity, but humanity according to its noblest and most generous ideals.

The alternative, so ran the theory on top at the time, was to let individuals go on as competing egos eternally preying on each other. A prospect to be avoided at all costs! And there was plenty of heavy hardware around at the time – under the 'Red Army', 'KGB', 'AVH', 'The Party' and other labels – to support the People in their historic avoidance. Even the inscrutable West played its part. Of course, enough time has rolled by since then to prove the theory – or at least the supporting hardware – to have been somewhat hollow.

Even then and even there, however, an individual unit of the 'People', just like an individual consumer or opinion poll sample here and now, could only live one life at a time. His or hers. (Neither the intellectual weight of prevailing theory nor the atomic weight of supporting hardware seems to have any discernible effect on this phenomenon.)

In our Imre's case, there were plenty of contributing factors and unfortunate circumstances that could have been considered mitigating. To start with, it seemed fairly certain that his boss had indeed been keen to squeeze one more load out of the lorry before it went in for a service. Also, there wasn't much doubt that Imre was simply at the bottom of a hierarchy whose sense of responsibility was not as Socialist as it might have been, but whose instinct for self-preservation could hardly have been more Capitalist even on Wall Street. Then again, it certainly did seem a touch unjust that Imre had not been accompanied to jail by any of his superiors.

On the other hand, he himself admitted quite frankly that he *had* gone on one more run instead of going in for a service and that he *had* stopped off to see a girlfriend and that he *had* tried to make up time by exceeding speed limits and that his brakes *had* failed on a bend and that he *had* got stuck halfway over the edge of a deep ditch. By all accounts, he was lucky to have lived to tell the tale.

Imre's negligence had undoubtedly cost far more time, money, work, machinery, energy, spare parts and lost opportunities than if he had put his lorry in for a service as prescribed. The people had also lost the services of an experienced heavy goods vehicle driver and the productive potential of an energetic and likeable young man. For no matter what he had or had not done, and in spite of the present absence of all those accessories by which people measure each other in everyday life, Imre was still, by every yardstick available to us, an adult, male, human being.

With chestnut curls and wide, hazel eyes, he was slim and wiry and his back was as straight as a poker. He had obviously cut a dashing figure careering around the countryside in the People's lorry and must have tickled the fancy of many a lass of the masses.

At present, however, his bearing was far from impressive. He had only just sunk down to our depths and was still feeling the effects of the change in altitude. Not that they ever really wore off, of course. Mind and body simply made as much adjustment as they could without snapping and

45

after that it was up to the individual to hang on as tight and as long as possible. Sometimes, bursting point would be reached. At other times, a man would lose his grip. Ultimately, some degree of deformation was unavoidable.

Imre was having a hard time, but we all knew what he was going through and did what we could to make things easier for him. But so many strings still tied him to the world above us that it wasn't easy for anyone to help him. For example, he still *felt* innocent inside. This kept him clinging to a picture of his boss begging him to deliver just one more load and promising to accept responsibility if anything went wrong. It was impossible, as yet, to make him understand that even if his boss saw this picture at all, he was unlikely to view it as fondly as Imre did.

He also clung to the belief that his excellent work record – only one employer since leaving school! – should stand him in good stead, as well as his widowed mother, two children and distinguished service in the factory water polo team. In short, instead of growing gills and learning to breathe underwater like any sensible person who feels him- or herself going under, he still panicked at the feeling of drowning and clutched at any straw no matter how fragile.

We soldiered on trying to cheer him up, but he steadfastly refused to let go of his cherished illusions. After a while, wiser heads than mine began inclining towards the opinion that we might do better to leave Imre to the tender mercies of the Great Healer, who would, after all, have plenty of opportunity to get more flexibility into his obstinate soul even if Imre made no effort to cooperate, because it would certainly be a tidy while before our man saw dry land again.

All of us in the cell were still awaiting trial. As we were not officially convicts yet, we all wore whatever clothes we'd had on when we arrived. With the passing of time, they became battered and shapeless beyond recognition. Everyone was still, nevertheless, unashamedly grateful for them. Anything familiar and personal was a comfort. The surrender of all intimate articles was not, perhaps, the end of the world. To us, however, it felt like a good first step in that direction. Time was not the only thing that men lost hold of as they were systematically reduced to those lowest denominators of existence whose only saving grace was that they were common to all.

One day, Imre was awarded a visit to the barber. Men more accustomed to the depths at which we lurked prized such breaks in routine as if they were gifts from the gods. Every moment of refreshing change was savoured to the full and every scrap of news was eagerly garnered. When Imre returned, however, his face was ashen, his lips trembled and he could look no one in the face for several days. Gone were the chestnut curls. All that remained was grim regulation stubble and memories of better times.

Imre became thoughtful and silent and gradually began to entertain ambitions a lot less elevated than acquittal. It was a process we had seen before. In an instant of rashness, rage or rotten luck, a man no more insignificant than countless others attracts the attention of that inconceivable immensity, THE LAW. A mighty wing flaps with absent-minded ease, barely flicking him with the furthest tip of its tiniest pinion. In that split second of contact, however, the man experiences a power so awesome that it thrusts aside everything that he has previously known and embeds itself for ever in the innermost recesses of his mind. Hurled headlong through the trapdoor at the bottom of society, he falls further than he had ever dreamed possible. Meanwhile, THE LAW, entirely oblivious of its microscopic victim, continues circling far above the toiling masses of mankind, soundless and invisible – but always up there somewhere. Imre went through all the standard phases of disillusionment and despair until, by the time his trial came round, he was a very quiet fellow indeed. His nerves were gone and he embraced the trial with open arms, eager for any definite decision that might put a stop to an infinity of 'ifs' and 'buts' and 'maybes'.

He came back with three heavy years on his back, but as cheerful as if he'd just got a load off his chest. I had a definite inkling that his peasant origins were going to get the better of his socialist upbringing no matter what, but I felt I couldn't just stand by and watch.

'It seems a bit stiff,' I began. 'You might as well start your appeal now. Before you leave here. You never know where you'll end up.'

He considered the suggestion politely and then shook his head. 'No. Thanks all the same. But I don't think I'll be putting in any appeal.'

I paused to assume the required tone of calm and reasonable disinterest. There is, after all, little point in panicking a person you are trying to help.

'It's standard practice, you know,' I ventured. 'You've got nothing to lose and, at the very least, you'll get a nice break from wherever you find yourself.'

'No, no,' he muttered. 'If I lose, they might give me another year. Or even more. Who knows?'

'Oh, dearie me! We're talking about a trial not a quiz show. You don't get penalty points deducted for guessing wrong. It's your Right. You have a Legal Right to make an appeal.'

But Imre clung to his sentence like a Christian martyr to his cross.

'No, no!' he groaned. 'You don't understand. I know for sure now. I know how long. I know when. I can see it coming nearer day by day. If I lost that, I don't know what I'd do! No, no! I'm not going to appeal! Not me. No fear!'

I could see it was hopeless. But I still called on the rest of the cell for support. 'Look, this is ridiculous. Come on, somebody say something! You all know this is just silly!'

Everyone looked sympathetic. But no one had anything to say. Everyone knew that no matter how ridiculous it was, Imre was now safe. He had passed into the comforting security of that limbo that lies beyond any reasonable doubt.

# 6

# For the Protection of the Public

The gentle hum of conversation and the unhurried thunkety-thunk of a volleyball told me that whoever I could hear outside could not be prison staff. Therefore, I reasoned, we must be very near the exercise yard. That is, if the prison did not contain some other yard that I didn't know of yet. Since men waiting for trial were only allowed half an hour of physical jerks at most and since these jerks had to be over well before noon, it seemed clear to me that whoever was outside must be convicts.

How calm their voices were! Perhaps now that the shock of arrest was over and the turmoil of hope was past, they had settled down to do their time as peacefully as possible. They were off the bottom now and, however slowly, floating upwards. One fine day, they would reach the surface once again.

After some time, it dawned on me that I knew one of the voices. It was Pista. Yes, it was definitely him! How he had tried to look after everyone in our cell. Cracking jokes, singing songs and chattering on and on to keep our spirits up. So, he was here. Well, that was a blessing. He was a local man and this prison was reckoned to be less hard than most. Quiet games of volleyball like this must surely ease the passing of the years.

My warder let out a yawn and looked at his watch. What we were doing in this dark corridor, I had no idea. But I'd been around long enough by now not to let this worry me. As usual, I had been marched off without a word and, as usual, no explanations were offered en route. Like the Will of God, the purposes of the Ministry of the Interior of the People's Republic were a mystery to be revealed only in the fullness of time. Much too late to mean anything to mere mortals like me. So there was clearly no point in worrying about being kept in the dark.

The screw guarding me was a big fellow who bulged out of his uniform and often had trouble keeping a tight rein on his energy. His face was hard, but not brutal. He didn't seem to have any sort of chip on his shoulder and had never shown much of a bent for bullying inmates. From time to time, he even seemed to show a sneaking sympathy for my case. Nevertheless, it never even entered his head that I might like to know what we were doing down here on this quiet afternoon, shifting from one leg to the other and from one daydream to the next.

Apart from a shaft of sunlight falling in through the vertical crack that ran the height of a nearby door that had been left slightly ajar, the passageway was entirely without light. Both ends were lost in darkness. Directly in front of me was a grubby, dusty wall that might once have been white. Only a short section of this, extending no more than a few feet to my right and left, was dimly visible. The rest was shadow, shading into deep shadow, shading into pitch blackness.

After a while, by steadily resisting the temptation to look at the shaft of sunlight, I gradually got my eyes accustomed to the murky darkness and began to get the feeling that the wall behind my back was not quite what it seemed. For a prisoner, the luxury of actually leaning against walls was taboo, of course, so it took me some time to realise that what I was standing so close to was really a row of iron bars.

As far as I could tell, these bars stretched from floor to ceiling and were at least an inch thick. Surely, this can't be for prisoners, I mused. Must be disused dungeons left over from the Hapsburgs or even the Turks.

No sooner had this thought crossed my mind than I heard a shuffling sound from somewhere behind me. A whiff of something fetid and pungent struck my nostrils. Big mammals in cramped cages. The smell triggered some age-old, deeply buried instinct and I stepped a long pace forward and, without asking permission, turned round to face the bars. Behind them a dim but towering outline leaned towards me from the murky depths.

The sunlight from the crack beside the door cleared my right shoulder and fell on the figure before me. A pair of vast hands grasped the bars in front of my nose and, a good metre above them, a face pressed itself into the gap between them. The figure seemed to be dressed in some long, form-less garment like a battered overcoat that reached all the way down to the floor. His hair was long and matted and bushed out around his head for at least a foot in all directions. Scars and pockmarks pitted and scored a broad face fringed by dense tangles of beard. The grime and filth that covered him made me feel pampered by comparison.

Although it was impossible to guess his age, the immense bulk of his frame and hands suggested that he was neither stripling nor pensioner. It also suggested considerable strength. His condition, however, was so low that the whites of his eyes were the dull yellow of old ivory. The stare he fixed me with was as baleful as that of a hungry man-eater. At the same time, there was something uncertain about his gaze – as if he were short-sighted or still half asleep.

'Ah, little csávó,' he wheezed. 'Don't be frightened of an old Rom!'

The voice was a chilling whisper stalking up my spine from dead of night and olden times. Each syllable touched some long-forgotten nerve, starting phantoms from subconscious nests like flocks of frightened birds. Shadows lurking in abandoned graveyards. Abducted infants. A blood-red moon above rituals unimaginably vile. Despite the bars, it took a real effort not to retreat another step or two.

'Come closer, little csávó,' he urged, as silky as a fawning tiger. 'Let me feel that fine jacket of yours! How fine it is! How fine! Never have I seen one like it.'

My jacket was quite threadbare from being worn every day since I'd arrived inside. Indeed, it had never been anything special even when it was new. On the other hand, to an east-of-the-Iron-Curtain eye, the fact that it came from the Free West was blindingly obvious and made it infinitely desirable even if it could only be touched.

'You stay where you are!' growled my guard. I had no intention of doing anything else. Quite suddenly, I found being in custody surprisingly comforting. The gipsy switched his gaze to the screw as if seeing him for the first time.

'Ah no, Honourable Lord, don't say that,' he wheedled. 'Don't deny a poor convict a last little mercy! Don't come between a suffering soul and a comrade in misfortune—'

'Shut your face, you pig,' snarled the screw.

At this, the gipsy went up in flames. He shook the bars like a frenzied gorilla and roared at the top of an immense voice, 'PIG? PIG? WHO CALLS ME PIG? Let him tell me his name so I may carve it on the handle of the knife I cut his liver out with! Let him stand before my face where my arm can reach him and say, PIG! What is this coward? Romanian? Russian? Bulgar? Pole? Ruthene? Magyar? Turk? Whatever scum he is, let him just come *here* and call me PIG! I'll stuff his filthy mouth with his own slimy entrails, piece by shitty piece ...'

Without pausing for even the briefest breath, he raged on and on with ever more graphic descriptions of his vengeance. Then, still ranting, he stopped shaking the bars and started running along them, first to his right and then to his left and then back again and again and again. As if somehow, by some demonic alchemy, this lateral motion might – if only he could build up enough velocity – be converted into forward motion and take him to the object of his hatred. Abruptly, he switched back to shaking the bars, but with redoubled fury now. Massive though they were, moreover, they seemed to me to be rattling in their sockets.

'Come here, Schmasser!' he bellowed in a voice even more deafening than before. 'Let me wring that fat neck of yours like a Sunday chicken ...'

Another torrent poured out of him. I couldn't help marvelling at the sheer energy of the man. He was like a volcano at full blast. Yet only a few moments ago he had seemed to be on his last legs. What must he have been like outside?

A fresh burst of rage boiled over into movement and he shot his arms out through the bars, straining at the guard as if the very force of his anger could bring the man within his grasp. Losing his composure at last, the screw raised his huge bunch of keys to smash it down on to one of the gipsy's outstretched hands.

A wild gleam of hope leaped into the yellowed eyes. Instantly, the gipsy brought his expression under control. But it was too late. With keys upraised, the warder grinned into the seething face and hissed, 'A horse prick up your hairy arse, gipsy!'

At this, the man let out a laugh like that of a drunken Cyclops and crooned, 'So why don't you smash me with the keys, Schmasser? Smash me here! Right here! Right on my hand! What's the matter? Scared of something? Scared you won't get them back, are you? Nice, new uniform! Nice, big bars! But an old, greasy Rom can still make you shit your knickers, eh?'

The guard merely grinned all the more and started jangling the keys in front of the ruffian's face, taking care to keep them just out of reach. This set the gipsy off once again and he started jumping up and down, shaking and kicking the bars, rushing from side to side, bellowing and roaring all the time in an agony of frustration. Meanwhile, the screw kept on teasing him with the keys. It was like baiting a demented bear.

Suddenly, the gipsy stopped erupting, reached down into the depths of his coat and brought out a 'bicska', the wooden-handled clasp knife carried by many Hungarians. The screw was as surprised as I was. The blade of a bicska is usually just cheap metal and never keeps an edge for long. But even so, I couldn't imagine how a man like this could have been allowed to keep one. Somehow, he must have kept it hidden. Biding his time. Instinctively, the guard switched the keys to his left hand and reached for his holster. Then he remembered the bars and relaxed.

'Come on, Schmasser,' whined the gipsy. 'Come and feel my little blade! What? Not playing any more? Scared, are you? Gun and all? Scared I'll slit your gullet like a Christmas pig? Like that big, meaty Cossack in Bukovina? And Kardos Zsiga? And Ion Dimitru? And Nyomó Laci? And ...'

Then, pretty much instantly and for no apparent reason, the huge figure seemed to go into a trance. He seemed to forget all about the screw, the keys, my jacket, where he was – everything – and spun round and round like a whirling dervish, dodging from side to side, leaping high off the floor, ducking into sudden crouches, slashing and stabbing and feinting at the air as if fighting off invisible attackers. All the while, he roared and raged like a frenzied gorilla, as he reeled off name after name after name ...

At first, he simply snarled them. Then his snarling grew into a roaring chant, which mounted by degrees into a bellowing, trumpeting dirge. The whole thing became a rhythmic combination of movement and incantation. The names seemed to spring from each and every one of the many peoples to be found between Budapest and the Urals. How many foes had been named or how many still remained to be called back from the dead, God only knows. For my part, I had already given up even trying to keep any sort of count of the ghosts that haunted the ruins of that gipsy's mind.

The fit called forth reinforcements. They came padding down the corridor with rifles unslung. Two leather-faced little Tartars with granite eyes and hands and feet as quick as a cat's. They halted in front of the bars and the older one shouted, 'Na, na, my little Zoli!'

'What are you up to, then?' cried the other.

'What's all this noise?' yapped the first.

'Manners of a PIG!' yelped the second, grinning like a death's head skull.

At that, the gipsy let out his loudest roar yet and hurled himself at the bars like a hurricane. Which was, of course, exactly what the Tartars had been fishing for. Cool, calm and collected, they swung smoothly into action. The rifle butts thudded a sickening one-two into the gipsy's knuckles and the younger one enquired cheerfully, 'Shouldn't you be more careful when you play with knives, Romaboy?'

The broken blade of the bicska protruded through the flesh between the index finger and thumb of the man's right hand. So great had been the force of the blow, that the blood was not yet seeping from the wound.

'Na, na!' chirped the second Tartar. 'Didn't your mummy teach you to answer when you're spoken to?'

The gipsy just glared down at them with the malevolence of a demon.

This time, the rifle butts thumped into the man's chest. Still he clung on to the bars and glared down at his tormentors. Once again, the rifle butts thudded in. The man's face blackened as if he were being possessed by some spirit of atavistic rage and he snarled, 'Dog-faced Tartars! Go and be men! Go stick your bayonets into babies!'

At this, the little men grinned even wider and the rifle butts took on a life of their own.

Time and again, they battered into the gipsy's chest and arms and shoulders. The man just carried on clinging to the bars. He neither stepped back nor took his eyes from his two assailants. Soon he started chanting his names again.

But the Tartars were by no means at a loss. They carried on hammering away with delicate precision until one of them suddenly switched direction and smashed the heavy butt of his rifle into the massive brow above him.

The big man's head jerked back and his knees buckled. He seemed about to fall. Then he shook himself and straightened up again. His eyes cleared and he stared challengingly down at the pair.

Their weapons coiled back into position and the Tartars stood poised and ready, staring coolly back up at him. For several moments no one moved. Then the gipsy let out a long sigh and nodded his head gently. His hands slid from the bars and he stepped back out of reach. Blood poured down his face. He stood gazing down at us for a long moment. Then, in a gesture of dishevelled, but vast grandiloquence, he swept an imaginary hat from his head, swung it in a graceful arc across his knees, bent forward in a low bow and shambled off into the depths of the cage.

The darkness made it difficult to be sure what he did next, but he seemed to squat down on his haunches, clasp his arms round his knees and start rocking himself backwards and forwards on his heels. On the other hand, the darkness in no way prevented us from hearing that he was singing to himself.

My warder glanced at his watch and growled, 'Come on!'

We strode off down the corridor and, after a good number of twists and turns, came out into the broad well-lit passageway that led to the main offices. I could not resist hazarding a question, 'What's he in for?'

My warder ignored the breach of regulations and grunted, 'Murder, what else? He's a mad dog. A born killer.'

'All those names?' I ventured.

'Who knows?' rumbled the burly warder. 'His present charge sheet's only got four. But we don't need any more to hang him. He's only got one neck, more's the pity. So any other sods he's done for will just have to be satisfied with that and rest in peace.'

'Executing him won't bring any of them back.'

My screw let out a rich chuckle and shook his head. 'You probably don't have monsters like him over in the West. Life's too soft and bourgeois, no doubt. But over here, we've got plenty so we know how to handle them. They're rough, coarse brutes. You pat them on the head and they'll rip your arm off. You've got to treat them like what they are – not like what some bleeding-heart at some decadent university hopes they might be. There's nothing you can do with that kind. Got to put them down. Like animals. The quicker the better. For the protection of the public. *Halt!* Atten-*shun!* Heels to-*gether!* Chin *up!* Eyes *front!*'

I straightened up and stared at the dusty pane of glass in front of me. The reflection there was dim and distorted by flaws in the glass. Try as I might, I couldn't really make out what it resembled most. Was it a member of the public in need of protection? Or a mad dog in need of being put down?

# 7

# Captive Audience

I had never told her that I loved her. Even though, for some time before my arrest, I had been fairly sure that whatever 'love' might be, that was what I felt. Our affair had developed of its own accord in the effortless manner of idylls and neither of us had tried to analyse what was happening.

For the first time I could remember, I had nothing to worry about. Work was under control and going well. Money, accommodation, car, everything was more than adequate. Spring had sprung into the finest of early summers. Our initial ups and downs had levelled out into a permanent rendezvous. Both of us were wary of overblown romantic imagery. Yet I found myself having to admit that I lived for the times we were together. We talked all day and half the night and still found we had more questions unasked and more thoughts unspoken than when we had started.

For the last few days I had been deliberately avoiding any mention of love, especially the variety with a capital 'L'. There seemed to be no point in labouring the obvious and

I did not want her to feel she was being pressured. Then one fine day it was suddenly too late and we had no further opportunities to discuss the matter.

Prison regulations permitted each man to keep contact with one person in the outside world. This threw me on the horns of a dilemma. I had no more concrete evidence of what she felt for me than my feelings for her. And my own, personal memories. Neither of which could be considered particularly objective.

It seemed to me that it could not be considered unreasonable if the change in our circumstances were to have some effect on our relationship. After all, who could blame her if the light she saw me in now was not as bright as it used to be? For my part, it was more than likely that I was hoping for more from her than she could reasonably be expected to be able to give. Anyway, it seemed quite clear that I could hardly take it for granted that she would welcome my attentions now that they were going to be more of a burden than a pleasure.

But I needed her. It was as simple as that. And there was no help for it.

Before, she had interested, entertained, encouraged, enlightened, aroused and exhilarated me. All of which I had managed to live through with some degree of equanimity. But now my longing for her was so imperious that the pain never left me for an instant. It was as much physical as it was psychological and almost unbearable.

I had never really been able to understand suicide. It had always seemed to me that life was short enough anyway, so what was the point of not hanging around long enough to at least find out how things would turn out. But now there were moments when I could see quite clearly how a person could get to a point where a pain just had to stop. At such a point, there really was no other way out.

After much thought and more debate, I arrived at a reason for doing what I had, of course, wanted to do all along. It was no more than the argument that if I respected her as an equal human being then I had no right to refuse her the right to refuse. I found this argument comfortingly difficult to refute, but I still wasn't entirely convinced that I wasn't putting her in an impossible position. Also I had a strong feeling that I was just passing the buck. But my cell-mates insisted to a man that I was doing the right thing.

So I put her name and address down in the appropriate box on the appropriate form and let the bottle float out to sea on the next tide.

Most of my time was spent thinking about what I would say if she came. There was not, after all, much point in dwelling on what I would do if she didn't. First of all, the meeting would not be easy. Of that much, at least, I could be certain. Apart from the uninviting decor, uniformed ears would hang on every word we said.

Moreover, meetings ran a regulation ten minutes and, not counting a regulation sixteen lines of regulation length on regulation notepaper, that was all the communication we could expect for at least a regulation month. In addition, she was not likely to know as much about all this as I had learned by now, so the ball would start in my court. I could not help feeling that an intimate tête-à-tête really needed more encouraging circumstances than these.

Perhaps it was wiser to drop the whole thing before it was too late? Not only wiser, indeed, but also more honourable. Why not spare her all this misery? But there was one thing from which I still could not escape. I had never told her that I loved her.

The more I turned things over in my mind, the more I kept going round and round in circles. There was no way out. Warder or no warder, I would just have to say what I felt. How could I do it? Where would I begin? Maybe I could start with a significant silence. Yes, that seemed promising. Then she could respond with a conclusive, 'I'm truly sorry, but please try to understand', if she wanted to bring down the curtain before things got too painful. Then that would be that and I would know where I stood at last.

What a laughable idea! If that was all she wanted to do, then why on earth would she bother to come at all? A touching scene of farewell before a captive audience? Not exactly an irresistible attraction for a woman in her position. No. If she turned up, there would be nothing for it but to make a clean breast of everything without the slightest hope of hiding anything, either from her or from anyone else.

There would be none of the time for reflection or room for manoeuvre that we all enjoyed outside. No second thoughts, no putting things off until the right moment. None of the many civilised alternatives so convenient for reducing the risk of rejection.

'Risk is everything,' I remembered her saying in one of those endless conversations that had so enchanted me. I had been trying her patience with my earnest misgivings about the unreliability of artistic life. Somewhat curtly, she had informed me that it was an artist's job to risk, and risk

64

everything – house, home and even rejection. The counsel of youth, perhaps. But as far as she was concerned, accepting risk was the first thing any tyro trying their wings had to learn. Every time an actor or actress went out on stage, every time a writer faced a blank page or a painter stepped up to an empty canvas, they were diving off the top of a high cliff and aiming for the tiny pool between the rocks.

'If you don't like the height, just come down and stop complaining!' How her eyes flashed when she was being tough! We had shared so many thoughts and ideas, so many jokes and memories, so many hopes and desires. Each shining in the light of fresh discovery or bathed in the afterglow of personal experience recalled. She had told me many things. And I? I had not even told her that I loved her.

Day followed day and still there was no news. My cellmates did their best to cheer me up, suggesting that as I had been too slow in putting down her name, I had probably missed visiting day for this month but would be all right for next. To a man, they were convinced she would come.

Hungarian women, they assured me, had hundreds of years of experience of visiting their menfolk in jails. It would not be such a big thing to her as I imagined. Most of them had heard of her and a couple had even seen her on the screen, so audience participation was intense. While they sympathised with my feelings, they enjoyed the situation immensely. I didn't really resent this. We were, after all, a little short on entertainment.

I suppose time may well have passed at its accustomed pace. To me, it hardly seemed to crawl from one heartbeat to the next.

On visiting days, every prisoner not under extra punishment was allowed to shave and to put on a clean shirt if he had one. The fact that I was included in these ceremonies did not, therefore, mean anything either way. Men went down to the visiting-room in twos and threes and from different cells, so it often took several hours before anyone knew for certain whether they had a visitor or not. Everyone was ready bright and early and we all paced up and down the floorboards smiling at each other and composing our thoughts.

When the screw finally poked his head round the door, the first person he pointed at was me. There were two more warders waiting outside and all three moved as one to accompany me. This left two less favoured souls from another cell completely unattended. The three screws stood glaring at each other with growing hostility.

After a while, the ferocity of their expressions could mount no further, so the two with the least kilowatts dimmed out and sloped gloomily off to join their charges. The victor beamed down at me as if I were first prize in a Party raffle, chucked me on the cheek with a ham-sized fist and turned on his heel in triumph. Taking care to pull ourselves up to our full heights and keep in step, all six of us set off in good order like a train of well-watered camels heading out for the next oasis.

She was even lovelier than I remembered and shone through the wire mesh as brightly as sunlight in a mirror. I stood there blinking for a moment and then a pang of horror shot through me as I saw that she was dressed to kill. A monstrous vision mushroomed up in my mind. She was on her way to Lake Balaton on the arm of an influential admirer and had merely stopped off en route for a few words with someone she used to know.

Later, it occurred to me she might have put on her finery just to give me the pleasure of seeing her look her best. At that moment, however, no explanation could have been further from my mind than that one. My knees turned to water and I gazed at her in speechless anguish.

Then drop by drop, the hideous cloud dispersed under the warmth in her eyes and we stood drinking each other in through every pore. A battalion of admirers could not have spoiled this moment! What could possibly have mattered beside the glorious fact that she was here? Time stood still beneath the sunrise of our smiles and might have hovered on until this very day were it not for a discreet cough from our guard.

He raised an eyebrow at each of us in turn to indicate that we ought to be warmed up by now so somebody would have to serve first. And so, as suddenly as a mountain spring gushing for the first time from virgin rock, we began.

I started stammering out my side of things, but didn't get very far before she made it clear that she had guessed what I had been thinking all along. She had been hoping against hope that I would not be so asinine as to try to spare her feelings. We agreed to imprint ourselves as deeply into each other's minds as we could, so that we might stand as much chance as possible of outlasting whatever was to come.

As I could not bring her a gift, I recited a poem I had composed. She told me some news of my grandmother in London. I lost myself in her eyes. She did her best to smile.

I told her a joke I had heard. She bit her lip and then shook down her long, auburn hair so that I could look at it. Our guard let out a gasp of admiration and the two screws supervising interviews to our right and left instantly abandoned their charges.

And so we went on for I don't know how long, until all three warders showered us knee-deep in bouquets of apologies and begged us to believe that they shared our feelings, but were powerless to prolong our meeting any further as their hands were tied. My victorious guard entreated her to rest assured that I would be waiting for her in the same place at the same time next month without fail. All three then joined as one to offer her their congratulations on everything in general and their condolences for me in particular.

Then we waved goodbye. My head was swimming and there were tears in her eyes. But I felt as if I were floating on air. She blew me a last kiss and the guards almost burst blood vessels choking back the 'encores' and 'bravos' rising in their throats.

As the two other prisoners had just enjoyed the unexpected windfall of the longest unsupervised family conversations they could ever have hoped for, our progress upstairs was more like the March of the Toreadors than a return to bondage. Since then, I have never been able to find it in my heart to completely condemn the rank and file of the Hungarian prison service no matter what they might be getting up to these days. After all, not every uniform in the world contains a really good audience.

The questioning eyes of my cell-mates set me off playing the meeting back in my mind in preparation for presenting my report. As I did so, I was stunned by a sudden realisation. I could hardly believe it. It couldn't be true!

Frantically, I ran backwards and forwards over image after image. But no matter how hard I looked, I just could not find the words. They were not there. They were simply not there. And now it was too late.

I had still not told her that I loved her.

# 8

# Tortoises and Auctioneers

Karesz clumped stiffly into the cell, his face carefully impassive. At once everyone clustered around him, eager to hear the news.

'Five years,' he grunted.

Someone vacated a wooden stool for him, while the rest of us either shook our heads at the length of the sentence or shrugged to indicate that it could have been even longer. Installing himself on the proffered stool, Karesz turned to accept our attention with the air of a man preparing to make the most of a meal that promises to be his last for some time.

A country lad who had learned to handle bulldozers in the army, Karesz had bettered himself on returning to civilian life by getting a job building roads and knocking down buildings. In his mid thirties, he was strong and sinewy with the rough, powerful, callused hands that result from hard manual labour and the broad, high cheekbones that result from many generations of Magyar peasant blood.

Although his family had worked the soil for centuries, they had never owned any land. Such a background was regarded as little short of ideal during the Dictatorship of the Proletariat. So Karesz had been arguably better off under Communism or Soviet Imperialism or whatever it will eventually come to be called than he would have been under any previous regime.

While his pedigree was ideal, his personality had evidently left something to be desired. By nature, he was inclined to let others worry their heads over such abstractions as International Socialism, Marxist Dialecticism, Marxism-Leninism, Historical Inevitability, the Glorious Example of the Soviet Union and so forth. He preferred just to get on with the job in hand. This made him a fine example of Working-class Man, but it also left him right at the bottom of the Party ladder. A position not without its advantages, of course, since it assured him a life that, while full of hard work, was mercifully uneventful and reasonably free of envious competitors.

Until quite recently, of course, when a difference of opinion with the local police had led to fisticuffs. The law had, so it was said, lost the first bout by a sporting margin. The return, however, it had taken with a vengeance. When he had arrived in our cell, Karesz had been black and blue and hardly able to stand on his feet.

For the next few weeks, he had been in a daze as if he could not quite grasp where he was or how he had come to be here. He was pathetically eager to discuss the events leading up to his fall, going over them time and time again and from every conceivable angle, as if the discovery of some previously unnoticed detail might have the power to change the past.

Any new suggestion, no matter how far-fetched, was received with enough gratitude to make a bishop blush. It seemed that he just could not understand how a man as simple and as straightforward as himself – a man who just minded his own business and got on with his job – could possibly have come to this.

For some time, he responded to the sight of a uniform with such utter servility, stood to such acute attention and marched about with such rigid precision that he might have been a prize cadet at a military academy. All to no avail. The magic wand that might have set him free never waved and he remained as firmly in the cell as the rest of us.

It was really after his wife's second visit that Karesz began to change. I had not been present at their first meeting, but this time only a few paces separated us as we faced the wire mesh. My own meeting wasn't serious, just a little extra arranged on some convenient pretext by my lawyer to get me out of my cell and check on the state of my nerves. So I had plenty of attention left over to take in what was going on next door.

Karesz's wife was one of those small, neat women whose features are too well defined and dark to be quite plain, but too anaemic to be really attractive. With just a little more ripeness, they would be sensual. Instead, they exude decency. Their eyes swim with righteousness as they do their duty as daughters, wives, mothers, grandmothers or, if spared the rigours of procreation, as maiden aunts. In all these phases, their faces wear no expression so well as that of martyrdom.

Indeed, after the brief garland of their youth has withered, they seem to wear no other expression at all.

Their dutiful little heads draped in demure kerchiefs, they seem to be most at home prostrate in abject submission before towering candles. Outwardly, they are doing their ultimate duty. Inwardly, of course, they find the posture delicious. The Latin Catholic world produces such women by the cartload and, although Hungary was never Latin and has only recently rediscovered Catholicism, it has always contributed its quota. I wondered how such a woman, even in her tiny prime, had managed to land such a down-to-earth, bona fide member of the proletariat as Karesz.

No matter how she had pulled that off, she now fixed her husband with her best beseeching look and they talked through the wire mesh in short words and long silences. No matter what you may feel, it takes a lot to really say what you mean under such circumstances. You have prepared for this meeting for so long and there may not be another until who knows when. The minutes are precious few and not a single one will wait while you think out what to say next. There is the iron room, the heavy-duty wire mesh and the eavesdropping guards. And so many hopes and memories jostling for the right to be heard. On such occasions, many a brighter pair than Karesz and his wife has stood tongue-tied as the seconds ticked past.

Brief though the meeting was, long before it was over, I saw the little brown mice in her eyes scuttling off to secret corners in search of some choicer morsel than the one they saw before them. I hoped Karesz hadn't noticed. It had, after all, been no more than a glimpse.

73

By the time we got back to our cell, he was in a sombre mood. Anyone coming back from outside was always given preference at the table and we sat ourselves down at the senior spots with the air of men returning from a military sortie of prime strategic importance and extreme peril.

'Doesn't take long, does it?' growled Karesz.

'What?' I muttered, taken aback by the uncharacteristic harshness of his tone.

'A man is only a meal ticket!' he rasped.

'I see,' I replied, still hoping that he had not.

'And if he's not on hand to bring home the bacon, he might as well be dead!'

'Ah,' I murmured. Now that I saw that he had, there wasn't really much to be said.

'Out of sight, out of mind.'

'Oh, I don't know—'

'You mark my words! Out of sight, out of mind! And not a bloody thing you can do about it. Once you had a family, now you don't. The gipsies have got it right – find 'em, fuck 'em and forget 'em! But especially, forget 'em!'

After this, Karesz lost interest in discussing his case or demonstrating drill. He stopped looking at guards as if they were really Fairy Godmothers in drag just aching for a chance to turn him back into Prince Charming. The days when he gave way to others out of natural politeness were also gone for good. He started learning the ropes and using them. His wife never visited him again and he came to know exactly where he stood.

'Are you going to appeal?' someone asked.

'Try and stop me!' retorted Karesz. 'Won't get anywhere, but it'll be worth a few visits from the defence – a few fags – a different wall; might even get a trip outside.'

'They usually hold the hearing at the court where you were first sentenced.'

'Make a nice change,' reflected Karesz. 'There's a lot of nice scenery between here and there.'

'Still, five years is a long time,' mused the previous speaker.

'Long? You don't know how lucky you've been!' broke in a grizzled old habitual. 'He wasn't himself this morning. You should have been up last week!'

Karesz grinned. 'Oh, yes? Did I miss something?'

'Not half! Over a hundred years he handed out. And it didn't even take him an hour! After a solid century and a bit, he was still early for lunch!'

'Wish they had to do one day – just one single day – for every year they dish out,' growled a sour-faced youth from over by the far wall. 'They wouldn't be so open-handed then!'

'If they could only take a few classes in here,' offered a bright smile from the opposite end of the cell, 'instead of having their heads stuffed with theory up at some University or Party College, what a difference it would make!'

'It sure would,' agreed Karesz. 'They'd give us double just to get even!'

'Well, at least they might stop thinking the whole thing's some kind of auction ...'

'Five, any advance on five? Ten, ten for the gent with the grey hair! Fifteen, anybody for fifteen ...'

'Pipe dreams! All pipe dreams,' cut in Karesz over the general laughter. 'Nobody gives a toss! Nobody ever really puts himself in anyone else's shoes. Not ever. Give a man a lucky break and it doesn't take him a week before he thinks he was born to it. Bigger, better, smarter, more in with God than all the other silly sods who are still stuck in the mud. Stands to reason, doesn't it? How could you ever get any bugger to be a soldier if he believed the name on the bullet was his? No! Everyone always thinks it's going to be the *other* feller! Never *ME!* That's human nature. Always was and always will be. The Party can talk about "Socialist Conscience" until it's blue in the face, but it won't change a thing. Maggots! That's all we are. A lot of squirming maggots. The only thing to look forward to is the day when we'll all have noshed each other and there's only one big, fat maggot left and that rotten grub finally starts gobbling up its own, bleeding arse-hole!'

The mood dampened while everyone digested that one. Our resident gipsy, Géza, sidled up to me. 'What do you say, Squire?' he mused. 'Do they hand out such heavy sentences over there in the Free West?'

Before I could reply, the door groaned open and a warder barked impatiently at Karesz. They had come for him already. He was now a convict and it was time for him to get into his stripes. Karesz got up from the table with deliberate slowness and stared the screw down.

'Don't talk about the Free West, Géza!' he chirped as he collected his things. 'That's Fairyland. They've got colour TV and telephones in every cell. So they have to keep the sentences short just to keep the phone bills down! Anyway, our lot don't really mean any harm. They just think we're tortoises. You know – we all live two or three hundred years anyway, so what's the odd five or ten between friends? Lets your blood cool down. Gives you time to think and take stock. Separates the men from the boys. No, there's nothing wrong with the Fraternal Socialist Peace Camp. We're just a bit short of telephones and a bit long on tortoises, that's all!'

With that Karesz swung his sack on to his shoulder and ambled casually towards the door. The guard opened his mouth as if to speak, but changed his mind. Karesz was just about to step out of the cell, when he turned and grinned at us.

'Seriously, though, you've got to give the Devil his due, haven't you? Our lot might not be worth a butterfly's fart as judges, but they're shit hot as auctioneers!'

The door slammed shut before anyone could laugh and Karesz was gone. Nursery School was over and University had begun.

# 9

# Toad, Rat and Hole,
# Hole, Hole …

One day, the 'Powers That Be' took it into their heads to do something about me. I had been left undisturbed for several weeks and I suppose I had grown accustomed to this state. Gradually, I had slipped into a familiarity with my cell and my comrades-in-grief that might even have been called 'easy'. Long hours and days had passed in reflection on my case and I had drifted into a sort of peace with both my external surroundings and my inner being. It was only to be expected, then, that something would happen.

What they had decided to do about me was next to nothing. A triviality. A mere fly-speck in the oceans of administration. Indeed, it was so insignificant as to be hardly worth doing at all. Unless, of course, you wanted to drop a pebble into a pool whose surface was too smooth and far too tranquil to be tolerated any longer.

The warder waited while I packed my belongings into a bundle. He seemed relaxed and cheerful. I thought this might be a sign that whatever was on the cards for me would be fairly minor. He had even left the door open so that everyone had a welcome feel of the little breeze wafting inwards and a free look at the passageway outside. There wasn't much to see, of course. But after the monotonous horizons of the cell, any change of scenery, no matter how invisible to an outsider, was a great relief to us. I swung my bundle up on to my shoulder and straightened up.

'Ready when you are then!' chirped the warder merrily. Everybody wished me luck and we marched out. We hadn't gone far before my companion stopped at a door and started jangling through his keys.

'Your new cell,' he offered encouragingly. So that was it! I felt both relief and unease at the same time. This was not the end of the world, after all. But then, what was the point of moving me just a few doors down the passageway?

Some clerk fitting heads to beds, I thought to myself with an inward shrug. Then the massive door clanged shut in front of my nose and I turned to face my new lodgings.

At first, I could hardly see anything at all. Then my eyes adjusted to the lack of light and I inspected my surroundings. The cell was very small and an awkward triangle in shape. The base of this triangle was the longest wall into which the iron door was set and its two sides were stone walls of roughly equal extent. Each of these was exactly filled by an iron-framed, double-tiered bunk. The window was a tiny slit just under the ceiling on the wall to my right.

It was high summer now and the cell was as murky as a morgue. Winter would mean complete darkness here. There was no tap, no sink and only a rusty bucket for excretion. The dank air felt chilly. How different from my old cell with its scrubbed floorboards and bright sunlight!

I couldn't make up my mind what to do next, so I stood there blinking at the shadowy walls. Down in the lower bunk to my right, something moved. I peered at it more closely. After a few seconds, I made out the dim figure of a man. He was sitting on the straw mattress, cross-legged and bent forward with his arms out in front of him so he was almost leaning on his elbows. He seemed immensely fat and his body looked soggy. His broad, pasty face trembled every few seconds and his jowls sagged down on to his chest. His eyes seemed to have a slimy cast over them. Every third or fourth breath, his wide mouth gaped open as his tongue, extraordinarily long, darted out into the air and then flicked back in again. After this his jowls quivered and bulged as he swallowed, like some great amphibian gulping down swamp insects. An odour of gently rotting vegetation wafted outwards from his lair.

The man thinks he's a toad, I thought. I wonder how long he's been sitting here in the dark?

I stood there for some time, drifting between sombre and formless thoughts.

At last, I wriggled up to the surface and spoke.

'Good day to you,' I said. This was a bit limp, perhaps, but it was all I could think of at the time. The toad made no reply, but simply stared right through me. He swallowed several more flies and, as I was unwilling to do anything until I had introduced myself properly, I tried again, 'Good day.'

A rustling above my head was joined by a high-pitched whisper. 'No need to take offence. He never answers.'

A figure scuttled into view on the top bunk. A thin, pointed face, crouched on elbows and knees under the low ceiling. Bony hands dangled loosely over the iron edge of the frame and sharp teeth gnawed frantically at a lower lip, making a long, thin nose twitch and tremble like the snout of a nervous rat. The eyes stared fearfully at some point several feet above my head.

'We don't talk much,' squeaked the rat. 'There's nothing to talk about.'

I hunted around inside my head for a reply but as neither of the cell's inhabitants seemed much inclined to listen I soon gave up. Not only was I lost for words, I also couldn't decide what to do next. I wasn't sure which bunk was supposed to be mine, there was no stool to sit on or table upon which to lay my bundle and it was too dark to see the floor. So I just stayed put.

How long have they been here? I thought. Don't the screws know what they're like? Perhaps they do, because they're both on their bunks and it's strictly against regulations to sit or lie on bunks during the day. But there can't be any point in trying to enforce regulations against these two. They're long past anything like that. Anyway, the floor space is too small to allow two men to move around on it at the same time. And they can hardly be expected to stand at attention all day and every day for God knows how many years on end! So, as the screws are *not* enforcing regulations, they *must* know what they're like. If they know, then this is a place where regulations don't apply – some sort of dumping ground, perhaps. A hole to hide the rubbish in. A hole, hole, hole ... Time was heavy enough before. But in here, it'll be like being buried alive!

I had no idea how much time had passed, but I still hadn't moved. What can I do? I thought. Which way shall I go?

It was only one pace to the end of the line in any direction, so the question was not exactly critical. Even so, I still could not make up my mind. I just didn't want to get on to a bunk. I couldn't clearly see whether the bunks opposite the Rat and the Toad were occupied or not but, in any case, I really didn't want to find out.

I felt the same fear of being on those bunks as I had felt in childhood about falling through a seal's breathing hole and being trapped under the ice in some desolate Polar sea. Why were they pushing me through this hole? Who had decided this? What made them think of it? How could they know about my childhood fantasies? What could I do? As I racked my brains for some idea, I noticed that I was moving.

I was taking short, chopped strides and walking across to the door. This took two paces. As I reached one bunk, I turned and took two steps to the opposite bunk. Then I turned and paced back again. Backwards and forwards. Backwards and forwards.

Now I know why the leopards and the other big cats pace back and forth across the bars of their cages at the zoo, I thought to myself. It's a sort of defensive reflex. They *have* to go somewhere, but there's nowhere for them to go. So they take the long way round. It calms them down. Lets them get lost in their own thoughts. Burns off surplus energy.

They always look so bored, but that's better than turning into a toad!

I don't know how long I kept on like this. I remember a warder coming in and holding me back forcibly. He said he'd told me to stop many times and wanted to know why I was ignoring an order.

I couldn't think of any explanation. So I just looked at him. He seemed to get anxious about something and let me go and went out. I felt uncomfortable. So I set off pacing again and soon felt better.

After a time, the warder came back, pulled me out of the cell and marched me off down the passageway. We kept going through corridor after corridor until I found myself in an office. It was warm and carpeted and full of old friends such as ashtrays, paperweights, bookshelves, box files and the like. It was inhabited by a bespectacled dwarf who, from the way he carried himself and the way he spoke, was obviously an educated fellow. He eyed the guard with some distaste and sent him out of the room.

'Now, then,' he said. 'What's all this nonsense?'

I was just about to tell him when it struck me that there was no point in talking about toads and rats and the comfort a leopard gets from pacing back and forth. He would simply consider that ridiculous. So I just said I had got used to my old cell and couldn't adjust to my new one. He was staring at me and I noticed that my cheeks were wet with tears. There was nothing I could do about that, so I didn't even try. He looked very ill at ease, even embarrassed.

'Why didn't you say so earlier?' he grumbled as he called in the warder and ordered him to take me back to my old cell.

The light was on. So it was evening, but not yet bedtime. The cell was wider and even more airy than I remembered. Everyone was very pleased to see me and asked me where I'd been.

They'll understand about toads and rats and holes, I thought. But I felt too tired to talk. So I just said, 'Oh, not so very far. I'll tell you tomorrow.'

# 10

# Filigree Flaming Fancy Free

Adjourned, broken off, delayed, discontinued, interrupted, passed over, postponed, reorganised and rescheduled, my trial had been kicked around like an old tin can for so long and so often that its credibility had become one big dent. Any connection between the legal proceedings featuring my name on its papers and what I actually did from one day to the next had become purely coincidental. By now, I wasn't even sure what my part in the play was any more and I had a strong suspicion that the rest of the cast was getting equally confused.

Originally, I had started out with an assumption that had, at the time, seemed fairly reasonable. I assumed that I had been cast as 'The Defendant'. This assumption soon proved to be not entirely unassailable.

The main factor limiting the scope of my performance was being confined to a cell without any practical means of communicating with the outside world. This worried me at first, as I couldn't quite see how I was going to assemble enough evidence with enough accuracy to be at all convincing when the curtain finally went up.

Compounding my anxiety was a suspicion that I found very difficult to shake off – namely, that this was deliberate. A ploy designed to make sure that, as the defence would never be ready, I would never get to trial. As there seemed, in those parts and in those days, to be no limits to the length of time anyone could be held in custody without trial, the prospects thus opened up did not encourage inner tranquillity.

After a while, however, I did manage to mature to the point of putting the on-off, stop-go situation down more to post-war reconstruction and centuries of political instability than to anything directed at me personally. A further mitigating circumstance was the fact that we were all suspended in mid-air in the middle of a Great Leap Forward on the road towards Socialism. To wit, the whole of the Hungarian Penal Code was, at that very moment in time, in the process of being overhauled and revised from top to bottom.

The proportions of this undertaking were undeniably epoch-making. Heroic patience, steadfastness and the revolutionary ability to rise above getting bogged down in petty details were clearly the order of the day. Especially for those on the receiving end of whatever was – or would be – inside those, as yet, unfinished volumes.

The only sensible course, then, seemed to be to stop trying to understand everything and just take things as they came. This is quite a simple proposition that probably holds true in most situations that a human being is likely to get stuck in. It was not, however, as easy to carry out as it was to propose. At least, it was a state of grace that had so far eluded me.

I could, for instance, still be taken by surprise. One morning, for example, I found myself being escorted down into the labyrinthine depths of the prison building. After mazing along long enough for me to lose not only my bearings but also my interest in getting them back, we arrived at a door cut in two horizontally across the middle so that its top half was a hatch. From the general dinge all around us, I took this to be the entrance to a storeroom for equipment of one sort or another.

After a while, the hatch opened and half a body poked itself out over the sill. It was the upper end of a dark, cadaverous young fellow who could hardly have been more than thirty and who immediately reminded me of an underfed raven. This mysterious bird let out a stream of high-pitched squawks that gradually resolved themselves into Hungarian words. The gist was that my application for release on remand pending trial had been refused.

I was flabbergasted. Indeed, I was so surprised that I couldn't stop myself asking what on earth he was talking about. Nor could I restrain myself from adding that not only did I have no recollection of ever having put in any such application, but it was also news to me that such applications were available for being put in for – at all!

That must have been going too far, because the raven now began hopping up and down on the sill with uncontrollable impatience, cawing loudly all the while that the crime I had committed was so serious that there could in no circumstances be any question of my being allowed out of prison to await trial.

I hadn't even started sorting out the implications of this before the hatch slammed shut, the raven was gone and the rot set in. The maggots of doubt gnawed away at my mind for days on end. As Lenin and every loyal Comrade since had predicted, bourgeois Western upbringing was proving to be a serious weakness. Especially mine. Obviously, I was still having trouble adjusting to being guilty until proven innocent.

Some weeks later, I did a little better in an episode that might well have been entitled something like 'Official Preparatory Hearing'. The two lay members of the 'Examining Committee' had taken their places on the stage, seated behind an item of furniture that was an ingenious cross between a pulpit and a desk. The Clerk of the Court, who was also doubling as Master of Ceremonies, read out their names and civilian occupations. Their manner seemed decent enough and they might well, for all I knew, have been creditable candidates for jury service.

Then, with suitable fanfare and flourish, our MC presented the star of our show: 'And Presiding Over the Right Honourable Preliminary Hearing Before the Worshipful Court of the People – His Honour The Presiding Judge, Comrade—!' When this worthy swooped in from the wings, I recognised him instantly. It was my old acquaintance, the underfed Raven!

I was bowled over like a nine-pin. Even so, I managed somehow to stay on my feet and very nearly resisted the thought that if this really *was* the Judge, then this really was *NOT* a Trial. And I did manage to resist saying a word out loud.

I felt I was beginning to grasp the basic principles of the game and I was certainly getting in a fair amount of training as well as occasional match practice. Sooner or later, I thought, both should prove invaluable. Indeed, although perfect equanimity still eluded me, I felt I was definitely improving with every outing.

One of my best efforts came one day when, after I had passed through the entire ritual of being prepared and served with every trimming due to the Dignity of Socialist Law, the Clerk of the Court kicked off by announcing that this hearing was hereby adjourned as one of the civilians on the Examining Committee sent his regards but was unable to join us that day as he had been unavoidably detained in Moscow.

I didn't turn a hair and instantly banished the thought that if the poor fellow really had managed to send such a message, not to mention his regards, then that was an act of courtesy of undeniably heroic proportions. People in Moscow, especially those 'unavoidably detained' in that city, were not known for being in any position to indulge in such niceties.

I did nearly as well at suppressing the suspicion that no human being with connections lower than Politburo or upper-echelon KGB could ever have hoped to get a telephone line from Moscow to Budapest in time for anything. And I soon smothered the feeling that if we had to wait for this paragon of resourcefulness and good manners to get back before we could resume the hearing, then this adjournment might not be briefer than the garland of a girl.

Instead, I concentrated on the compensations. It really is an ill wind that blows nobody any good. You just have to keep your head calm enough to tell good from bad and vice versa. After all, and in spite of everything, I had been getting out of my cell more often and meeting friends and well-wishers more frequently than anyone could possibly have expected.

Also, I had been to the edge of the abyss so many times by now that I had got quite used to the prospect of the drop and no longer felt an overpowering urge to jump out of my skin at the mere sight of it.

Every day, I was becoming more and more like the old, Russian peasant woman waiting for the train. Some time just after some Revolution, or some war or other, confusion reigns and no one has much idea about the arrival of the next morning let alone the next train. But the old peasant woman has heard that one is due some time soon. In view of the size of the country and the difficulty of the times, this information is as specific as any reasonable person has any right to expect. Being at least as reasonable as anyone else, the old girl gathers up her bundles of food and all her necessary bits and pieces and stations herself beside the tracks.

The only way she can be sure of catching the train is to be there when it arrives. The only way she can be there when it arrives is to be there all the time. There may not, of course, be a train at all. Her strategy has, however, taken account of even that eventuality.

All she has to do to find out if there will or will not be a train is to wait long enough! How long will that be? Who can say? The train might, after all, turn up just after she has left and then all her waiting – no matter how long it may have been up to then – will have been in vain. Not a lot of certainty about this plan, one may well sniff. But then you never can be completely sure of anything in this life. Except that it takes a very long time indeed to outwait an old, Russian, peasant woman.

At first, she huddles between her bundles, watching intently so as not to miss the first puff of smoke on the horizon. Days lengthen into weeks, weeks into months and months into years. The old woman feels quite at home now. She sows and reaps her little crops, tends to all the tasks of every season and keeps the weeds from overgrowing the rails so that the engine driver will have no difficulty in knowing where to stop.

She is neither happier nor more unhappy than she was before. Each day delivers its allotted share of joys and sorrows and she finds great comfort in recalling her old village and reciting the names of her relatives. If you ask her when the train will come, she just smiles, shrugs her shoulders and gets on with weeding the railway tracks. And, for all anyone knows, she's waiting there still.

Like me, she ended up no longer going anywhere. Like her, I no longer got steamed up about it. Of course, things might have been different if she had been relying on a bona fide timetable or if I had been counting on a genuine trial. As things were, we had both got beyond cudgelling our brains over things too deep for either of us and had settled for just keeping the weeds down.

Instead of hoping for justice, I looked forward to a few moments with friends. Instead of poring over evidence and sifting through arguments, I savoured morsels of news from the outside world. Instead of sighing for long-lost landscapes, I enjoyed every detail of even the slightest variation from my cell.

There was, I realised, absolutely nothing I could do about anything outside my own head. Everything out there was entirely in the lap of whatever gods were presently in office. Being utterly powerless, I was also absolved from all and any responsibility. Once I had learned to stop worrying about it, this absolution gave me a surprising amount of comfort and relief.

Furthermore, it was not just a matter of feeling better simply because I had stopped banging my head against a brick wall. Soothing though such relief from impact undoubtedly is, it is more the minus of a minus than a true plus. What I had gained, however, was genuine enough. Since I no longer had to contend with the outside world and all the uncertainties of my relationship with it, I had gained the freedom to concentrate on my inner space.

To me this came as something of a revelation, but to my colleagues in both the cell and the wing my discovery was nothing new. More seasoned souls than I, they pointed out that this was undoubtedly, more or less, the path trodden throughout all history by those who had withdrawn from this vale of tears to free their minds for the contemplation of eternity.

That struck me as a bit far-fetched, but my colleagues just shrugged and insisted that there was not much to choose between our respective situations. Had not those who had passed this way before us given up all material possessions? And did not few people possess less of anything than we? Those earlier pilgrims had surrendered all vestiges of temporal power. There was not a lot we could do about anything, either. They had submitted themselves body and soul to the Will of the Almighty. So, all in all, had we.

Of course, it was quite possible to argue that there were differences between us. Our exalted predecessors had, presumably, chosen their courses, for whatever reasons, of their own free wills. Few of us, however, had exactly volunteered to come in here.

On the other hand, as my colleagues were quick to point out, once anyone has run further than the first few laps of the great race of their lives, how much freedom of choice, let alone will, do they really have? How free are they to decide what they truly want to do or have or be?

Is not life, when you get down to the nitty-gritty, just a process of eliminating alternative after alternative until, in the end, there are no more left? For anyone. No matter how high or how low.

I could think of no way of denying this and had to concede that, perhaps, after all, it was not unlikely that those saints and stylites, apostles and acolytes, monks and madmen of old had had no more control over their destinies than we had over ours.

Different heads in different traps spawn different theories of the Universe with the fertility of frogs in spring. Everything is relative, of course, but some theories do seem to work better than others. For a while, at least. This one did a lot of good in our neck of the galaxy. Anyway, whatever its pros and cons, it was what kept my chin up as I approached the end of that long and winding road leading to my trial.

Not that anyone could really tell when anyone's trial would actually arrive, of course. Even so, the consensus in the cell had grown to feel that there was nothing much left in my case but to reach an official verdict. By now, even I had understood that an unofficial verdict had been reached long ago. Especially when I remembered the Raven. There was nothing to be done about that. However, there were two things I could still manage.

For my friends and supporters, both inside and out, fears could be soothed and worries could be eased by what I said and how I behaved. For myself, like a squirrel fattening up for winter, I could greedily gobble as much as possible of the sights and sounds I loved and enjoyed.

I would have to filter out everything around me that was irrelevant to this purpose and concentrate on the cream. This would, I hoped, be helpful to those who mattered to me. If I succeeded, however, the person to benefit most from this manoeuvre would undoubtedly be me. By simply marshalling my innermost thoughts and keeping the territory of my mind intact, I would be gaining the scarcest of all commodities in my present circumstances: freedom – if not of body then at least of mind.

I would see the world as I pleased and respond to it according to my own judgement. As all the forces that I had been surrounded by ever since my arrest were still combining to make me do the exact opposite, I felt it would be no small victory if I carried it off.

A bright day. Brimming over with sunshine and summer heat. Heavy shadows in the courtroom. Cool inside with restful gloom. Faces. Some closed and blank. Others beautiful with sorrow. Eyes aglow with doubt and hope.

A friendly rumble. Town traffic coming in through the walls. Rare visitor of late. The smell of melting tar. Unmistakably Eastern Europe. Uniform shirt bulging and billowing over rippling back muscles. Michelangelo, to the last curving line and bulky shading.

Laughing blue polka dots flirt and tease a bald and manly pate of solemn sienna as they dance up and down on the fluorescent white of a mopping handkerchief. Pat, pat – tee-hee-hee! Enough, enough! Still they peek cheekily out as their bald beau banishes them to a breast pocket.

Flickering typewriter keys lick eagerly at the fingers of an olive-skinned secretary with high cheekbones and jet-black hair. Old Cuman blood. Oblivious to the excitement of the keys, she preens herself for all to see her at her buxom best.

Fragrant whiffs of ladylike perfume. Fresh on green maids, fruitful on grown women, comforting on matrons of maturity.

A shine glints deep on leather shoes like newly dropped horse chestnuts. Why, the place is packed with gems today!

Presiding Judge presides on and on. Easy to ignore. Much more convincing as that Bird of Doom – the Raven of the Dingy Storeroom!

A window to my left. Tall and narrow. Rich light flooding in. But also a tree. Small, with an odd, elongated, oval crown. Poplaresque. Perfectly framed in the window. What luck! Leaves of the darkest and deepest green. Each leaf exquisitely shaped and drawn as sharply as the finest filigree. Latticework against the light. Like those legendary trees in medieval paintings. And blossoms of bright orange flaming between the leaves. It hardly seems real, yet everything else pales away beside it.

I drank in every second of that perfect tree. Gazed at it without blinking to bounce its brightness against the back of my eyeballs. Filtered it through my lashes to frame it in soft focus. Clenched my eyes tight shut to crush its colours against my mind. Shot them open suddenly to let it burst brilliantly into view. Closed one eye after the other in quick succession so it skipped skittishly from side to side. Stared at it as hard as I could and then, jerking my head round swiftly, projected it on to the wall behind the court officials. Again. And again. And yet again. Each time it glowed, obedient and proud, above the vague and mumbling crowd.

Abruptly, everyone stands up. It's all over. Fifteen minutes to talk with friends. The skin I'm in laughs and jokes and urges everyone to keep their spirits up. The look in their eyes replies that they're not certain I'm all there.

Well, wherever I am, I feel in the best of health and I can – and do – honestly say I have never enjoyed their company more.

This must get across as everyone cheers up and sparkles and grins and hugs and has a lovely time. The warders stub out their butts, button up their shirts, adjust their hats. A last tear. A fond farewell. And off we trot. Leaving everything behind.

Or so they all think. What a pity none of them can see my gay and carefree tree! Sunlight streaming through its latticework of leaves and bursting from its blooms of orange flame! It blazes upon the air brighter than a crest upon a brand-new shield. And I'm as happy as can be, following as it leads the way, dancing along in front of me – one step, two steps, three steps, four – ONE, two, three – ONE, two, three – ONE, two, three – ONE …

# PART TWO

# Second Thoughts

# 1

# A Warm Night in Budapest

From outside, the building looked much like many another chunk of Hapsburg Urban. But inside, it sprawled inwards, upwards, downwards and aroundwards for more floors, landings, corridors, catwalks and staircases than were possibly imaginable from the street. It also teemed with life.

Inmates and warders, relatives and lawyers, officials and outsiders hurried and scurried hither and thither behind protective frowns of deep concentration. I recognised the scene at once. Big City! I nodded to myself. Everything passes through here sooner or later. Even Me. Where, oh where would we be without centralisation?

This line of thought was nipped in the bud when the little file of which I was a part was sucked abruptly into the general current of activity. A dapper uniform steered us swiftly up and down staircases, in and out of doorways, round corners, through vestibules and along passageways until we sailed suddenly out into clear daylight. Morning exercise. We were just in time.

The yard was a small triangle, crushed awkwardly between towering walls. Generations of captive feet had tramped and stamped and scraped its cobbles until they had become a patchwork of dips and bumps and furrows that, by causing our exercises to be performed at impossible angles and in unpredictable positions, lent them the welcome spice of variety – not to say, even novelty. It was in one of these unpredictable positions that I came face to face with a singular example of that sophisticated and mordant wit for which Budapest is still justly famous.

Round and round rolled my head, following instructions and swinging a small patch of clear sky backwards and forwards like the weight at the end of a pendulum. After a while, the novelty wore off and my attention slipped back down the tunnel of confining walls and stuck at some objects I couldn't quite identify.

They looked like small figures of some kind. A whole flock of them. Perched at irregular intervals and varying heights. At certain moments, it looked very much as if they were watching us. Birds? But they stood stock still. Not a preen, not a pout, not a shuffle. No hint of a coo or a song. Not even the ghost of a peck or a chirp.

I had almost given up trying to work out whether they were real or just visions resulting from the revs of my head, when a bellow from our guard switched us all over to arm-waving. I could now continue my observations on a more even keel.

Realisation dawned and my heart went out to the mind behind it all. The figures were human forms, frozen for ever in a riot of grotesque postures that were spitting images of our own. They were all imitating the daily rituals they had overseen for so long. It must have been many a year since both sculptor and architect had been laid to rest. Yet the sense of humour still enshrined on those walls was, if anything, even more telling now than when this joke of jokes had first seen the light of day.

We would never meet in what is usually meant by 'real' life, but the contact between us was real enough nonetheless. For anyone with eyes to see, they had left behind sparks of understanding unquenched by passing time and a good laugh no regime had been able to stifle. From where I was waving my arms, you could hardly ask for anything more.

All over the world, housing shortages seem to have become an integral part of city life and Budapest – both outside and in – was no exception. By normal standards, our room was of noble dimensions, but it sheltered forty-two of us by nightfall and every scrap of floor space was gone. Our guardian architect, however, had not abandoned us even here, because his ceiling was so lofty that it accommodated no fewer than five tiers of bunks beneath its canopy.

Newcomers started at the top with plaster hardly a foot above their noses when lying flat on their backs. For anyone fatter than a rake, rolling over was a serious problem. Even for a rake, sitting up in the middle of the night to take a leak was an instant headache.

As predecessors passed on to other ports of call, promotion flowed downwards. It was the same old hierarchical structure all over again, but this time in reverse. The top was the bottom and the bottom was the top.

101

Mercifully, however, turnover was rapid and the incessant toing and froing created an atmosphere more reminiscent of a railway station than a state prison. The door was also something of a windfall. Instead of the usual solid slab of heavy metal punctured by a peephole that could only be operated from outside, it was no more than a row of iron bars, two metres high and set in an iron frame.

This meant we could see everyone who passed along the passageway outside and the traffic was steady enough to provide continuous entertainment. Moreover, due presumably to the general overcrowding, the cell also doubled as a visiting-room and meetings were conducted through the bars of the door.

The blessings of this were twofold. First, everyone had a share, no matter how small, in any visit that anyone received. Second, the warder had to supervise from outside in the passageway where all the comings and goings and wheelings and dealings continually distracted his attention. The first was very good for morale. The second was absolutely wonderful for business.

The net result of all this was, predictably enough, that the best address in our part of town was the bottom bunk directly opposite the door. Even more predictably, like most desirable residences anywhere on Earth, this address was already occupied.

The property in question did not simply boast the best view. It was also the focal point of commerce, information and culture. The cornerstone of its importance was its position. But its life-blood was a permanent and practically non-stop game of chess.

The proprietor of this attraction was a short, beefy fellow with glistening curls like a bunch of black grapes and a glance sharp enough to cut shoe leather. Most people think of chess as a combination of concentration and patience in more or less equal parts. Our champion, however, could hardly ever be bothered to even look at the board.

More contrary still was his habit of continually holding court with all and sundry, while at the same time dabbling in everything from gossip to barter. As he lobbed piece after piece carelessly into place almost before his opponents had finished making their moves, chess seemed to be the last thing on his mind.

Also, unlike most chess players outside the Grand Master circuit, he played strictly for money. Our coin was, of course, the standard currency of lower depths everywhere: cigarettes, tobacco, food. But if you had anything at all, no matter how useless the object would have appeared outside, it could usually be traded for something down here. At worst, it could always be gambled away for excitement.

The 'Chess King' was a bird that had become very rare on the wrong side of the Iron Curtain – a fully-fledged professional crook. Not your standard bent politician or a Party apparatchik out to feather a nest, but an honest-to-goodness working criminal. I never even heard tell of another.

Nationalisation, uniformity of earnings, scarcity of cash and valuables, superabundance of police and informers, lack of protection under the law and unfair competition from those in high places had all conspired to render professional crime a dying trade.

Furthermore, if you did not circulate in elevated Party circles, there wasn't much you could do with any gains you might manage to achieve. You certainly couldn't indulge openly in the life of luxury and ease, which was, presumably, the whole point of professional crime in the first place.

Add to this the fact that the severely reduced land surface and sealed borders left precious little room for losing pursuers or getting lost in the crowd and it was not difficult to see that Communist Hungary was no place for self-respecting members of the alternative society. Indeed, our own Grand Master harboured grave misgivings about how much longer even he could scrape by under such conditions.

This was doubly ironic as he had all the makings of a star. In more favourable circumstances, he would undoubtedly have hit the big time as easily as short-game cricketers now hit sixes. As it was, this was clearly neither the time nor the place for individuals of exceptional talent.

By and large, the right to be held in custody without trial and for an indefinite period of time is a serious millstone round the neck of anyone under arrest. More than almost any other quirk of law, constitution or custom, it is this one that has come to be considered the benchmark of barbarism throughout the world. Individuals actually in such custody usually find it very difficult indeed to salvage anything from the situation. Our chess player, however, managed to pass though the eye of even this needle, day in and day out, with an ease that was little short of impudent.

Despite a solid record of previous convictions, he was in for something quite minor this time and reckoned he couldn't be due any more than three or four years. This prison was his local nick and all his relatives knew who was who and had the routines off backwards. The place was very big and very busy. Amid all the hurly-burly no one noticed a few extra visits here and there.

Then, as he was only in custody and not yet serving a sentence, he was still, technically, innocent. While this usually made no discernible difference to the treatment a detainee received, it did mean that he was allowed to remain in civilian clothes. The upkeep of these was still the responsibility of the individual not the State. For someone who knew the ropes, this boiled down to underwear and shirts being washed and changed as often as relatives could arrange. For our Chess King, this meant regular deliveries, which regularly included much else besides clothes.

As the Administration had its hands full with the population as a whole, it had little time for particular individuals. So the atmosphere here was much lighter than in more concentrated centres of correction. Furthermore, the lively turnover of inmates assured continual new customers and continuous prosperity for the Chess Game. All in all, our man was more than content to stay put.

Consequently, whenever his trial came too close for comfort, he sacrificed a pawn. He would allow some dispensable, but not entirely insignificant, item relating to his case to be unearthed. Some detail that the Prosecution would find interesting but that he did not really need. Something that had previously been, somehow or other, overlooked.

This move had so far won him half a dozen adjournments and he had already crossed off over two and a half years from whatever he was eventually going to get. With a bit of luck, the clock would more or less have stopped by the time they finally got him sentenced. He explained the ins and outs of all this while dispatching an errant knight and serving a couple of customers.

'Of course, things are easier for me in here,' he admitted, sliding home his lethal queen. 'Being a pro, you know. It's not the same thing as being a social misfit or on the "X" list or political or anything like that.'

He passed round his winnings with absent-minded bonhomie and we all lit up.

'Nobody seems to take my game seriously any more,' he mused, more in sorrow than in anger. 'Strictly speaking, no matter which way you look at it, it *is* against the law. And I mean real law, old ones; not laws that just got invented to cover up Party fleecing operations. But even so, my game's no threat to the Revolution or the State or the Proletariat – or whatever it is they're so touchy about. So they don't seem to be bothered. Once upon a time, of course, the boot was on the other foot. In those days, pros like me got the ton of bricks on the bonce and politicals got the writing paper and the amnesties. That was a kind of insurance, I suppose. You know, just in case today's dirty rat becomes top dog tomorrow. Anyway, times change and you just have to take the rough with the smooth, don't you? In those days the game was well worth the candle, as long as you didn't get caught. These days, it's hardly worth the bother – unless you do!'

Thoughtfully, he patted his curls back into place and started setting up the board for the next optimist. We all wondered how long it had been since he had actually lost a chess match. His other games were a different matter, of course. Dying professions are notoriously difficult to resurrect. Not even a man as talented as our Chess King could be expected to do much about historical inevitabilities.

'If things are so tough,' someone asked him, 'why don't you join the Party?'

'Good move,' grunted the Chess King. 'Very good move. But I dunno. It doesn't feel right to me. Up to now, I've always held back – on moral grounds, you know.'

His expression remained perfectly serious.

'Yes,' he continued. 'You've got to draw the line somewhere and somehow, I've always felt there was something just a bit too, sort of, underhand about playing with a deck so totally stacked in your own favour. On the other hand, times do change, you know, and you have to remember us Hungarians have got a kind of knack for getting caught on the losing side of almost any conflict – even when we're doing our level best to swallow anything just to get on the right side. So,' he sighed, 'if those Americans don't hurry up, I can see the day coming when I might have no option but to put in for my little Red Book, just to make sure of a comfortable old age.'

Many games later, the weather if not the times had changed and the evening was as hot and sultry as only Budapest at the height of its very own kind of heatwave – the 'Kánikula' – can be. The air gets trapped in the basin enclosed by the hills of Buda and not a breath of a breeze stirs for day after day throughout the whole of Pest. On such dog days the very Danube seems to sweat and even a sopping-wet, cold towel wound round the head brings no more than a moment or two of relief.

From asphalt to armpits, the city was melting and, for once, we were grateful for thick, dank, stone walls. No one either in or out of uniform had enough energy left to move a muscle. Lights Out never meant much in this nick and tonight it meant nothing at all. Everyone, no matter what their problem with the world might be, was taking life easy.

Summer had been in full swing for some time outside and had already stirred its full quota of youthful pulses. So those with all their lives before them were well represented among us.

With so many people in such a small space, all of them too lethargic to move and with nothing better to do than talk, the cell had become a vertical version of one of those literary cafés that distinguished Budapest in its heyday as the city caroused its way out of the nineteenth century and into the twentieth.

I had already been promoted down a bunk and the one above me was now filled by a long, handsome youth who lay sprawled on top of his blanket with the effortless grace of early manhood. He was concentrating on breathing in the steamy air.

The fact that I was English had leaked out and ardent fans of Western pop music had started pumping me for news and gossip. The lad above tried to maintain a lofty indifference to our idle chatter, but eventually could hold back no longer. As far as he was concerned, the Beatles were the only thing in life that made any sense. The world, he felt, would do well to meditate upon the abstract realism of 'Loossing in Ze Skay Viz Diemondz'!

The silence was long and humid. Our pop fans waited for me to come up with a Western insider's response to 'Abstract Realism'. I waited for inspiration. The boy above just waited.

After a while, I gave up trying to figure out anything relevant and thought I might as well make do with explaining what or, strictly speaking, who was really up there in the sky with those diamonds. Then I had second thoughts. After all, 'Abstract Realism' was no more way-out a concoction than the song itself and might well be just as valid a response to pop music as any other. Especially considering where we were at this moment in time. What was the point of bursting such a bright bubble of youthful imagination with such a dry pin as linguistic accuracy? Which did we need more in here, anyway?

The young man above me was steeped in a musing melancholy that was so relaxed as to be the very quintessence of the Californian concept 'laid back'. Neither of us knew the phrase at the time, of course, but if he'd lain back any further the boy under the ceiling would have slipped right off the edge of the world and disappeared under the horizon and into infinity without so much as raising a ripple.

Our three-dimensional conversation flowed gently back and forth, up and down and from side to side. The lad had been arrested that afternoon. He'd been caught red-handed in a silly burglary. He hadn't bothered to take even elementary precautions against getting caught, nor had he checked whether the place he was breaking into contained anything at all worth lifting.

Furthermore, he'd been out on parole at the time. His Parole Officer was a young tutor in French at the University, a lady from the highest circles with lots of good connections. She was also his mistress. Or vice versa.

This was his fourth trip inside. He'd been fifteen the first time. Yes, she would probably be upset. But she'd understand. No, he didn't feel he was wasting his life. In the Universe as a whole it really made no difference at all whether he was here or there. Or anywhere else, for that matter.

Miss her? Well, not yet. It was too soon. Maybe he would when the weather cooled down. Anyway, sex didn't really mean that much – not really. After all, it was fundamentally just a reflex biochemical reaction. Basically the same thing time after time. Not much more than knee-jerking in pairs, when you got down to it.

What would he do when he got out? Why, his best – yes, he'd do his best.

But he didn't hold out much hope. Casually and in a world-weary drone he intoned a few lines of verse,

> *Mais mon coeur, que jamais ne visite l'extase,*
> *Est un théâtre où l'on attend*
> *Toujours, toujours en vain, l'Etre aux ailes de gaze!*

The effect of this was electrifying. In other circumstances it would certainly have brought his audience to their feet. Had it not been so hot, even I would have applauded. I can't even hazard a guess at what it was that moved the surrounding youth so deeply, especially as Baudelaire was not likely to be on any Communist secondary-school curriculum and, anyway, none of the lads present spoke a word of French.

For me, it was not so much the poetry, nor even the unexpected expenditure of energy. It was the accent. It was downright startling. Not just impeccable. It was so rich you could practically chew it. Effortless street Parisian from some old 'film noir'. Jean Gabin to a rolling 'r'. Stunning. Particularly when you remembered his English. Where had he got it from? Was his well-connected Parole Officer up to something more than boy-toying, after all?

I tried to sound him out. What did he feel when he was caught? Well, relief – yes, relief. Burgling was very tiring. Wasn't there anything he wanted to do in life? Well, not much. Just, you know, take one breath after another. And take things easy. As easy as easy can possibly be.

I paused to weigh things up. But I hadn't got very far before he started singing. In a nasal falsetto that was slightly off-key. His Beatle-ish was incomprehensible, but mood and rhythm oozed out of him and his performance was almost as moving as his French.

In the humid darkness, I picked out the youths around me gazing up at him in fervent admiration as he lounged above us, chanting softly and with infinite longing the words of 'Loossing in Ze Skay Viz Diemondz'.

A breath of air strayed in through the high window and felt around between the bunks, cool and soothing as a loving hand. Voices flickered out one by one, like the lights of an apartment building after midnight. A car coughed itself awake outside and spluttered off into the hushed murmur of the streets.

111

I billowed out over the hazy borderland of sleep and was filled with the calm certainty that if I could just become relaxed enough, if I could only lie back far enough, if I could listen with my inner ear for just one more moment, I would hear the whispered secret of the city and glide under her concrete skirts to lie hidden, safely and for ever, from the prying eyes – from the prying eyes – from the prying eyes – from the ...

# 2

# Red-Haired Man Out Shopping

Of all the spaces and places in the entire Hapsburg sprawl, my favourite was the Entrance Hall. And this was not just because it was, from our point of view, also the Way Out. The main reason why I enjoyed it so much was because it was so absolutely enormous. The ceiling was high enough to provide room for even the most epic flights of fancy and the tall, narrow windows let in veritable floods of sunlight.

Convicts were never allowed to get near enough to those windows to really see out, of course. But sunbeams needed neither permits nor patronage to slip in through the glass and cheer us up. No matter what was happening anywhere else in the world, they were always here for anyone who needed them. Since their real nature was invisible to anyone in uniform or even indirectly on the payroll of the State and since sunbeams did not make any noise, the Authorities had not yet noticed what they were up to. So there were no regulations in force against them.

I was getting better at being invisible myself. As far as any passing guard could see, I was a quiet bundle of striped canvas standing more or less to attention. In fact, I was a piebald yearling and had been stretching my legs frolicking in that lovely space and browsing on refreshing Kentucky blue grass drenched in dew for quite some time. I was just breaking into a canter to vault an inviting brook when the small door cut into the heavy oak portal became an oblong of blinding light and a uniform let in a silhouette from outside.

The door thunked back into place, the light dimmed until it was no longer blinding and the silhouette turned into a tall, well-fed young buck, sporting a crest of unruly red hair and a carefree smile. His expensive leather jacket, blue denim shirt, horn-rimmed specs and brand-new Levi's announced that he belonged to that stratum of the new society that was beginning to rise above the daily grind of Building Socialism. The way that he displaced considerably more than his fair share of air and the sheer volume of his self-confidence reminded me more of a youthful Etonian arriving to take up residence at, say, King's College, Cambridge, than a young Hungarian arriving at a somewhat less august institution of self-improvement.

'Lovely afternoon, Comrade!' chortled the young buck.

'Hmmn,' growled the bulldog at the desk, apparently unprepared for being addressed by a gentleman.

'Well now, shall we cross the t's and dot the i's, then?'

'Dot the i's?'

'That's what I'm here for, Comrade!'

'Is that a fact, Comrade?'

114

The red-haired man's young, brash, bounding bounce met the old, dull, stolid lump of the guard at full tilt and head-on. They glared at each other. By both nature and nurture, they were exact opposites and evenly matched. But the guard had the uniform and the desk. So he held the higher ground. The red-haired flame began to burn a degree or two less brightly.

'A fact! That's just what it is, Comrade.'

'Is it?'

'You see, the thing is – there seems to be some mistake.'

'Does there, now?'

'No question about it, Comrade—'

'Papers.'

'What?'

'Papers, Comrade.'

'You mean my identity card?'

'No Party Card, then, Comrade?'

'I only came out to do a bit of shopping.'

'Notification of Sentence.'

'Notifi— No, no. I mean, I never got one—'

'But you have been up on a charge?'

'Charge? Well, yes. But that was nine months ago—'

'What was it?'

'What was what?'

'Not the month, Comrade.'

'Oh, I see! Ha, ha, that was a good one, Comrade! Very pat—'

'The charge.'

'Oh, come now. It was nothing, really, just a bit of horse-play. Lads out on the town—'

'That would be Riotous Behaviour, Disorderly Conduct – or Disturbing the Peace. Which?'

'What?'

'Much damage?'

'Oh, hardly anything at all. Trifles, bagatelles—'

'Riotous-B plus Dis-Con plus Drunk and Dis *and* plus Wanton Des of People's Prop, I expect.'

The red-haired man was lost for words. The guard contemplated him darkly.

'So what did you get?'

'Well, that's just it, you see. There's obviously some mistake—'

'Oh, yes?'

'Well, there was never really any definite decision—'

'Was there not?'

'I mean, after all, the whole thing was just a storm in a teacup, just a bout of high spirits, and taking everything into account, my background, my educa—'

'What did he give you?'

'Who?'

'Father Christmas, Comrade.'

'What? Oh, yes! Ha-ha-ha—'

'Well?'

'Well, I got a lecture, you know—'

'And?'

'And, ahem, let me see, now, there might have been some mention—'

'How long?'

'Long?'

'Years and months, Comrade.'

'Ah, well, I see, yes, there was something, but I can't be sure. There might have been something about, perhaps—'

'Two years?'

'Two years! Oh, no, no, no! More like eighteen months, maybe—'

'Eighteen months? All right. That'll do for now.'

'But, of course, there was nothing definite and, in any case, whatever it was, it would be suspended, of course—'

'Would it, now?'

'Well, it stands to reason, doesn't it? It's standard practice. I mean, it was all a joke and a man with my qualifications – what's the point of wasting them in some jail when they could be doing something useful for Socialism …'

'That's all been taken into consideration; you can rest easy on that score.'

'But there's been no further communication about the case since then.'

'No?'

'Not a word. It did seem a bit odd, at first. But then we just put it down to the usual thing. Too much paperwork. Suspended sentence. No hurry—'

'Well, never mind. You're here now.'

'What? Ah, yes! But I only dropped in at the station out of a sense of duty – Socialist Conscience, you know! Just to dot the i's and cross the t's. Then they sent me on down here. Actually, I've only popped out to do a bit of shopping. I told my wife I'd be back for lunch.'

'I wouldn't expect it to still be warm if I was you, Comrade. Not by the time you'll get back.'

'Now look here! There has to be some mistake. Where's the paperwork on this?'

'Where it should be.'

'Well, what does it say?'

'Mind your own business!'

'What do you mean? Whose business is it if not mine?'

'Now, now! A clever cadre like you can't really think Officers of the Penal Service of the People's Republic go around discussing official business with every Tom, Dick and Harry, now, can you?'

'But this is a special case—'

'Every case is special these days, Comrade.'

'Ah, yes, of course! But we had no idea—'

'Well, we have now.'

'What?'

'So why don't we stop wasting the People's time, Comrade, and just get on with it?'

He opened a huge ledger and picked up a pen. Then he glanced down at something hidden from view in the drawer of the desk. Satisfied, he looked up again.

'Right. Takács, Zsigmond Vilmos. Is that you, Comrade?'

'Well, yes.'

'Of Zugliget Square, 14a, B.P. XII?'

'Er, ah, yes.'

'Good. That's the spirit, Comrade! Valuables?'

'What?'

'Rings, medals, watches, fountain pens, biros, propelling pencils, manicure sets, shaving gear, personal photographs, penknives, bracelets, cash and so on.'

'But look here! What on earth is going on?'

'Inventory. You want them back when you get out, don't you?'

'Am I to understand you're taking me in, then?'

'No, Comrade, I'm going to give you a massage.'

'But we've had no warning—'

'Lucky for you; less time to grow an ulcer.'

'But we've had no time to get ready! I mean, a year and a half. One should have some time to get things in order.'

'Things never get in order, Comrade. A fact of life.'

'Look here, Comrade, at least let me make a phone call! My wife doesn't even know where I am!'

'She'll work it out. Given time.'

'Oh, come on! Please, Comrade! Just one phone call!'

'This is not a General Post Office. The People's Regulations are very clear. One letter per month and one visit. *If* you keep your nose clean. *No* phone calls.'

The red-haired man stared at the guard in disbelief. Then he turned and gazed longingly at the door cut into the massive oak portal of the main entrance. It was obvious what he was thinking. But the area beyond that door, through which he had come in only a few moments ago, was, as he knew full well, crawling with uniforms, all of which carried guns. Our man wilted visibly.

'Now, why don't we register your valuables?'

The leather jacket looked a lot less dashing now and beads of sweat trembled on the freckled brow.

'Couldn't I just write a note? Just a few words. It won't take a minute.'

'Let's start with your wristwatch. You won't need to know the time where you're going, Comrade.'

Motes of dust danced in and out of the long, straight shafts of sunlight falling in through the windows like golden spears. Sunbeams tickled my nose and radiated cheerful messages – that it was warm outside and sunny, that it was good to be alive on such a day as this, that it was a lovely day for doing anything at all, even for going out shopping.

I took them at their word and made the most of every sunlit second. I was having a wonderful time. So were the sunbeams.

To the red-haired man unbuckling his watch, all this was, of course, still invisible.

# 3

# Come Fly With Me ...

All morning the heavy truck bumped and banged from stop
to stop. It let off one man here and two there, until in the
end all that was left was the hard core. A handful of
Hungarians and me. Conversation dwindled. We were tired.
It had been a long trip.

Not that we had gone very far. There wasn't very far we
could go.

Hungary had lost two-thirds of its land territory in two
rounds of friendly Peace Treaties after two World Wars. So,
in every direction, a heavily fortified, overmanned and thoroughly mined frontier awaited the traveller at no distance
at all. One of the many advantages enjoyed by modern,
Socialist Hungary, surrounded as it was on four of its five
sides by Fraternal Comrades in the Camp of Peace, was that
national man-hours wasted in travel were reduced to a
minimum. What was wearing us out was not kilometres. It
was the long drawn-out agony of the heavy truck as it lurched
along as laboriously as any pre-Socialist-era ox cart.

We had no idea how long we would have to hang on like this, since we never knew where we were going next, nor how long we would stop at wherever we pulled up on the way. There was nothing unusual about this, of course. We all knew perfectly well that it was not in the nature of consignors anywhere in the world to discuss itineraries with cargo. So there was no real reason why we should have found this trip particularly exhausting. Today, however, energy seemed to drain out of us with each new stop and start.

At first, it had been a tonic to peek out of the small windows in the doors at the back of the vehicle. Then city streets had given way to countryside, our ranks had grown thinner and thinner and someone had guessed where we must be heading. After that, there wasn't much to say.

With every bend in the road, the inevitable became more and more inescapable. The more certain we became about where we were going, the more fully we realised how little we could do about it. The road that flowed from under the wheels of our truck was as implacable as the lines of destiny that the Fates were, in ancient times, believed to spin for every man. No mortal had the power to hold them back – or to alter their course.

The looks on the faces around me left me in no doubt that this eternal truth was as clearly understood by my companions as by any stoic Greek or noble Roman of antiquity. The same looks, however, told me that we were not quite as good as the Ancients were reputed to have been at accepting our lot with a shrug and a grin. In the end, we just sat there for mile after mile, making the worst of getting nowhere.

Lurching and groaning like a reluctant camel, the truck heaved its bulk up on to a kerb. It wasn't driving in anywhere. Just stopping in the street. The heavy doors grated open and the guard waved his rifle. We dropped out one by one, our clumsy boots clanging on the pavement like magnets on a gong. As we straightened up and stretched the stiffness out of our joints, we used the interlude before being rounded up to steal a good look at the outside world.

The morning was even brighter than it had seemed from inside our iron womb. The street was deserted. Sleepy. Hushed. Expectant. A border town in a Spaghetti Western in the last moments before showdown. A huge wall ran the whole length of the street. Smooth and featureless. Not a window or a gutter to be seen. Plastered from top to toe in plump and creamy stucco. Clean and gleaming. Spared, by some strange freak of chance, from the all-enveloping grime of Socialist Industrial expansion. The wall was warm and bland and not uninviting in the Panavision sunlight. An imposing composition. Stark and simple. Unexpectedly exotic. A wall fit for Tropic Isles or the High Sierras. It would have been no surprise to have seen the Jolly Roger flying from its ramparts or a sombrero in siesta against its base.

A growl from the guard broke the silence and the image faded. We all clattered round to the other side of the truck and lined up facing the broad arch of an iron-studded gateway of massive timbers that had been screened from our view behind the vehicle. Bolts thundered back and a small rectangle cut into the timber swung open. Lowering our heads and picking up our feet, we stepped inside.

An archway, wide and low, with a pleasant, Moorish air. God bless the Turks! Coolness and shade. And depth. The wall through which the archway ran was either very thick indeed or else it was not a wall at all, but some kind of building with no windows on the outside. The gatekeeper looked us sternly up and down. He must have been satisfied with what he saw, because he grunted to our guard, who grunted to us, who – without a single grunt between us – marched off and out into the sunshine.

An elegant and spacious square appeared before our eyes. Not in fact square in shape, it was really a large and noble oblong. The low building folded around its perimeter was plastered in the same material and painted the same colour as the outer wall. The main gate was now behind our backs. In front of us, at the far end of the square, we could see a small path leading off somewhere.

The impression of cloistered tranquillity was vividly reinforced by the neatly fitted carpet of pampered grass that filled the entire centre of the quadrangle. English lawn it certainly was not. But it was very decent grass all the same. Despite the parching heat, moreover, it was an arresting green. Lush and refreshing.

This was surrounded on all sides by a strip of pink dust, which was stamped firmly flat and which separated the green of the grass from the cream of the walls with satisfying crispness. The scene had the simple clarity of a Piero della Francesca and we studied its unruffled calm in unhurried silence.

It was obvious enough that we would not stay lined up at this end of the square for very long. It was equally obvious that it was likely to be some time before any of us passed this way again. The squalls and gales of arrests and trials, the buffeting gusts of vanishing faces and floundering hopes – even the stormy terrors of conviction – had all blown over. From now on it was going to be a long, slow haul. We were all newly outward bound and a lot of water was going to flow under our keels before we sighted land once more. I eased myself back under my cap and soaked in as much as I could. The sunlight. The green. The pink. The cream. The air. The open sky.

'Atten-*SHUN!*'

The command was firm and sharp, but carried no real sting. Our new guard was just telling us what to do, not what we were. He inspected us, nodded to his predecessor and took us over. We right-turned and swung off at an easy plod, tramping along the pink until we got three-quarters of the way up the right-hand strip.

'HALT!'

One at a time, we peeled off the line and ducked through a door in the cream and into an inner office. Here we handed over the odds and ends of personal belongings that had previously been deposited at the jails where we had been held in custody. It was a real pleasure to see my watch and shoes and wallet again, even though they were only passing from sack to locker, barely pausing long enough for me to acknowledge each in turn.

The officer filling in the blanks was a grizzled veteran close to retirement. He worked with a frown and a growl and there was nothing personal about his questions. He didn't even look up as he entered the appropriate answer in

125

the appropriate space on the appropriate form. Routine – nothing but.

It was comforting to note that there was as little of me in these personal details as there was of him. It struck me that all I had to do was match the tone of my replies to the timbre of his enquiries and we would be through before he looked up. I would be gone before he knew what the facts and figures on his form looked like in the flesh, and the guard in charge of the line outside would be ignorant of my vital statistics. I would slip through, if not entirely unnoticed, then at the very least incompletely catalogued.

I warmed to the thought. This was next door to being invisible. The officer's pen scratched on. He showed no sign of looking up. His sack-emptying assistant showed every sign of nodding off. The true significance of the scene flashed upon my inward eye. This was no low dungeon. This was a seasoned establishment with long traditions. They were used to handling all kinds of cases here, right up to the very highest. As high, indeed, I seemed to remember, as the present Head of State when he was in his Socialist Martyr phase. In a place like this, small fry like me would hardly rate a second glance.

The officer sniffed and squinted down his nose at the form in front of him.

Oh, joy! For him I didn't even rate a first glance! I felt an overpowering urge to reach out and point my index finger just where his nose would bump into its tip if he turned his head to look at me. The urge was so strong I had to grab hold of the rough cloth of my left trouser leg to keep my hand otherwise occupied and had to grasp so hard that I almost let out what might well have been considered to be an unseemly expulsion of air. I got a grip on myself and calmed down. After some moments, the danger of exposing myself passed and I felt safer than I had for weeks. If one couldn't quite manage being truly invisible, then surely the next best thing was utter insignificance.

Outside, there was a long and lovely wait while every single man went through the formalities. There was no talking. The guard was very relaxed, but very alert. In any case, we were all in the same mood and had no need of words. None of us had tasted so much fresh air or seen so many bright colours in ages and all of us were intent on making the most of it. It was the quiet concentration of emigrants watching the coastline of the old country slipping away over the horizon.

Stamping up the pink again, we turned left at the top right-hand corner. Left-right-left along the short, top end of the green. A glimpse of outhouses on our right. Flowerbeds in full bloom. Deep in the background a large building. Impressive proportions. Wrought-iron stairs. Glass portico. Rambling and stately as the mansion of some ante-bellum planter in the Deep South of the Empire of Rotting Capitalism. Its yellow stucco glowing like a sunlit buttercup, it disappeared over our right shoulders.

An old lag sprouted up from tending his blossoms. Tanned, leathery face. Weather-beaten furrows. Expressionless eyes. Taking his time. Not even a peek out of the corner of his eye as we passed. On to the left-hand corner, then down a quarter of the square to another arch. As wide and as low as the first, it looked deep enough to swallow a regiment.

'HALT!'

Our boots slammed together in surprising unison and we waited at the near side of the arch while a pack of important-looking uniforms swept out through the tunnel. As they drew level, our guard's arm swung smoothly into a soldierly salute. A large, florid face at the centre of the troop delayed returning his salute until the last possible moment and then instantly quickened his stride.

His attendants bobbed up and down like puppies as they scrambled to keep up with him. The pecking order of pips on shoulders and braid on caps dictated that the pups had to wait and see if Top Dog acknowledged our guard's salute before chancing their arms. Well-timed acceleration, however, had left them no time to follow suit without getting left behind. Doubtless, all omissions had been duly noted. Top Dog had served a clean ace.

Our guard's face remained impassive, betraying nothing. Quietly, he waited until the passage was free, let his arm swing back down to his side and herded us into the tunnel. It could not have been more than twenty-five metres long, but the air was noticeably chilly here and our footfalls rang distinctly hollow.

The space we came out into was really quite square and was considerably smaller and more shabby than the last. No grass here, just pink dust. Still settling from its recent trampling. The walls were higher and packed with small square windows, heavily barred. On each corner of the roof sat searchlights and machine guns. From behind us a heavy shadow fell over much of the compound, turning the pink of the dust into a sombre mauve. The machine guns shifted idly to get a better bead on us.

The Hungarians shuffled off to my left and disappeared through a massive door at the far end of the compound. The guard followed them in. I was left unattended and alone with the walls, the shadow and the silent eyes above me. Not having received any orders, I stayed put.

After watching the light cloud of fine, pink dust settle down again grain by grain, I studied the machine guns on the two corners of the roof facing me. They sat quite still. The muzzles of their barrels were neat circles that never wavered. They seemed to be trained on a spot that appeared to me to be remarkably close – if not, indeed, exactly spot on – to where I was standing. I began to feel disquiet.

Summoning up as much surreptitiousness as I could muster, I stole a glance out of the corner of my left eye. There was no one to my left. After a suitable pause, I stole a glance out of the corner of my right eye. My heart sank. My worst fears were confirmed. The compound contained no living being large enough to merit a bullet. Apart, regrettably, from me.

There could no longer be any reasonable doubt. The chest those machine guns were trained on was unmistakably mine. I stifled a sneeze and stayed as put as I possibly could. For what seemed a very long time, the machine guns remained perfectly still. So did I. So did time.

Suddenly, this eternal moment was cut short. A sound spilled out from nowhere. It echoed and re-echoed from wall to wall until it reverberated away over the rooftops. So unexpected was this interruption and so distorted was the noise that it took me some moments to realise what it was.

It was music and it was pumping out through one of those antediluvian public address systems that were standard

issue throughout army camps and other establishment insti-
tutions of many countries for many years after the Second
World War. They seemed to come with the Nissen huts,
barbed wire and concrete shower blocks. No matter how
much you tinkered with them, they always produced the
same sound. A No-Fidelity metallic jumble, full of wows,
flutters, feedback and interference of all kinds, decomposing
and re-composing in infinite and impenetrable permutations. No announcement or soundtrack had any hope of
survival. This example of this equipment sounded as if it
was, at last, squawking its last.

I had no clue as to what was being played, but the noise
of the system itself was familiar to me. I recognised it from
boarding-school days in East Anglia. The boys at my school
had always assumed the whole contraption was a special
scrambling device designed to prevent the enemy from
finding out what film we were watching. Even with the help
of moving pictures, the film was often over before we could
find out ourselves.

It took me several moments to identify the voice lurching
so painfully from note to note. I couldn't believe it! This
had to be some kind of stupendous practical joke! Was it
possible that Communism could have produced – in only
two decades – a mind at once cosmopolitan enough, devious
enough and painstaking enough to have perpetrated a trick
like this?

And if it had, how come said mind hadn't been called to
either some distant Gulag or the Politburo long ago? And
what about my utter insignificance? Was that also just another
illusion? But even if it was, how could I have come to warrant

130

a salute like this? And most unbelievable of all, how could such a recording possibly have got here just in time to make this moment?

These questions and more I turned over and over in my mind, while the public address system twisted the sound round and round in my ears. But there was no denying the fact of the sound. It was definitely and excruciatingly here. The more I pieced the tortured phrases together, the less I could doubt the result. Crackling through the rarefied air of mid-afternoon – in the mid nineteen sixties – in middle Europe – behind the Iron Curtain – was none other – than Frank Sinatra! Heavily disguised soundwise, of course, and not yet the eternal Minstrel of the Lonely Heart that he would one day become. But, nevertheless, certainly from a Kremlin point of view, already high on the Soviet black list of major Capitalist-Imperialist-Hyenas of Decadent-Western-Musical-Brainwashing.

The number he was singing was, I need hardly add, although quite new then, already, quite clearly, not exactly destined to become a Kremlin evergreen.

I was sure of this because, by now, I was quite certain that the song being extruded from the melody-mincer was that outrageously appropriate number 'Come Fly with Me'! I stole a peek at the three machine guns I could take in without actually turning round, in the hope that some non-regulation grin or twinkle or twitch might give me a clue as to whether all this was deliberate or just sheer coincidence. No muzzle betrayed a tremor, nor any stony face a smile.

It dawned on me that the most likely explanation for this situation was that the old scrambling device was still as impenetrable as ever. I became absolutely certain that even if there was anyone else within earshot who understood English, no one could have the foggiest notion as to what we were actually listening to – no one, indeed, but me.

Suddenly, I found this very comforting. Clearly, if no one knew what we were listening to, my cover was still intact. I was still insignificant and very probably utterly so. In which case, no one could attach any meaning whatsoever to any expression that might cross my face. So I could rest the iron mask for a while without risking perforation.

Throwing caution to the winds, I settled down to wallowing in the song on my own and in perfect privacy. For all the world as if I was playing my personal record player, after enjoying a nice, unlimited-hot-water shower, on a quiet Sunday morning in my flat back in West London.

To me, Frank had never sounded more twentieth century, nor the band more all-American. Even the scratching, the hiss, the flutter, the wow and the feedback came from the sunny side of the street. I felt as cheerful as a GI putting in at a cushy, overseas posting. Devil-may-care, I shifted from foot to foot, nodded my head to the rhythm and even worked my jaws, pretending to be chewing gum – all quite openly.

Who could ask for anything more? Practically invisible, not behind bars, not under guard and, courtesy of Ultra-Low-Fidelity sound, intimately in touch with the Other Side! Right under the noses of loaded Marxist-Leninist machine guns – all on the same day!

I didn't feel in the least bit tired any more.

# 4

# A Striped Bow Tie

Karl was born in *Old* Hungary. That is to say, the place where he entered this world was located on a strip of land that had been known since Roman times as the 'Partium'. For almost a thousand years, this Partium lay in between what is drawn, on most present-day maps, as Hungary and what, on most present-day maps, is no longer drawn at all – that is to say, Transylvania. Although his family had lived inside Magyar territory since time immemorial, the blood that flowed in Karl's veins was pure Teuton.

However, he was a grown man before he got any nearer Berlin than Budapest, so Karl remained a chip that had landed quite far from the old block. On the other hand, having first seen the light of day in the last year of the First World War, he was also a relatively new chip. In character, however, he was a genuine Prussian of the Old School.

His family was one of the many pillars of solid German stock that had always held 'Hard Work' and 'Common

Decency' sacred. Such families had kept economic life going, throughout Mittel Europa and as far afield as distant parts of tsarist Russia, for centuries. Generation after generation had stiffened the backbones of the bourgeoisie from the Black Sea to the Baltic.

In certain regions, such as Transylvania, for example, they had been an established part of the social fabric ever since they were imported to repopulate villages and towns decimated by the ravages of the Mongols – mainly, the fabled 'Golden Horde'. This made these Germans considerably more native to that region than the Romanians who now ran it and who were presently eking out their version of an economy by making life as hard as possible for ethnic Germans and then selling them off to the Federal Republic for a going rate of about 12,000 D-marks a head.

While Karl was growing up, Germany went from abject defeat to rampant inflation to National Socialism. Hungary, meanwhile, went nowhere and had a very hard time doing that. What was left of Karl's country lay flatter than its Great Plain, the proverbially flat Puszta. His compatriots – both those inside Hungary's new borders and those stranded outside them – ached beneath the crushing weight of the Treaty of Trianon and its WWII sequel.

After five years of Romanian 'administration' (according to some commentators, Trianon did not, actually, give them the right to annex Transylvania – they were merely supposed to administer it as a more or less autonomous territory), Karl's family decided, having spent seven centuries on the same soil, that the time had come to up roots and retreat back over the new Hungarian border.

Bilingual in Hungarian and German, fluent in Romanian and bursting with the vigour of youth, Karl went to school in a land-locked rump of a country run by an Admiral who declared himself to be a Regent, made no secret of his 'irredentism' and, even at the height of Nazi power, fished for an alliance with Britain.

Apropos of this last, Hungary's Admiral seemed to be deterred neither by the fact that Britain was one of the co-authors of the Treaty that had well and truly pollarded his country nor by the fact that 'Perfidious Albion' also bore much responsibility for the straightjacket out of which the Germans were at that time well and truly bursting. When toppling the bloody Communist Regime of 1919, Horthy was rumoured to have got help from – or via – a certain shadowy Brigadier Maurice, reputed to be an agent of British Intelligence. This might offer some explanation for the old Admiral's prejudice in favour of the English. As a Royalist, he might also have felt a good deal of sympathy for the greatest of the Constitutional Monarchies, upon which the sun of Empire had, at that time, not yet set. On the other hand, as an old salt suffering from lack of access to the ocean wave, he might simply have found the siren song of the sea – as rendered by the descendants of Drake and Nelson – irresistible.

Unfathomable as his Admiral may have been, Karl was not the boy to let his head get muddled by such quixotries. His motherland might well be Magyar and he might well feel the pain of her losses as his own, but his clear, grey eyes were firmly fixed on the upraised arm of an ex-house-painter who was leading his Fatherland from one resounding triumph to the next. While the Admiral dillied and dallied, the house-painter redrew the map of Europe. While the Allies hummed and hawed, the Germans got on with the job.

The point was not lost on Karl. As, indeed, it was not lost on the vast majority of the German electorate in the heyday of the Third Reich. As far as Karl was concerned, the most natural progression in the world was that the two countries should go forward arm in arm and side by side. In his experience, which was quite extensive for his years, the world was a tough place and Adolf Hitler an unusually forthright and far-sighted man facing up to the harsh realities of existence with refreshing directness and commendable vigour. Many years later, when his experience was very extensive indeed, he was still faithful to the convictions of his youth.

In the Second World War, Karl had served the cause with might and main. The outcome had been a bitter disappointment to him. After the German surrender, he stayed on in what was now 'West' Germany and became a spy. While ostensibly serving new masters, Karl kept his opinions intact and largely to himself. By the time our paths crossed he had the patter down to a fine art. When pressed on a specific point, he would express himself with disarming charm. All sweet reason, but firm as steel.

The whims of history had forced Karl to shelve the banner for which he had been fighting. (Temporarily, of course.) But they had not forced him to shelve the banner he was fighting against. The Dragon of Communism was clearly in his sights. No sacrifice was too great in the campaign to bring it down. And Karl's particular sacrifice was by no means negligible. He was doing sixteen years for espionage and had so far served ten. Like most spies, he had also been sentenced to deportation as soon as he had done his time. So in his case, remission was not applicable. It was going to be sixteen years to the last gasp. No quarter asked or given. It was a state of war.

Karl conducted his campaign from the fortress of a will as indomitable as that of Milton's Lucifer. No less unshakeable in the righteousness of his cause than the fallen Archangel, he developed his strategy with the impeccable logic of a Grand Master. He calculated that the worst his enemy could do to him was to kill him. If, however, he valued his life less than his enemy did, then this threat would be rendered empty.

So he came to feel – to the very marrow of his bones – that if the Authorities fell into the trap of killing him, he would win three battles at a single stroke. First, whatever plot his opponents were hatching against him would be stopped dead at his death. Second, whatever time he still had left to do when he died would instantly be commuted into remission from his sentence. And, last but by no means least, he would finally be granted the supreme honour of joining all those comrades-in-arms who had been more fortunate than he and had fallen on the field of battle. His victory would then be complete and glorious and he would rest in eternal peace with the clearest of consciences.

Having thus nullified his enemy's ultimate weapon, Karl was free to concentrate on the details of day-to-day combat. His main effort here centred on being a shining example of everything he stood for. He felt that if he could keep this up through the worst that his enemies could throw at him, then his very existence alone would be a mortifying humiliation for them. Every aspect of his appearance and behaviour was, therefore, employed to this end.

He was of medium height and slim build with hair that was still dark, and had steely grey eyes that were quick and lively but held on a tight rein by rigid self-discipline. Somehow, his hair was always neatly trimmed and his moustache clipped to the most demanding military specifications. Furthermore, he never seemed to appear unshaven, while his convict's uniform of striped denim actually seemed to fit. He had even succeeded in engineering a shine on the archaic and formless bundles of untanned hide that did service on our feet in place of boots.

Naturally, his complexion was paler than it might have been in less sheltered climes but, unlike most of us, he radiated health. Of course, he had his own routine of special exercises which, it goes without saying, he kept up without fail, day in and day out.

So successful was this regimen that imprisonment seemed to be seasoning his constitution as if it were prime timber. His body gave the impression of getting tougher and more resilient with each passing year and more and more impervious to outside influences of any kind.

Towards warders, he maintained a manner of detached and often amused contempt, insulated beneath an armour of punctilious correctness that was both shock- and fool-proof. To the rest of us, he was a stern but understanding superior, commanding respect from even the least kindred of spirits. Whatever anyone thought of his political convictions, there was no denying the way he carried his sentence. At times, it was difficult to believe that he had already kept this up for a whole ten years. On the other hand, anyone could see that he might well keep his colours flying for another six.

The screws had long since given up trying to dominate him. Indeed, most of them had even given up pretending to be his equals. As he remarked once with a steely twinkle in his eye, 'When it comes to years of service, I'm a long way senior to most. And those poor screws who've been here longer than me – all three of them – look burnt out. Not a spark left. They'll soon be saving the Government a lot of pension money. I don't expect them to live long once they leave here.'

None of the staff could match either the force of his personality or the speed and adroitness with which he dispatched anyone who tried to bully or humiliate him. By the time I had the opportunity to see him in action, his technique was masterly. He never lost his temper and was never quite reportable as insolent. Nevertheless, all the screws to a man had come to feel in their bones that, aside from the purely fortuitous and probably temporary imbalance in their relative positions on the social scale, none of them rated high enough even to tie his boot thongs. Not one of them could handle him face to face and none of them could quite put their finger on why this should be so. Consequently, most of them had arrived at the subconscious assumption that Karl really was, in some undefinable but nevertheless undeniable manner, superior. Whether this was true or not, it worked.

From this point, it was but a short step to grudging respect and even admiration. It had become established practice that when the Authorities wished to communicate with Karl, some screw or other dutifully delivered the message. They were equally dutiful running in the opposite direction.

This is not to say that Karl succeeded in avoiding punishment. Indeed, this was not even his aim. Far from it. Punishment was, in fact, an essential element in the 'Master Plan'. It was the springboard for counter-attack. '*Der Bumerang-Effekt*' was what the German contingent called it.

This had been evolved over a number of years, during which Karl had established by repeated experiment that the Powers That Be were never going to be quite dense enough to grant him the privilege of martyrdom. Since the ultimate Big Stick was thus out of bounds, Karl calculated that he could win the next round, too. All he had to do was prove that he was impervious to pain, hunger, thirst, exhaustion and anything else that could be thrown at him.

To this end, he subjected the prison Governor's office to a ceaseless barrage of strategically timed and ingeniously irritating messages and demands. These were varied by riots, disturbances, fasts and other provocations. All were designed with Hungarian inventiveness and carried out with German precision.

Karl had spent hundreds of days in solitary confinement with no sanitation, no light, no clue as to when he might get out, and every dietary variation from bread one day and water the next to nothing at all till whenever. Each time, he emerged paler, dirtier, skinnier and bloodier. But quite unbowed.

Though the opposition tried various forms of beating, they stopped short of such refinements as the nail-plucking and tooth-pulling that were so fashionable in the fifties. Karl explained this by pointing out that it was, as usual, just a question of doing your homework and understanding your enemy.

The key was that the present Head of State had only been in prison for four years, instead of fourteen, like his predecessor-but-one. So his wounds had closed more quickly and he had fewer scores to settle now that he was out and on top. It was also common knowledge that he was by nature unusually lukewarm about the physical measures so enjoyed by his predecessors. This tended to take the edge off staff enthusiasm.

Furthermore, most of the old guard that had rendered such sterling service when the Party's power was young had either cleared out during the exodus of 'fifty-six or fallen by the wayside in the clean-up that followed, or reached retirement age. The bulk of what was left was a younger generation that was woefully short on the kind of experience that was indispensable for any serious torturer.

This was backed up by the overview. Signs had been filtering down for some time that the regime was trying to acquire a more humane image. While these signs did not signify anything as radical as the turning of a new page, they did give reason to believe that the top dogs no longer felt able to be quite so free with their old tricks as they used to be. Especially if there was any chance that news of what they had been up to might get broadcast back into the country via their bête noire, Radio Free Europe.

Another consideration reining in the old ways was the simple possibility that the scalpel might slip. This could be inconvenient, since if the patient failed to recover, a pawn at the very least would be lost from the store the Communists always kept for swapping with the Other Side. And since no one could tell for sure which particular pawn the opposition would fancy in any given deal, it was best not to deplete your stocks unnecessarily. (The 'Other Side' was, of course, us. So I couldn't help wondering occasionally what *we*, in the meantime, were doing for pawns.) Anyway, on account of such factors and dizzying combinations thereof, Karl didn't lose any limbs and the beatings achieved just about as much and as little as the solitary.

The little was what the Prison Authorities got. A little target practice, a little steam let off and a little blooding of new recruits. Karl's team, on the other hand, got the much. In the first place, the respect in which the rank and file of convicts held Karl rose to new and gratifying heights. In the second place, the confidence with which the screws approached him fell to new and even more gratifying lows. Punishment had become a kind of promotion and Karl had reached the rank of Field Marshal at the very least. By common consent, he was the undisputed Commander-in-Chief of our wing.

'*Der Bumerang-Effekt*' had also produced another result, which, though perhaps less immediately eye-catching, was arguably of even greater importance than Karl's promotions. It did not hail the hero anew each time he returned from the front, but it accrued steadily year after year, like interest. While the odds might, by any conventional assessment at least, still be in favour of the home side, a subtle shift in the whole pattern of play had taken place. Without anyone – including even Karl – being able to pinpoint exactly when or how it had happened, the initiative had changed hands. Having secured his position among the prisoners and undermined the effectiveness of the screws, Karl had at some point or other been able to go on the offensive.

He now used disturbances actually to manipulate and, to a surprising degree, control what went on in our part of the jail. His objectives were varied. Sometimes, all he was after was a break in routine monotony. At other times, he might be changing men round between cells, enlisting the allegiance of a newcomer or carrying the propaganda war to the enemy. But always, his every move had purpose.

It was never just a question of keeping our own morale up and the guards of our guards down. News of what went on in our wing – the HQ of the 'Foreign Legionnaires' – leaked out to the rank-and-file Hungarians who filled the rest of the prison. Karl was well aware that they followed every move he made as avidly as football fans follow the moves of their favourite striker.

He also knew that men were never more susceptible than when they were in despair; that he had his audience entirely, exclusively and continually to himself; that the comings-in and goings-out of the ever-changing tide of Hungarians was as ceaseless as the ebb and flow of the sea itself, which meant that news of his exploits could and would travel far and wide, and that the consequences of his machinations bid fair to being little short of incalculable. This did not displease him. Karl still took what he called his 'wider responsibilities' very seriously indeed.

Higher-ups and lowly warders had both become uncomfortably aware of this situation. As, indeed, it had always been intended that they should. The uncertainty and suspicion with which they viewed Karl and his manoeuvres – not least when he seemed not to be up to anything – frequently blossomed into outright paranoia. The more they tried to work out what he was really up to, the longer their reaction time became. The longer their reaction time became, the less effective were their counter-measures.

Karl, meanwhile, went from strength to strength. His understanding of his opponents and his anticipation of their moves became uncanny. This left him free to devote less and less time to thinking about what they might be doing and more and more time to devising ever newer and more subtle schemes for their discomfiture.

Nevertheless, he was careful not to let success go to his head. He never lost sight of the fact that his opponents were operating from strength, while he was manoeuvring from weakness. Yet he remained firmly convinced that this very weakness was his strength. For, as he never tired of pointing out to us, he had nothing to lose but his head, while his antagonists had a whole world of other things to worry about.

It was a classical strategic situation, he insisted, and cited many examples from Nature, Ancient History, World Literature, Folklore, Homer, the Bible, the Koran, the French Revolution, *Mein Kampf*, Current Affairs, Military Theory and Hollywood to prove his point.

All his time, which was plenty, and all his intelligence, which was also far from scant, was devoted to mulling over every conceivable possibility from every conceivable angle. Somebody once urged him to hold his horses for a bit for fear the Authorities might decide to pull the thorn out of their flesh and simply send him packing to another prison.

'What a good idea!' chuckled Karl. 'But there's not the slightest chance of that, worse luck! No. They've figured that one out all right. If they ship me out, I start up again somewhere else. Meanwhile, back here, the memory lingers on and some of the boys are now beginning to get the hang of tactics. Also, they're getting pretty fit. I've been training them for years. So no peace and quiet here and big trouble elsewhere. More eyes seeing, more ears hearing, more heads thinking, more worms turning. In the end, they have to send me to another prison – and maybe a boy or two from here, too. It becomes a pincer movement and then we get sent to yet another prison and then another one and so on. I still have six years left. In six years I could infect a lot of prisons. And this is the only place they keep heavy Westerners. Everywhere else, it's all Hungarians and other sub-cultures. I'd be out of quarantine. Just think of the information, the propaganda, the contacts! My God, it would be a national epidemic! But there's not the slightest chance of that happening, I'm afraid. These Commies are dumb. But not quite *that* dumb. They won't give me a free tour of the entire underground country. I am in for spying, you know. No, they'll swallow the bile and contain the pain here.'

Karl's tone was sometimes flippant. But his position had not been bought cheaply. He had paid for it with real courage, undeniable suffering, endless patience and year after year of his life. Many of us in the West – the territory of the Allies in the last World War plus Austria and the Western part of Germany – had grown up in an atmosphere coloured by the belief that all Germans were Nazis and all Nazis were Baddies, Brutes, Beyond The Pale and totally Unthinkable. All-purpose villains for all seasons.

Yet if you took a good look at Karl and then took an equally good look at his opposition, it was hard to see how they were the better men. Of course, it was possible to argue that his burning conviction in the rightness of his cause was misguided. Also that a Fanatic is still a Fanatic, no matter how brave he or she may seem to be. Nevertheless, no matter how ill-gotten Karl's coin may have been, there was no denying that he had certainly paid his dues.

His war, moreover, was far from over. The enemy still held an overwhelming territorial advantage from which it was unlikely to be dislodged. There was also the inescapable fact of his remaining six years. On the other hand, no matter how much he tried to deny it, Karl had already held out under fire more than twice as long as the Führer himself. A comparison Karl found entirely odious, of course.

The High Command was stationed in a comparatively spacious, three-man bunker strategically located in the centre of the wing. The benefits of this arrangement extended well beyond mere comfort. Since the only two points of access to the row of cells containing his HQ were the stairs at the opposite ends of the iron catwalk outside them, Karl had the earliest available warning of any approach by the enemy and the longest time to take evasive action before the enemy reached his position. Thus Karl was as safe as he could possibly be against being surprised by a random raid. The same strategic siting also gave him the best lines of communication in both directions.

Karl had built up his own General Staff. This was an elite corps of handpicked German-Hungarians. They were, in the main, large, solid, agricultural types, also in for spying. Most of them, however, were so straightforward and unimaginative that I often wondered how their previous employers had expected them to do a job which had always seemed to me to call for at least *some* degree of deviousness. The only explanation I could think of was that they were intended to serve as pawns.

Whatever they might have lacked as spies, however, they were made to measure for Karl. Working for him they were energetic, efficient and loyal. Nothing the Authorities could do seemed to shake this allegiance. Which was not entirely surprising as Karl had, after all, given them a job, a cause and a reason for living when they had reached rock bottom and had also shown them how to carry the massive weight of their sentences with dignity and honour. Because of him they felt more like men and less like pawns. All that Officialdom was able to muster against this, was stone walls and punishment.

The General Staff gave Karl unhesitating obedience and affectionate admiration. They called him 'Iron Charlie' and believed every word he said without question. His men were posted at key points throughout the wing so that he could get things done quickly and neatly. He shared his HQ with a taciturn hulk with spade-sized hands, who seemed to be both bodyguard and batman, and the soft remains of someone known as 'Rotting Franz'.

Franz was a shortish fellow with blond hair, a boyish smile and a tan. Or rather his smile *seemed* boyish and his skin *looked* tanned. It came as something of a shock to look at Franz more closely and see that his boyish smile flitted on and off his lips without ever reaching his baby-blue eyes and that his tan was more unhealthy than the most deathly of pallors.

He had a habit of holding his hands clasped together in front of him with the fingers firmly entwined and rubbing them incessantly against each other like a house-fly cleaning its mandibles. Most of the skin had been worn away and the flesh of his fingers was not only raw but also putrefying. There was no way to stop his interminable rubbing short of cutting off his hands. No one had gone that far yet, so he just rubbed and rubbed and rubbed.

He also suffered from severe digestive problems and ate very little. He found it difficult to concentrate for long enough to finish chewing anything anyway. His tan was neither dirt nor sunburn, but some kind of fungoid infection. The stench he gave off from all sources was permanent and sickening. He muttered at random in snatches of French, German and Hungarian, occasionally reaching patches of clarity during which he would converse with startling calmness and lucidity.

Apparently, he had also been a spy once, though no one seemed to know when or for whom. All that was really left now of whoever he had once been was a mop of surprisingly youthful blond hair. His sentence was twelve years. He had served eight. No one expected him to get through another four. He was taken out of the cell at regular intervals for some kind of medical treatment. At least, that was the official story. Karl had won him in his last campaign. This had been mounted in response to breaches in security.

For some time, events had revealed that the Authorities were getting better informed about what was being said and done in the wing than could reasonably be put down to normal seepage. Suspicions had narrowed down to Franz, who was at that time in a different cell from Karl. He was not thought to be a deliberate informer. Not unless he had unimaginable talent as an actor, coupled with the dedication of a saint. One look at his fingers and a single whiff of his stink was enough to convince anyone of that.

What it all boiled down to was a matter of jelly. That, over the years, was what Franz had become. If prodded long enough and hard enough, he would split open and spill out anything that happened to be inside. It was even possible that if someone learned just how to prod and where, he might spill whatever someone was after with some degree of predictability.

On the face of it, Franz did not look as though he could contain anything worth much prodding. From time to time, however, his usually incoherent ramblings would coalesce into the most unexpected renderings of conversations preserved verbatim or reports of events replayed down to the last detail.

When the tally of Franz's changes of address reached a total too high to be put down to mere serendipity, Karl decided it was time to act. The permutations on who was in which cell with whom had evolved to a point at which there were only two new Franz combinations left.

If our blond jelly really was the leak, the moment of truth had arrived. So Karl gave the word. Orders were accordingly disobeyed, disrespectful remarks duly dropped, warders suitably jostled – with everyone in the central cells involved with impeccable timing and clockwork precision.

There were only two three-man cells in the wing. They were next door to each other and right in the middle. One made as good an HQ as the other. So it didn't matter to Karl which of these he was in. What did matter, however, was that one of his companions – in whichever cell he occupied – should be Franz. He could then keep him under permanent observation and, in the fullness of time, most of what was left inside that blond head would have been put there by Karl himself.

One hundred and ten days after the start of this operation, the last to emerge from solitary confinement were Karl, his bodyguard and three retainers. And surprise, surprise, who should be returning at just that precise moment from medical treatment so extended that his old bunk had in his absence – oh, so unfortunately – been allocated to someone else? Why, who but Rotting Franz, of course!

Six men. Two three-man cells. Franz could be billeted with either two high-ranking Staff Officers – or the Commander-in-Chief. Karl had never, even for a single moment of his one hundred and ten days, been in the slightest doubt as to which temptation the Authorities would find irresistible.

Peace and quiet had reigned for some time. One morning, we all filed out of our cells as usual to be inspected, counted and lined up for going down to the yard. Karl appeared at the head of his retinue as usual. As usual, Franz was immediately behind him, with the hulking bodyguard bringing up the rear. The bodyguard was silent and watchful – as usual. But amid all this normality – there was one thing that stood out like the proverbial sore thumb.

At the collar of his convict's tunic, Karl sported an absurd and unmissable object – a very large bow tie made of the same striped denim as our uniforms. The duty guard was a dark-jowled bruiser who had only just arrived from another prison and had not yet had time to clock up any experience under fire. He took in the bow tie for a long moment. Karl took him in for just as long. Eventually, Blue Chin could hold his larynx back no longer and snapped, 'What's that?'

Inclining his head courteously, Karl replied, 'With respect. If the officer could be more specific?'

'More what?'

Karl let his gaze get a couple of notches more penetrating as he allowed the guard's ignorance to sink in.

'What – exactly – do you wish to know? Sir.'

'That. On your neck. What is it?'

Karl's tone became distinctly drier. 'Do you mean my skin?'

'No, no! That!' And the screw jerked a stubby finger at the bow tie.

Karl fixed the indicating digit with a look of distaste: 'I'd say it was nicotine, Sir. What else could turn it so brown?'

The gangway rocked with laughter, while the screw turned this way and that, hardly knowing where to look next.

'Young man,' said Karl kindly in a convenient pause in the merriment, 'what you are probably trying to ask me is – what is *this*?' And he adjusted the bow tie for emphasis.

'Yes, yes!' blurted Five O'Clock Shadow, relieved to get off the hook at last.

'Why, don't you know?' replied Karl mildly. 'It's a bow tie.'

Applause burst out on cue, dashing the beefy guard's hopes of an early peace. Unable to beat a retreat, the fellow became even more confused than he already was and his basic instincts got the better of him. Throwing caution to the wind, he snarled, 'It's not regulation issue!'

'Perhaps not,' replied Karl, still more mildly. 'But it is customary to dress for important occasions.'

'Important occasions? What's so important about now?' our man ground out with dark distrust.

'You are Hungarian, I presume?'

'Hungarian!' bellowed the screw, falling in head first. 'Hungarian! What the hell do you mean, you kraut? Of course I'm Hungarian! There's no Hungarian more Hungarian than me and don't you forget it!'

'Then I need hardly remind you what day this is.'

'Day?'

Karl skewered the man with a look of withering disdain. 'Why, man, surely you can't have forgotten that today is the twenty-eighth anniversary of our glorious re-occupation of the sub-Carpathian Provinces stolen from us by the cowardly Czechs?'

The screw stared at Karl in bewilderment, while gales of laughter buffeted his ears.

'Surely you remember? No true Hungarian could ever forget. Ungvár, Munkács, Beregszász, Szolyva, Ilosva, Huszt …'

Another voice snatched up the refrain, ' … Tecsó, Rahó, Késmark. Lőcse. Kassa! Pozsony! Újvidék! Temesvár! Arad! Kolozsvár! Nagyvárad.'

It was Franz. He was standing stiffly to attention and chanting the names of the many once proud Hungarian cities that had been chopped off the nation by the treaties of Trianon. The litany had crossed most of Hungary's present-day borders, got well into double figures and showed no signs of slackening when Karl's bodyguard slipped his arm solicitously round the chanting blond and began murmuring soothing nothings into his ear as if comforting a delirious child. At this, Franz clicked his heels with surprising force, raised his arm in an unmistakable and entirely illegal salute and burst into song with the passionate intensity usually reserved, in these latitudes, for 'The Marseillaise'.

What he was singing, however, was a rousing marching song from the heyday of resurgent Hungarian Nationalism in the late nineteen thirties. Very moving, very unsocialist and very much against regulations. The screw didn't know where to put himself.

Being at heart a Hungarian, the lost cities and the lively song hit him smack in his spiritual solar plexus. He went red in the face and could hardly stop himself being swept off his feet by a wave of emotion.

Being, at the same time, a paid servant of the Hungarian People's Republic, this was the last thing he could be seen doing. Conflicting emotions raced through him like rip tides. At one moment he looked as if he were on the point of returning Franz's salute. At the next, he seemed about to punch Franz in the face.

The entire wing fell about, hooting with laughter. Meanwhile Franz, entirely oblivious to everything around him, carried on saluting and singing like a true-blue patriot.

Standing beside me, one of Karl's henchmen clutched his sides, shrieking with merriment through streaming tears.

'Iron Charlie!' he croaked. 'Iron Charl-he-he-hee! Breaking in the new boy! With a striped bow tie! A striped bo-how-tie! Oh, Go-hod in Heaven! A stra-hiped bo-how-ta-hie ...'

The light in his eyes showed quite plainly that this moment would carry him over many a long month, no matter what happened next.

# 5

# The Twins of God

They arrived right out of the blue one bright, sunny morning. So meek and mild, so clean-cut, so upstanding and stepping out so neat and nimble (and oh, so self-conscious about it all!) that they might well have been parading in their Sunday best instead of sporting convict stripes.

As like as two peas in a pod, their shape, size, weight and colouring conformed exactly to every known spec for all-American seedlings of purest Pilgrim stock. They sprang from Idaho or Utah or some such upright and God-fearing Garden of the Great Far Eden.

'Students of Divinity', they proclaimed themselves to be, before bursting loud and long into Hymns of Praise, interspersed with Joyous Scripture. Their minds were unsullied by knowledge of even one word of the Hungarian language – and were, thus, immune to even the possibility of corruption through the insidious medium of the serpent's tongue. They shared, moreover, the impenetrable shield of a sublime faith in the utter inviolability of their souls.

This innocence was not, however, simply an instrument of defence. From every pore of their unblemished skins poured that most offensive of all auras – the unshakeable certitude of being absolutely in THE RIGHT and exclusively in on THE TRUTH. The screws, exposed to what seemed to them to be never-ending earfuls of incomprehensible tirades, quickly gave them up as a lost cause and flung them into the first cell to hand.

This only had room for two and was already occupied. The sitting tenant was our Trusty. His name was Heinz and he was by nature an accommodating chap. His mind had for some time been concentrated on earning full remission and getting through what he hoped might turn out to be the last year of a very lean seven. Hence his natural desire to please had been rendered even more servile by his desire to avoid blotting his copybook in any way whatsoever.

Keeping his nose clean meant a lot more to him than simply keeping his remission. He was a bona fide German from the wrong republic, so he was, of course, a nasty Nazi. On the other hand, he had not a drop of Hungarian blood in his veins, so he was not a traitor-to-the-Motherland nor a viper-in-the-bosom nor anything similarly unspeakable. Most mitigating of all, his sins were merely criminal. So he did not have the Deportation Order out against him that would certainly have been hanging over his head had he been a spy or otherwise political.

This meant, in the first place, that he was of no value as a pawn and would, therefore, not find his release delayed indefinitely on the off chance that he might prove useful in some swap or other. In the second place, it also meant that when he did, eventually, get out he would *not* – automatically – be dumped over the border.

All this was very important to Heinz, because somewhere along a long line of creative manoeuvres in the alternative economy, he'd struck up a relationship with a local beauty. His creative manoeuvres had left him stranded down here with us, but the local beauty had stood by him. These unexpected twists of fate had sobered him up so thoroughly that he had rediscovered his faith in humanity and was all set to go straight when he got out.

Heinz's heart yearned to settle down in a little nest with his little wife – in Hungary. The Federal Republic was out of the question, of course, since it was not the policy of the People's Republic to let any of their people pop over to the decadent West at will. Even athletes and actors with impeccable working-class backgrounds and bona fide invitations or participating in major events, festivals or performances usually had to leave behind hostages – babies and very young children were best – and even then, they would have to be accompanied by trustworthy Party cadres. For Heinz, it was either Socialism with wife or Freedom without.

Heinz had made his choice and now the great day was practically in sight, each passing moment of each passing hour made him more and more aware that all it needed was one slip – just one foot wrong – and his remission could evaporate into thin air. Equally swiftly – he was not, after all, Hungarian – a Deportation Order could materialise. So at this particular point in time, the last thing that interested our Trusty was taking chances.

157

Just one short year away, Heinz could see the light gleaming at the end of the tunnel and he was bending over backwards to make sure of reaching it. He agreed whole-heartedly with anything and everyone, prostrated himself beneath any punishment in ecstasies of submission, jumped to obey any command, revelled in abuse, sprinted from chore to chore when anybody else would have walked and was generally winning hands down.

Heinz had enough charm and had done enough hard time for no one to resent him having become a Trusty, nor to harbour a grudge against him for being so well on the way to getting out so soon. However, the continuation of both these desirable situations depended quite as much on maintaining favour with Karl as on keeping in with the screws. So Heinz's spirit of cooperation was as all embracing as his trips around the prison were frequent. No matter who called upon him to do no matter what, Heinz was more than happy to oblige.

His Hungarian was very serviceable and he welcomed every duty the guards dumped on him with a servility that would have done credit to a Western politician currying votes. Fortunately for him, it had entirely escaped official notice that wallowing in humiliation was the key to Heinz spending far less time inside his cell than out.

For several days now, he had been luxuriating in his cell alone. This perk had blown his way because his previous cell-mate had been seized by a sudden phobia against uniforms, which had manifested itself in an irresistible urge to piss on them at every opportunity. Urine-soaked guards had remained steadfastly unamused and said cell-mate had been rapidly removed to solitary accommodation in which urinating in any direction without drenching oneself was practically impossible. No replacement had yet been found and we'd all read the situation as being a kind of bonus to Heinz for being such a good boy.

When the bonus stretched into a week of privacy, even Heinz's head started turning. Seized by something very akin to hubris, he started dropping epigrams about his recipe for success as an underdog. Indeed, he more or less insinuated that he had evolved a sort of Credo. Apparently, he expected *us* to believe that *he* believed that if you learned to rejoice in humiliation you would be delivered from feeling humiliated; that if you really enjoyed insults, they were no longer really insulting; that if you could match guffaws with whoever was laughing himself silly at your misfortunes, they'd soon stop finding you so funny; that if you could feel gratitude in direct proportion to your degradation, even the most nauseating of tasks or situations would soon become remarkably exhilarating.

It was all, he maintained, simply a matter of seeing things in their true light. Normal human responses, he insisted, were not normal at all. They were merely reflexes conditioned into you as part of being brought up according to the accumulated conventions of society. If you could get conditioned, he argued, you could also get un-conditioned. All it needed was the right motivation. Freed from the burdens of unnecessary and useless reactions, your soul felt a lot lighter, time passed a lot quicker and you could keep your mind on whatever mattered to you most.

He called this philosophy, 'Transcendental Masochism' or 'Turning Both Cheeks to Let the Enemy Bugger You Until

He Drops from Exhaustion, Boredom or Satiety, Whichever Comes First'. We all saw his point, but drew the line when he suggested he had arrived at this revelation via the New Testament and reflecting on the life of Christ.

Everybody knew full well that Heinz had been born as resilient as a rubber cheque. It was simply his nature to bounce back on to his feet no matter how hard he fell – that was just our Heinz. Divine Revelation had nothing to do with it. Besides, others had arrived at conclusions that were no less practical than his without needing to invoke such an obvious *deus ex machina*. Heinz, however, stuck to his guns with a straight face. So when the Twins landed in his cell, we all thought it was pretty much poetic justice.

'Talk about the Holy Twinity!' lamented Heinz only a few mornings later. 'You know they practically sleep hand in hand? Wouldn't hear of taking the bunks and being more comfortable than me, but neither could bear to suffer less than the other, so they both ended up on the floor. And you should hear the noise! Prayers, hymns, psalms, sermons morning, noon and night! I can't understand a word, thank God! But the non-stop boompety-boomp and natter-natter-natter are killing me! If I couldn't get out to scrub some floors or do a bit of decent grovelling every now and again, I don't know what I'd do!'

We couldn't help grinning at the length of Heinz's usually cheery face. Our grins stiffened quite swiftly, however, as the Twins began feeling their calling ever more strongly and set about the salvation of the rest of their fellow men.

They had no idea where they were, who was who or what was what. This deterred them not a whit. They assumed spiritual responsibility en bloc for the entire wing. Guided by the conviction that no soul was so black as to be utterly beyond Redemption, their boundless Mercy embraced even the screws. As their linguistic endowments stopped short of actual dialogue, the Twins spread the Word by gesture and mime.

Touching tableaux proliferated all over the compound as they clasped convicts by the hand or clapped caring arms round sinful shoulders in paroxysms of Brotherly Love. Business ground to a halt as Psalms exploded into ears at the precise instant the latter were pricked to pick up the crux of a deal or a vital nub of inside information or the nitty-gritty of a news update. The profound sympathy with which they gazed into a man's eyes – just when he was on the point of meeting someone else's – was little short of excruciating.

Morning exercise, which had been so painstakingly refined to a high degree of efficiency, was reduced to chaos. Even Karl, adept though he was at turning any setback to his advantage, was at a loss. Everything had become such a shambles that the Twins couldn't even be used as a diversion.

There was no escape from the deluge of hymns and the radiance of Divine Forgiveness even for the prison staff. They had as little idea of how to deal with the Twins as we had. Their only weapons, after all, were brute force and firearms. Such passing vanities had little hope of piercing the armour of all-American Faith.

At first, we found some consolation in their confrontations with Authority. But, since the Twins emerged from each one radiating even more Loving Kindness than before, our consolation was all too brief. Never was ignorance more obviously bliss.

The most exquisite trials, however, were reserved for the handful of inmates who spoke English. We were regarded as chosen disciples and for us there was no refuge or respite whatsoever. Even worse, we could all see what tremendous mileage the pair was going to get out of this escapade once they got back Stateside.

They would be Daniels returning from the lions' den, from the innermost lair of the Great Satan himself. They would have carried the Cross through the very Fires of Communism and back to the Promised Land intact and unbowed. From staunch Seattle to the bayous of the Bible Belt, the Land of the Free was paved with excitable old ladies and exciting new marketing opportunities. 'Hallelujahs' and 'Amens' would ring in a glittering career just as soon as the Twins were redeemed. Indeed, they stood a very good chance of getting their own TV show.

It was all too obvious that any hope I might have harboured of escaping salvation, even for a few minutes, was going to be in vain. So I decided there was nothing for it but to bend with the wind. The philosophy of Heinz might even, with a bit of luck, lead me to find out how long it might be before the dawning of the Day of our Deliverance.

So, at the earliest opportunity, I responded to the twin smiles with heartfelt joy and sincere repentance. Their halos positively glowed and I was instantly clasped to the bosom of Abraham. It soon became clear that Heinz was right. Not only was I now taking the heat off my fellow prisoners but, judging by the grins on the faces of the warders, I was also getting the seal of official approval.

Far from making any effort to stop me talking, the screws actually took to nodding encouragement as we passed. Most miraculous of all, the Twins themselves became noticeably less militant as they revelled in the chance of concentrating on a single sinner undefended by any barrier of language. At the same time, purely incidentally, of course, they talked about themselves. It took no more than two and a half turns round the compound before I found out what the whole wing was aching to know. The news was not so bad. The Almighty seemed inclined towards Mercy after all.

Next morning Karl slotted himself in beside me as soon as we reached the yard. Demonstrating bravery far above and beyond the call of duty, Karl's men melted into positions to form a human barrier between the Twins and me. Under the thunder of Morning Service, it was just possible for us to hear ourselves speak.

'How long? How long?'

> 'I CRIED UNTO THE
> LORD WITH MY VOICE—'

'Three months.'

> 'WITH MY VOICE UNTO THE LORD—'

'Three months?'

> 'DID I MAKE MY SUPPLICATION.'

'That's what they said.'

'I POURED OUT MY
COMPLAINT BEFORE HIM—'

'Some hopes!'

'I SHEWED BEFORE HIM MY TROUBLE.'

'You don't believe it?'

'WHEN MY SPIRIT WAS
OVERWHELMED WITHIN ME—'

'Too good to be true.'

'THEN THOU KNEWEST MY PATH.'

'Smell a rat?'

'IN THE WAY—'

'Never heard of a sentence that short.'

'WHEREIN I WALKED—'

'Could be a trick!'

'HAVE THEY PRIVILY LAID
A SNARE FOR ME.'

'You sure that's all they got?'

'I LOOKED ON MY RIGHT
HAND, AND BEHELD—'

'Their charge sheets – I saw them.'

'BUT THERE WAS NO MAN
THAT WOULD KNOW ME—'

'So tell me!'

'REFUGE FAILED ME—'

'Disorderly Conduct in a Public Place.'

'NO MAN CARED FOR MY SOUL.'

'Pull the other leg!'

'I CRIED UNTO THEE, O LORD—'

'You know those "Hands Off Viet Nam" posters?'

'I SAID, THOU ART MY REFUGE—'

'The ones they let me out to admire every weekend?'

'AND MY PORTION—'

'Sorry, I forgot. Bit after your time.'

'IN THE LAND OF THE LIVING.'

'One of them crossed out the "U S A" –'

'ATTEND UNTO MY CRY—'

'– on the wing of the bomber –'

'FOR I AM BROUGHT VERY LOW—'

'– and wrote "U S S R" above it instead.'

'DELIVER ME—'

'Sounds likely – but why are both inside?'

                        'FROM MY PERSECUTORS—'

'Maybe the sentence was *six* months.'

            'FOR THEY ARE STRONGER THAN I.'

'God Forbid!'

                    'BRING MY SOUL—'

'But they couldn't tell them apart –'

                        'OUT OF PRISON—'

'– so they just stuck them both in and divided by two.'

                    'THAT I MAY PRAISE—'

'Not long now, anyway, so cheer up!'

                        'THY NAME—'

'St Marx must be developing a sense of humour in his old age.'

                        'THE RIGHTEOUS SHALL
                    ENCOMPASS ME ABOUT—'

'It's almost enough …'

                    'FOR THOU SHALT DEAL—'

' … to make you believe …'

                    'BOUNTIFULLY WITH ME.'

'In miracles?'

'A-A-A-A-A-H-MEN!!!'

Two and a half months later to the day, they were gone. Everyone breathed a sigh of relief. Especially Heinz. He even found it in his heart to forgive them – not so much for getting out before him, but rather for the implacable, all-American meekness with which the Twins were certainly – even at that very moment – making doubly sure of inheriting the Earth.

# 6

# Don't Forget the Wheat!

Round and round the yard we tramped, describing circle after circle with our feet. Eyes to the front, hands behind backs. Everybody exactly in step. The rhythm of our rawhide boots as rock steady as the rhythm of a train riding its iron rails. It was a route march to nowhere.

At the same time, it was also a marketplace, news service, advice bureau, gossip column and strategic HQ. Men flitted up and down the line at every opportunity, passing information, airing opinions, spreading rumours, hatching plots and clinching deals with admirable brevity and impeccable timing.

All this was possible because of the self-evident but, nevertheless, much underestimated fact that a line composed of twenty-five pairs of men is considerably longer than one composed of one single screw. This fact remains true even if said screw carries a sub-machine gun. More to the point, one pair of eyes can never be everywhere at once and one head, even if crowned by a big hat of high office, gets a lot more bored watching fifty bodies tramping round and round in endless circles than fifty pairs of eyes get watching him.

The rooftop machine guns were always with us, of course, and, naturally, the possibility that they would come into play could never be entirely discounted. There was always the possibility of some guard getting itchy fingers or flipping his lid or even something serious happening, such as a break-out attempt or a riot or whatever.

Of course, the last time a break-out had actually been attempted was back in 1956 and the situation that had prevailed then was pretty special and highly unlikely to arise again. In any case, travel was not in our stars. Where, after all, might anyone break out to? All that lay outside our prison was a tiny country, riddled with security organs, populated by informers and tightly sealed at every border. Not to mention, never less than 300,000 fully equipped Russian troops.

Apart from which, the machine-gunners were too far away to pick up details. Even if they did, what could they do about them? It was the old problem of having nothing but a howitzer with which to swat a fly. Furthermore, there was rarely, if ever, anyone up there on the roof to keep an eye on the men manning the artillery. On reflection, we soon came to the conclusion that the guards must be as clear about the relationship between flies and howitzers as we were. They must know full well that the roof guns could not really open up at every flit and grin and wink and nudge.

In all probability, then, and despite the menacing muzzles of their armoury, most of the guards must have come to regard roof duty as a sort of perk. A well-earned rest from the daily grind on the ground. A siesta in the sky. To be disturbed by nothing short of counter-revolution down below. All in all, they were probably quite happy simply to keep the conduct of ground-level business within the bounds of decorum.

So, then, as long as we bore in mind the fact that the ears up there couldn't hear a word being said down here and we didn't let the barrels pointing down at us make us lose our nerve, we could regard the machine guns as being more in the way of ornament than armament and make the best of a nice hour of business and pleasure.

This micro-climate was quite healthy for economic affairs and seemed, on further consideration, to be amply supported by the macro-economic parameters of the situation. This again seemed to favour underdogs. Authorities and prison staff were, on the whole, if not in every particular case, quite well aware that there was more to most appearances than met the eye.

Nevertheless, there just wasn't too much they could actually do about most things without resorting to extremes – such as mowing down an entire morning exercise in order to ensure the elimination of the odd chatterbox or, failing that, employing enough guards to physically outnumber convicts.

The first alternative – the wholesale and often cold-blooded liquidation of an entire group of fellow humans for reasons of real or imaginary necessity – is, of course, by no means unknown in human history. Even so, it has usually required extraordinary circumstances to make its employment feasible. Without wishing to insult memories or belittle anyone's suffering, we could hardly claim comparison with

Carthage at the close of the Punic Wars or with Herod's infanticidal Judea or with the Teutoberger Wald and Varus or with the Burial of Attila or the sack of Albi or the field of Mohács or Katyn Forest, My Lai or even with Budapest in 1956. We did not, as a group, feel we were in any real danger of imminent extinction.

The second alternative – physically outnumbering those you wish to sit on – may, at first, appear more feasible. It has, if nothing else, the advantage of appearing to create employment. However, the most important single factor in the practice of industrial-scale imprisonment is still, predictably enough, what it always has been – Cost Effectiveness. This obviously declines pro rata as the per capita ratio of guards to prisoners increases.

The *reductio ad absurdum* of this process would result in one half of a population being continuously employed in guarding the other half. Such a situation is also by no means unknown in human history. On the other hand, even Egypt and Rome, for all their cultural advantages, eventually had problems keeping the economics of this feat in balance. In modern times, few states have found it possible to sustain enough production to support either the guarding or the guarded half of a population indefinitely.

Anyway, the general rule these days seems to be that not even the most exalted Powers That Be find it worthwhile to justify the overwhelming cost of this measure, especially if they can't really put their finger on any specific ill to be cured by it.

So, bathed in the protective halo of the macro and the micro, we trundled on, round and round the yard, sorting out the business of the day. The basic match-up on the

171

ground remained what it always really had been, a man-to-man affair. Mano a mano. Stripes versus Uniform. One pair of eyes watching fifty moving targets. Fifty pairs of eyes watching one potential trouble spot. Every single screw has to blink sometime. A long line of eyes does not.

The duty guard was as keen as mustard, a raw recruit eager to make his mark. It was only too obvious that he was determined to run a model exercise. Instead of nodding off to the rhythm of the feet like his elders and betters and his rooftop back-ups, he watched us like a hawk.

It was no contest, really. The line had far more experience of playing Mouse than he had of being Cat. One or two pairs of feet, doubtless considering his attitude a bit uncalled for, were even turning a trifle cheeky. They took to shifting places just a fraction of a second too slowly to go entirely unnoticed, yet a smidgeon too quickly to be identified for certain. Voices drifted up through the threshold of audibility for tantalisingly split seconds and always from the end of the line furthest from our screw.

This goaded our beefy, young herdsman like horseflies stinging a bull. He reacted in more or less the same way. His looks became blacker and blacker and he charged up and down the line, bellowing, 'No talking there!' in his most bellicose voice, stamping his boots and shaking his sub-machine gun with great gusto.

But the more he glared, the less he saw. Waves of conversation started flowing up and down the line with the insolent grace of a matador's cape. As pass followed pass, the suspicion dawned that the cape of unpermitted conversation was being embroidered with sequins of unheard-of mockery.

Our screw got red in the face and hot under the collar. He kept clicking the safety-catch of his sub-machine gun absent-mindedly on and off. This was all the more menacing for being so obviously unintentional. One or two of us began feeling that things might be getting a bit out of hand. A bull with a gun is, after all – and no matter how silly he may look or how favourable the micro and macro parameters may be – still a dumb brute toting a lethal weapon. Furthermore, unlike the four-legged half of most corridas, this toro was fairly certain to live to fight another day.

Just then, a gust of provocative gaiety swirled up from the back of the line.

Our screw charged past, snorting fire. As he thundered out of view behind me, the unthinkable happened. The rock-steady rhythm of our tramp-tramp-tramp faltered and broke. A strange sound, midway between a retch and a groan sprang, quite undeniably, to the ear. This was followed immediately by an unequivocally painful-sounding thud. The two added up to an extremely convincing impression of some form of heavy and horrifying impact. Leaping up before my inward eyes came the tragic likeness of a broken matador bleeding in the sand beneath the baleful nostrils of a monstrous toro.

With a presence of mind no less admirable for being purely instinctive, the line hauled itself in and wheeled round to see what had happened. A figure lay in the dust beneath the guard's lowered head. It was Robert, our one and only Canadian. He was clutching his abdomen and the contortion of his body told us he wasn't kidding.

By now, we had neatly surrounded the pair and we pressed in for a better view. Robert's face was twisted to one side, his tongue protruded far out of his mouth and a malevolent bruise swelled vividly up on his forehead. A purple tinge seeped steadily into his features second by second. His body bounced as he was racked by another spasm. Then he lay still, frozen in a posture of extreme tension. The Bull bent over him, glaring downwards in triumph.

'So it's you, is it?' he bellowed. 'You're not getting out of this one! Jump to it, now! On your feet!'

Robert replied with another gut-wrenching groan and stuck his tongue out even further.

'Come on! You can't fool me! Get up or face the consequences!'

'Shouldn't you just, er, shoot him, sir?' enquired a voice in tones of measured solicitude. The Bull's head swivelled round in ferocious amazement.

'Put him out of his agony. After all, he's practically dead already,' continued Karl reasonably.

'What?' snarled the guard.

'Heart attack, sir,' explained Karl courteously. 'Have you never seen one before?'

He gazed coolly down into the screw's upturned face, until the man straightened up in bewildered exasperation, dangling the sub-machine gun from one hand like a forgotten toy.

'You're right!' said Karl with sudden conviction.

'What?'

'Absolutely right! What kind of Socialist Sense of Responsibility would waste the People's hard-earned bullets on a Capitalist Swine that's as good as dead already?'

'What?' gasped the guard, completely off balance and finding the helpful sincerity of Karl's gaze at least as confusing as Robert's frozen agony.

Karl allowed a long pause to make sure the steam had finally fizzled out of his man and then launched the counter-attack proper. Leaning forward, he murmured confidentially into a hairy ear, 'Apart from which, sir, don't forget the wheat!'

'What?'

'The *wheat*, sir. *You* know!'

The screw stared back at him, his face utterly blank. Karl squinted conspiratorially up at the rooftop machine-gunners as if their earthbound colleague's refusal to twig were leaving him no option but to disclose something he would rather not have aired in public. Then he leaned even closer.

'Whe-e-e-at,' he pronounced in a whisper so sibilant as to be completely audible to everyone present. 'Five-year plan. Shortfall. Government negotiating. Very Delicate. Top level. To buy – wheat. From – the *Canadians!*'

The officer's eyes bulged as he strained for comprehension. Karl glanced furtively round the yard, as if to check the clarity of the coast once again. Then he turned back to the warder, raised a hand and cupped it over his nose to make it clear that he was masking his sibilant whisper.

'He's the only Canadian in here. A corpse could be – embarrassing. International incident. End of five-year plan. Party unhappy. No more nice uniform. Big hat kaput.'

The picture cleared and our man looked as if he'd just stepped under a waterfall. Sweat spurted out of his brow and he blushed crimson.

'Don't want to put our foot in it, now, do we, sir? Not so early in our career.'

The screw gazed wildly from face to face, utterly at sea in the world of high diplomacy. Karl coughed delicately and ventured, 'Massage, sir?'

'What?' blurted el toro, throwing variety to the winds.

'Massage. You might try massaging his heart.'

Understanding flooded into the heavy features like sunrise on the Day of Resurrection. The strapping figure dropped his gun, fell to his knees, flipped Robert over as if he were a rag doll and started pummelling away at that part of his chest in which he, apparently, imagined the Canadian's heart to be lodged.

Carefully, one of Karl's men reached a hand out towards the firearm now lying forgotten on the ground. The line froze, paralysed at the thought of the impending blunder.

Karl, however, was equal to the moment. Without batting an eyelid, he crunched the heel of his boot slowly but firmly down on to the outstretched fingers. Manfully, their impulsive owner swallowed a groan.

'A little lower down, sir,' suggested Karl, helpfully, while quietly grinding the offending fingers deeper into the hard dust.

'What?' came the familiar refrain.

'A little lower down. That's his breastbone, sir.'

The screw turned back to his work with a will. Whatever the actual state of Robert's heart might have been, these muscular ministrations seemed to be having an effect. Quite probably, it was simply a choice between being pounded to death or recovering as fast as possible – and the body, in its wisdom, merely opted for the less painful way out.

Anyway – and for whatever reason – Robert suddenly gave a sigh like a sounding grampus and opened his eyes. Joyfully, the guard thumped him on the chest with the full force of a ham-sized fist. With a wheeze like a punctured bagpipe, Robert flopped back against the ground and his face filled with alarm. Instantly, he rolled his eyes, pulled his tongue back into his mouth, relaxed his muscles and started getting his natural colour back. The screw pulled back his fist. Robert shook his head vigorously, swallowed hard and looked a lot more healthy. He seemed quite conscious now, though somewhat pale and still as shaky as a new-born calf.

'You should walk him round, sir.'

The warder replied with his customary monosyllable.

'You have to walk him round a bit,' explained Karl patiently. 'So he doesn't get another fit.'

At the mention of a possible encore from Robert, the screw snatched the Canadian up as if he were an underfed infant, thrust his shoulder under the invalid's armpit and set off trundling him round the yard at the double.

'Not so quickly, sir!' called Karl.

'What?' boomed the head under Robert's arm.

'Slow down! Don't shake him up!'

Instantly, the broad back obeyed. For several minutes, the pair tramped round and round the admiring circle of the line, keeping in step with commendable precision. Once or twice, Robert introduced a bit of variety by faltering or tripping. But the screw was on his toes and adjusted his stride to the inch. It was a flawless display.

Eventually, Robert recovered enough to start beaming fondly down at his saviour. The guard greeted this with huge relief and trundled Robert back to the starting line for Karl's approval.

'See if he can stand on his own,' said Karl thoughtfully.

Releasing his charge, the screw waved his massive arms in encouragement like a fond parent egging on a much-loved but sickly child. Robert responded nobly, putting one leg gingerly in front of the other and smiling shyly for approval between each step. His benefactor beamed at him proudly, with his big, round hat pushed casually to the back of his head and his hands on his hips. Robert had almost reached the other side of the yard when the moment of truth arrived.

'Yours, sir, I believe,' said Karl, holding the sub-machine gun out in one hand. Quite by chance, its muzzle pointed straight at its owner's heart.

'WHA-A-A-T!' screamed the uniform, consistent to the last.

'Oh, there's nothing to worry about, sir,' added Karl. 'It's not loaded.'

And, raising his other fist aloft, he opened it, so that everyone could see what he held in the palm of his hand.

# 7

# Sunflower by a Wall in Sunshine

'Respectfully reporting, cell number twenty-six – two heads – all present and correct, *sir!*'

Gimlet glare grinds out grim scrutiny. The harder the stare, the higher the authority. Supposedly. Two iron bunks, two straw mattresses, two straw pillows, two wooden stools, one tap, one bucket, two aluminium bowls, two aluminium spoons, one aluminium lunchbox, two striped denim caps above two striped denim uniforms, standing quietly to attention.

Glare, stare, scowl, frown – and a one and a two and, 'Cell number twenty-six, carry ON!'

Turn, stump, clump, out, slam – gone ...

Peter let his long, weedy frame flop against the rough stone wall and relaxed. He looked even more blanched and fragile than on most mornings. After a few moments, his right hand drifted out like a lost cloud, fumbled around under his pillow and floated back into view, bearing an object that was a combination of modern precision engineering and

179

old-fashioned granny glasses. Springy coils of prehensile steel gave a firm grip on the ears, while the miniature binocular barrels were minutely adjustable for brilliance and focus. These were Peter's spectacles.

He had been allowed to keep these because he was going blind and, since blinding was not part of his sentence, the Authorities wanted no blame to attach to them if Peter's light happened to flicker out while he was still in their custody. The feeling filtering down from on high seemed to be that Peter's possession of his glasses constituted incontrovertible evidence that the goods were already damaged on arrival. The official line seemed to be that as long as he had his glasses, no one could have any grounds for blaming the Hungarian People's Republic for anything that might happen to Peter's eyesight.

He fiddled around with the adjustments, slipped them on and leaned his round, balding head back against the wall again. By easy stages, he picked up his pattern of even, shallow breathing more or less where he had left off to present us for inspection. Every millimetre of his long frame was utterly relaxed. With the twin turrets of his glasses aimed upwards at the darkness of the ceiling, Peter concentrated on saving his strength and staying alive with the least possible effort. So soon after inspection, conversation was out of the question. So I drifted off into contemplating his case.

Peter was a German from East of the wall. He had spent regular periods in prison there until he had escaped to the West with his wife and one child. After what had seemed to him to be a suitable interval, he had gone back alone for their second child, a boy of six. All had gone well, until they had been caught on the Hungarian–Austrian border.

The boy, innocent even in Socialist Law, had been sent back to East Germany. Peter, however, had been tried and sentenced in Hungary. This was very lucky for him, because his previous convictions and Democratic Republican – that is to say, East German – origin would have weighed very heavily against him, indeed, if he had also been sent back. As it was, he had got off lightly with two years straight.

There might have been any number of reasons behind this clemency. One of the strongest of these was, quite simply, that Hungarians were not German. Hence, they were not motivated by any overwhelming urge to get even with their more fortunate kinfolk on the Western side of the Iron Curtain by, among other things, taking every opportunity to severely punish anyone who tried to go and join them. Also, they had not been the principal villains of the last war. Hence, they did not feel they had to expiate endless guilt by proving that they were more Red than even the Russians. Then again, the embers of 'fifty-six had been thoroughly damped down by now. The Hungarian regime seemed to feel that they were quite firmly back in the saddle and their overriding priority no longer seemed to be the demonstration of utter loyalty by demonstrations of utter ruthlessness. Such reasons for the clemency accorded Peter so, apparently, fortuitously were probably reasonably obvious to most reasonably well-informed watchers in the Free West.

On the other hand, many things that did not exist to Western minds or, if they did, were no more than obscure footnotes to distant history might also have played a part in

Peter's good luck. Since those most westward wanderers among the ancient Horse People – the Magyars – strayed into Christendom over a thousand years ago, they had had long experience of life as underdogs. After their dubious conversion to Christianity, they experienced many catastrophes verging on obliteration. There had been the ravages of the Golden Horde, the long occupation by the Turks, the long subservience to the Hapsburgs, the humiliations after 1848 and the crippling loss of territory and people imposed upon them under the Treaty of Trianon and repeated after the Second World War. Such things and their consequences – so misty to minds of the West – were very real facts of life to many Hungarians.

Most, including even some of those sitting in office or passing out sentences, had close relatives in Transylvania or in what is now Slovakia or just across what was then the Soviet border or in Vojvodina. Consequently, they often felt at least a sneaking sympathy for Germans like Peter. Also, not being Hungarian, he was, of course, not really skin off their nose.

Some combination of all the above – plus a tendency already taking shape among younger members of the Party in Hungary to take out a little insurance for the future, to begin again the old game of playing both sides against the middle, as well as who knows what touches of personal sympathy aroused by his long and skinny but uncomplaining figure – had added up to a humane two years for Peter.

This was mellowed further by the absence of a Deportation Order and recognition of his new, Federal German nationality. He could qualify for as much as six months' remission and could end up repatriated to the homeland of his choice. Naturally, these possibilities had not been entirely absent from his calculations when selecting the border he would try to cross.

Peter had attained perfect tranquillity. His breathing was now imperceptible. His twin turrets were utterly immobile. I hoped his heartbeat was still strong enough to keep the blood moving round his veins. It would be a pity if it were not. For, not long ago, he had heard that his patron city of Hamburg had raised a sum of money sufficient to compensate the Democratic Republic for allowing one small boy to find his way out to the West.

This curious practice – a sort of modern version of the ancient Germanic 'Blood-Money' or the Medieval sport of 'Capture and Ransom' of which the most famous example was, probably, Richard the Lionheart – was followed by many West German cities at the time, though, for obvious reasons, it was kept as quiet as possible. So despite his doomed eyesight, deteriorating health and rapidly evaporating career – Peter was, of all things, an opera singer! – he was at one with the world and at ease with himself. He felt that things had turned out better than any normal human being had any right to expect. All he had to do now was simply bide his time as quietly as possible.

His mind was clear and straightforward and utterly without bitterness. He knew that the chilling mass of the stone walls and the spartan conveniences weren't doing his lungs any good, but he was convinced they were no worse off than if they were breathing the polluted air of his native city. He accepted the fact that the prison diet was not keeping up his strength. But then, he felt that his nerves were not being undermined by a diet of indigestible propaganda, either. He saw full well that the question mark hanging over him ever being able to sing professionally again was growing bigger with each passing day. Nevertheless, now that his family was safe and sound, he was in no doubt that the future he had secured for them was well worth the price he was paying.

He had reached a high plateau of serenity – a long, emaciated Buddha, benignly watching eighteen little months glide by. Even if these were somehow to prolong themselves to the full two years, Peter would not complain. His son would just be a little bigger and a little stronger by the time they met again. Nothing anyone could do – certainly not any screw – could force that fragile smile from his face.

Today was the day for Peter's treatment. At his trial, he had managed to get the need for regular medical treatment recognised as a mitigating circumstance. It had been duly included in his sentence. So every two weeks, he had a trip to Sick Bay. As none of the staff there had graduated beyond the quick pill-or-plaster school of medicine, the ophthalmic benefits of this outing were open to doubt. The change of scenery, on the other hand, definitely did his soul a power of good.

For some time now, Peter had been trying to dream up an excuse for me to go along with him. I had no hope of being granted a regular excursion, so we decided to try to save my trip until it would really count. Accordingly, we held off putting in a formal request until it felt as though time was standing stiller than the stone walls around us.

We couldn't devise anything really wrong with me, apart from my way of life, so we plumped for something mysterious.

My rawhide clodhoppers had worn a hole in the skin of my left shin. As I still had to sport this footgear every day without fail on pain of being adjudged improperly dressed, this wound, though minor, never got a chance to heal. It was not particularly painful and didn't seem to be inflamed. But it had grown a dry scaliness all around it, which, we thought, looked promisingly repulsive.

I had also evolved another whatnot on the same leg, just below the knee. The most likely cause of this seemed to be an absent-minded tendency on my part to scratch the spot on the not infrequent occasions when I wasn't actively concentrating on not doing so. We had no idea what prompted this habit, though one or two old hands hinted darkly at some kind of obscure maggot vaguely connected with the straw in our mattresses.

We took the beast to be legendary, especially as whatever the whatnot was, it did not spread. All it did was form a neat mound of bruised purple surrounded by a hinge of flaky scar tissue. We were fairly confident that the two fluorescences ought to be worth one outing.

A week before Peter's next scheduled treatment, therefore, we had respectfully requested the warder on duty to examine my leg. As we had surmised, he had no idea what my whatnots might be, but his head was as full of legendary maggots as any inmate's so he wasn't very keen on getting too close. This suited us fine as the further the distance of inspection, the less risk there was of a genuine diagnosis.

After that, we repeated this demonstration every morning with straight faces and humble persistence. I even developed a suitable limp in the exercise yard. So today we were not a little curious to discover whether our labours had brought forth fruit. At the allotted time, the bolt slid back, the hat poked in and we were on our way. Together.

The only other man apart from Peter undergoing regular medical treatment in our wing was Rotting Franz. As the treatment he was getting was both personal and private, Peter and I were on our own. My long companion really was very feeble and could only muster the gentlest of shuffles. In addition, he would come to a complete halt every now and again to adjust his glasses to cope with real or imaginary variations in the brightness of the outdoor light.

I held my limp down to a compatible amble, buoyed up by the thought that at this rate the trip would take all day. Our screw was already having trouble finding a stride short enough to avoid leaving us behind. Clearly, his patience was fraying, but we were spared the retribution this would normally have brought because Peter's fragility was so patently obvious and because the restraining influence of the Sacred Cow of Medical Treatment was so strong.

After the limitations of our cell and the unvaried circling of morning exercise, it was wonderfully refreshing to have just the two of us tottering along like ailing octogenarians enjoying a constitutional by the seaside. Every now and then, Peter would stop and lean on my shoulder to catch his breath or adjust his glasses. The limpid air of morning was marvellously still and calm.

We tottered across the packed, pink dust of the inner compound and out into the cool shelter of the long archway leading to the outer square. Our footfalls, echoing against the walls, sounded delightfully clear and melodious. As we came out into full sunlight, Peter clutched my shoulder and fiddled with the adjustment rings on his glasses with his free hand.

We stood quite motionless while Peter engineered a pause entirely for my benefit by pretending to steady himself with a cycle of deep breathing. The oblong of grass seemed an even more brilliant green than I remembered. The pink path split the cream and green even more crisply than before. The warder paced backwards and forwards, swinging his keys but keeping his thoughts to himself.

A swallow darted across the wide-open sky. We drank in the scene like parched soil soaking up summer rain. We could have gone on standing there till God knows when, but our guard suddenly let out a snort and seemed about to boil over. Making a supreme effort, Peter straightened up and lurched forward again. Exquisite timing! Admiration smiled inside me.

We pottered up the side of the square and across its top, past beds of bounding nasturtiums and startling cornflowers, along walls overwhelmed by regiments of roses and on, step by step, until we arrived at a point where the neat oblong of the square was broken to our left by an untidy path of crushed gravel. With the lumbering gait of a heavy roller, our custodian crunched up this and we tagged along behind in grateful silence.

Past corrugated iron sheds and up a short, rocky slope we wandered, until an edifice of imposing proportions hove into sight like a ship of the line under full sail. Rigged out with wrought-iron trellises and balconies and porticoes of glass, skylights and solariums and parapets and verandas, it billowed out majestically on all sides. Like the ocean swell embracing a proud hull, mounds of jumbled rocks covered with vegetation bulged around its base.

As we approached the galleon containing the Sick Bay, Peter's knees buckled so convincingly that I glanced up involuntarily to see if he was all right. Steadying himself on my shoulder, he breathed a long sigh and wound himself up for another effort. Inch by inch, we wobbled on until we were almost at the top of the rock garden. By now our progress was so slow our guard was practically walking backwards. As we reached the summit, Peter hovered in mid stride for several bars with the agonised ecstasy of a great conductor prolonging a phrase of lingering regret. Then, in a dying fall of infinite gentleness, he collapsed slowly right on top of me.

Gritting my teeth, I struggled in silence to save his elastic length from measuring itself on the gravel. Bracing the boot of my bad leg against an outcrop of rock, I glanced upwards and saw the barrels of Peter's binoculars glinting in the sunlight above my head. Though their wearer appeared to be on the point of expiring, the twin turrets never wavered. Taking care not to unwedge myself from beneath Peter, I swivelled my head in the direction in which his specs seemed to be aimed.

There, soaring above the foliage and rocks, was the most gigantic sunflower I had ever seen. Its mighty stem reared up and up until its head cleared even the high outer prison wall that stood behind it. Its colossal, yellow face blazed against the aching clarity of the bluest sky of the finest of fine summer mornings.

Peter pressed tenderly downwards. I pushed doggedly upwards. Unable to bat an eyelid between us, both of us stared straight at the splendid immensity of the sunflower. Our guard was out of sight and out of mind. For all the advantages of his rank, the poor fellow would never have the faintest inkling of what we were up to at that moment. Not even, perhaps, if the wheel of fortune turned far enough one day to let him see the world from our point of view. For where would this loveliest of sunflowers be by then?

Meanwhile, we sipped the sight of that heavenly bloom, like hummingbirds draining nectar. So vast and so yellow. So high in the sky. So clear against the blue. The yellowest of sun-drenched yellows. Dripping with buttercups and corn-fields and brown-limbed maidens stacking sun-dried hay. Bursting with ripening apricots and standing maize and glistening horses, chestnut, black and bay. Greeting us with blessings from the summer and the fertile soil and the innocent land.

# 8

# Regulations Re: Bedsprings, Swallowing Of

We hurried through the bowels of the building until we came to a place that looked like an underground bomb site. The floor was bare concrete, cracked and shattered as though a squadron of tanks had rumbled over it. The crumbling brick walls were no less battered. Dust and grime lay everywhere, blurring outlines and muffling sound. Dank, musty air hung heavy and still as in a mine shaft or a catacomb. The warder seemed anxious to spend as little time down here as possible. He rattled open a rusty iron door and bundled me in.

The semi-darkness was kind enough to cloak details, but the cell felt as rough inside as it had looked from outside. The same battered brick walls, the same shattered concrete floor and no window. Just a small metal grating for ventilation. It seemed unlikely that this section of the edifice had ever been intended to house living beings. Storage, probably.

Building materials, heavy-metal bits and pieces, perhaps. In any case, either the place had never been finished or it was already being demolished. To judge from appearances, however, even the latter had been given up as a bad job long ago. Nothing suggested itself as being something to sleep on. I started nosing around to see if there was anything in the way of toilet facilities.

'Unlucky, mate,' growled a voice. 'You piss in the corner. Or you wait for the bucket. They bring one round in the morning. Unless they forget.'

I peered into the corner from which the voice seemed to have come. In the depths of the shadow there was a recess the size of a small broom cupboard. Inside the broom cupboard was a man. Squatting on his haunches, he was neatly wedged between the walls which supported him firmly on three sides. Clearly, the best armchair in these quarters was already taken.

We introduced ourselves. After that I pissed in the corner. The dry rubble and deep dust soaked up the urine like cat-litter and prevented it from flowing out over the rest of the floor. I reflected that few things were entirely without some usefulness and looked around for somewhere to sit down. The corner furthest from the lavatory and opposite the armchair seemed the most inviting.

'Where you from?'

'Vác,' I replied. The man grunted.

'And you?'

'Hospital.'

I made myself comfortable and stretched out my legs. My rawhide clodhoppers rested on the rough fragments of

191

masonry without getting damaged and kept my feet safe and snug. Yes, indeed, I thought to myself, yet again. Nothing is entirely useless. I was tired. It had been a long day.

'Bit short of bunks down here,' the man ventured. 'Transit depot. Got a full house. Lots of bodies travelling through. No room in First Class.'

I peered more closely into the opposite corner, but it was too dark to see whether my companion was wearing a grin or not.

'Grub?' I suggested.

'Didn't you bring any?'

'A bit.'

'That's your lot, then. Might be some coffee in the morning. With the bucket. If it comes.'

'And if it doesn't?'

'Tough shit. Nothing personal, of course – but we don't belong to them. We're just passing through. So they make no provision. How can they? Never know who's coming or going. They just wait for the trucks. Same as us.'

It must have been long past Lights Out, but there was no electricity in the cell and I assumed that, as we had not been blessed with light in the first place, we would not be bothered with the usual ceremony for extinguishing it. It seemed a safe bet that we would not be disturbed till morning. So I thought I might as well have a bite to eat before turning in. I opened my bundle and pulled out my 'csajka' – the basic aluminium bowl that was standard issue in Hungarian prisons in those days. It was light, durable and endlessly useful for many purposes including containing anything and everything. At present, mine held my food. I still had a fair supply. A hunk of bread, two winter apples and a chunk of what Hungarians call 'szalona', Germans call 'speck' and the English prefer not to recognise by any name at all. A sort of solid lard or bacon fat, it reminded me of whale blubber or candle grease. I found it almost inedible, but in Central and Eastern Europe as a whole, and behind bars in particular, it was much prized.

'Care for some supper?' I offered.

'Thanks all the same, but I'm not hungry.'

'I've got some szalona.'

'Szalona, eh?'

'Plenty to spare.'

'Well' – I could almost hear the man's saliva dripping – 'thanks again, but I don't eat much these days.'

'Please yourself.'

I whittled myself a slice of bread, half an apple and a thin sliver of szalona. Just enough to lubricate the dry bread, but not enough to trigger off nausea or heartburn. I was already putting my store back into my csajka, when my companion piped up again.

'Maybe you'd like some tea, though?'

'Some what?' I could hardly contain my astonishment.

'Tea. Maybe you'd like some.'

'Cold tea?'

'Naargh! Tea – not cat's piss! Tea as tea should be. Hot.'

I savoured the thought for a moment. Cups of tea from Lyons' Corner House and Covent Garden caffs, from Irish building sites and maiden ladies' flats and even from my grand-mother's kitchen table flooded into my head, dancing and flirting with the full-bodied shamelessness of Impressionist cancan dancers. I clearly heard my grandmother chortling, '*What's* better than a nice cup of tea, dear? *Another* cup of tea, silly!'

Lovely, lovely, long ago ... Back on Earth, I wondered how my companion was going to make good his offer. A pipe dream, of course, but well meant. How could I turn him down without showing him I thought him a liar? Oh, well, what was there to lose?

'A very good suggestion.'

'Nothing picks you up like a nice cup of tea, does it? Might as well brew up as sit around loafing,' twittered the man like a house-proud sparrow. 'Haven't done a stroke all day!'

He untied his bundle, rummaged around inside it and pulled out a tin of boot polish. Twisting off the lid, he held it in both hands and then pressed with his thumbs against the inside surface. Two slits had been cut into the metal to form a cross. When he pressed against them, the four points formed by the intersection at the centre of the cross opened outwards and protruded vertically from the lid. He screwed the lid back on to the tin and set it down on the floor. Reaching back into his bundle, he then pulled out a rag, which he proceeded to unfold. It was filled with little bits of cloth which had been torn up small and charred black. With great care, he placed the feather-light fragments on the floor beside the tin of boot polish. Then he took off his cap, felt along the seam of the brim and extracted a tiny piece of lighter flint. Pulling off one hide boot, he grunted, 'Lend me your bicska, will you?'

It was a bit odd that he didn't have one of his own. My doubts must have shown on my face, because he reached his boot out towards me and growled, 'All right! Just cut me a little nick, then. Just there!' And he pointed to a spot in the back of the heel, a millimetre or two higher up than the surface of the sole.

Opening my little wooden-handled clasp knife, I did as he asked. Then he wedged the flint firmly into the nick, knelt down and set about striking the heel of the boot against the bare concrete. Sparks showered up, piercing the gloom, and a couple of them nestled comfortably among the charred rags.

Bending low, my companion now cupped his hands round the charred fragments of rag and blew into them until they glowed bright red. Then he scooped them up in one hand and dropped them into the tin of boot polish through the four-pronged opening in the lid. Quickly but carefully, he blew into the tin until the wax or paraffin or whatever the flammable element in the polish was caught fire and blossomed into low, quiet flame.

Reaching into his bundle again, he took out a small canteen, pulled out the cork, poured a little water into his csajka and then placed this gently on top of the tin of boot polish. It stood neatly on the four prongs protruding from the lid, while a wispy flame nuzzled playfully against its aluminium base. I was lost for words. The contraption was as fine a little camping stove as you could have wished for. Certainly, you could not have asked for anything better in a place like this.

My comrade straightened up and turned his attention to his left hip with all the gravity of a surgeon embarking on a major operation. Cupping one hand under his trouser pocket, he drew out the lining slowly and steadily with the

195

other. As the material of the lining unfolded, tiny scraps showered into his waiting hand. When he had shaken every last one out of the lining, he reached over and sprinkled the scraps into the csajka. Then he stood up, stuffed the lining back into his pocket, slapped the dust off his knees and rumbled, 'Give it a stir, will you!'

I took out my battered aluminium spoon and, while he stowed his charred rags and flint away in their respective hiding places in bundle and cap, I stirred away with gusto and a straight face. Dropping the bundle neatly into his corner, he turned back to the stove and sat down to put his boot back on.

With a couple of deft flips, he wrapped his foot in the square of threadbare cotton with which we were all issued instead of socks and which I had originally taken to be scraps of old sheets. If these were folded perfectly, they were surprisingly comfortable. One false fold, however, and – no matter how small the wrinkle thus formed – walking became a blistering experience. I never did get the hang of them, but from the way my companion worked his, I could see he was an old hand. Peasant background more than likely. I'd heard they still used these 'foot-kerchiefs' in many rural areas. Anyway, whatever his background, he certainly wasn't a pampered intellectual. By now, my curiosity was killing me.

'Where did you get all that?' I asked.

'Hospital,' he grunted. 'Good place. Give you tea instead of coffee there. Say it soothes the gut.'

'So they gave you enough to take with you, did they?'

'No fear! I had to dry out the leaves after every breakfast.'

'What about the flint?'

'The orderlies are pretty easy-going up there. Not like real screws. Young geezers. Educated. Come and sit on your bed and talk. Try to straighten you out. All smoke Western cigarettes. All got lighters. Never been inside, though, so they're not too careful.'

'And the rags?'

'Got to think ahead, you know. Never waste your last match. Always make some kindling. If you've got kindling and a spark, you can always make fire. You can tear endless amounts of kindling scraps off just one old foot-wrap, and still have plenty left for your foot. Try doing that with your modern sock. Why, these new materials don't even char properly!'

For a few moments I thanked Providence for having had the wisdom to keep modernisation of Convicts' Footwear out of the last five-year plan and offered my apologies for ever having looked down on the lowly, ancestral foot-wrap. Then I thought I'd better clear up the last loose end.

'What's the dope on the boot polish?'

'They insist on giving you that. Regulation issue. Inspection after inspection in Hospital, you know. Show place. Spit and polish. Shave every other day. Haircut once a fortnight. Showers. Sheets. The lot.'

I finished my supper and took out my cigarettes. I still had some tailor-mades. Tipped cigarettes, called 'Fecske' in Hungarian. In English, the word means 'Swallow'. The bird, not the verb. It was a popular brand. I offered one to my companion. Lovingly, he examined the striped paper and loose, dry tobacco.

197

'Thanks, mate. Don't see many of these down here.'

He bent down and lit up from the friendly glow in the tin of boot polish.

Taking a deep drag, he savoured the taste and then exhaled with a satisfying rush, chopping up the smoke as he muttered, 'Couple more stirs and it should be ready.'

I complied dutifully, licked my spoon and put it back into my bundle. He rolled over on to his knees, lifted up his csajka and blew out the flame. Pouring half the brew over into mine, he set his bowl down on the ground, got up and stood on the tin with one foot to press the prongs back into place. Then the tin went back into his bundle and out of sight. There was no doubt he was an old hand. He took no unnecessary risks and left nothing lying around. Even down here, you never knew when some screw might barge in unannounced.

He sat down in his armchair again and we settled back for our tea and cigarettes. The tea was only lukewarm and, by London standards, it was undoubtedly weak and hardly a choice blend. Nevertheless, we sipped it as delicately and as thoughtfully as connoisseurs savouring their favourite brew. I leaned back against the wall and sighed contentedly.

'That's a good trick, that. With the boot polish.'

'Not bad.'

'Can you use the tin again?'

'Should be a few more burns in it. If you don't try and get the water too hot.'

'Can you still use it for polishing boots?'

'If you give it a good mixing with plenty of spit. Flame dries it out, you see.'

198

'Of course.'

'Anyway, that's just a big joke. You can't get a shine on these lumps of old hide, no matter what. Polish makes no difference to them. They just give us a tin to make them feel as though they're doing something. You know, cross something off a list.'

'Yes.'

'You say you were in Vác?'

'Yes.'

'Didn't they tell you in the button factory you can get fire out of them, too?'

'No. They never let me near the place.'

'No?'

He paused to weigh this up. Not working meant drawing hard time. Usually a sure sign of a stiff sentence. And/or a hard case.

'Well, anyway, I've heard you can get those buttons to burn like a real little campfire. Never had a chance to try it myself. Never got near any real buttons. These metal things on our jackets are no good and we never have any buttons on the shirts we get in Kőhida.'

'That where you're heading?' I murmured. I had heard of the place. The name meant 'Stone Bridge' in English. Its reputation was not good.

'Suppose so. Never tell you a thing like that, though, would they? That's where I've always gone before, so that's where I'll end up again, as like as not.'

I let the thought drift round the dark cell for a few moments and then got down to the nitty-gritty.

'What got you into Hospital?'

My companion puffed his Fecske for a few moments, then lurched forward on to his knees and waddled nearer until I could see him fairly clearly. He unbuttoned his jacket and pulled up his shirt.

'This, mate,' he growled.

I stared at his stomach in the dim light until I was sure I was seeing what I was seeing. A long gash started just below his breastbone and ran down his stomach to below his navel. It gaped open like a toothless grin and I couldn't understand why there was no dressing of some kind on it.

'Here!' grunted my cell-mate, grasping my free hand and placing it right on the wound. It was dry and hard and the edges were firm and scaly. I snatched my hand back and gasped, 'What is it?'

'Won't close up any more, mate. Flesh has got hard. Like old shoe leather. Can't knit properly. Been cut open too many times.'

He stuck his cigarette into the corner of his mouth, stuffed his shirt back into his trousers, waddled back to his 'armchair', still on his knees, and wedged himself back in again.

'Yes,' he mumbled through his dog-end as he did up his buttons, 'they do their best. But it won't knit together any more. Hard as old boots inside. Cut too many times in the same place. Last little bit still holds, but as soon as they take the stitches out, the rest opens up like a rose. "Calcification", they call it. Cal-ci-fi-ca-tion.' And he nodded sagely. 'That's the word. This time they told me if they have to do it one more time, the inside won't close either. Can't hold anything against them, though. They do their best. I was there over six months this time. Touch and go for the first couple. Still, you've got to take the rough with the smooth, that's what I say.'

'Why do you have this, er, problem?'

'Problem? What problem?'

'I mean, how does it happen?'

'Oh, there's nothing to it. Once you get the knack.'

'The knack?'

'You bet. The best thing is a bed-spring.'

'A bed-spring?'

'That's best. You know – the coiled springs that join the wire mesh under the straw mattresses to the iron frames of the bunks. A spoon will do sometimes, if it's not too big and you can fix something to it. A string, if you've got one. Or a strip of cloth, if it's strong enough. It can work if you jiggle it round. But nothing beats a bed-spring.'

I puffed at my cigarette, thinking furiously. Odd conversations were not unusual in these nether regions. Neither those above the law nor those below it could always be relied on to restrict themselves to talking normal common sense as understood in most parts of the world outside. Still, this conversation was turning out to be odder than most.

'What do you do – with such a bed-spring?'

'Well, you take the bed-spring out of the frame and you straighten it out. Takes a bit of time, but you can usually manage if you keep at it. The main problem is if the screws check the bed before you finish. They check all the time nowadays. Sometimes, they even take the bunks out and just leave the mattresses. You can get a bit stuck then.'

'Mmm, yes. But why do you want to do this – to the bed-spring?'

'Why?'

'Yes. What for?'

'To swallow it, of course.'

'Pardon?'

'To swallow it.'

'To – swallow?'

'That's right.'

'Uh-huh.'

I puffed my cigarette for a few moments and racked my brains. Things did not get any clearer.

'Uh – how?'

'How?'

'Ah – yes – how – swallow?'

'Well, you're a rum bugger and no mistake. You're drawing hard time in Vác and you're trying to tell me you don't know how to swallow a bed-spring?'

'I'm afraid I don't.'

'Jeezus Mary! What *is* the world coming to!'

'I'm sorry, I must have missed out on something. You see, I wasn't born in Hungary.'

'Oh, well, that might account for it, then.'

'I suppose so.'

'Can't be helped. Don't let it get you down.'

'I'll do my best. But what about the bed-springs?'

'Right. You might need to know this some time, you know.'

'That's always possible,' I agreed, offering him another Fecske.

'Well, there's nothing to it, really,' he began, going carefully through the entire ceremony of lighting up. 'You just twist a nice little hook in one end,' he explained, giving me a light from his glowing tip. 'Not too big and not too small – and then you slide it – hook first – down your gullet. It can be a bit retchy at first, but if you take it nice and easy and don't panic, it'll go down all right.'

'Down where?'

'Down your gullet, where d'you think?'

'What do you do when it's in there?'

'Well, you've made sure it's long enough so there's a bit still sticking out of your mouth even when the other end gets right down deep in your guts, of course.'

'Oh, of course.'

'Then you wiggle the inside end around a bit to make sure there's plenty of guts on all sides – and then – you give it a few jerks ...'

'A few – jerks?'

'Just until it catches good and proper—'

'Catches? In what?'

'In your guts, mate, not your bollocks! Not unless you're all hollow down below – ha-ha-ha-ha!'

For several moments, my companion chortled happily in his corner. I took advantage of his mirth to turn what he'd said over and over in my mind. Once he calmed down, I pressed on.

'But what – catches in your guts?'

'The hook, my sweetheart, the hook you put in the end of the spring when you was straightening it out.'

I kept silent for several minutes to let everything sink in. 'Why would you do something like that?'

'Why? To get out, why else?'

'Out?'

'Of course. The Hospital's a lot better than Kőhida, any day of the week!'

'Yes, I can believe that. But doesn't it hurt?'

'Of course it does. But not half as much as staying where you are.'

'How many times have you done this?'

'Oh, I've lost count by now. Enough.'

'But you said that soon it won't heal up at all.'

'So they tell me.'

'So you can't do it again.'

'Says who?'

'But if you do it again – even one more time – what happens then?'

'Don't ask me, mate. Doesn't matter anyway, does it? You can't help yourself when you go over the edge.'

'You've got to be joking!'

'Come off it, mate. Stop taking the piss. You're in Vác, aren't you? Confined to cells? You must know the score. You can take it for just so long. Then something's got to give. Anything. Doesn't matter what.'

'But you could be dead!'

'So what's so different about that?'

'You can't think like that, man!'

'Can't think at all, mate. Not when it comes over you. Just got to get out. Doesn't matter how. Just – out.'

I thought hard for several moments, but I couldn't think of anything to say. So I took out my cigarettes again without even working out how many I had left. I decided to skip the business with the charred rags and showed my box of

204

matches. As we relaxed again, the man unbuttoned the top pocket of his jacket and pulled out a grubby scrap of paper.

'You're a bit green, mate, but you sound like you've got a bit of education,' he said, holding the paper out towards me. 'Can you read Hungarian?'

'I used to be able to.'

'Do me a favour, will you? Read this for me.'

'Where did you get this?' I asked as I unfolded it.

'Hospital. Gave it to me as I was leaving.'

Puffing on my cigarette, I read in the glow. It was an extract from a directive from the People's Ministry of the Interior, Department of Correction and Penal Administration, paragraph such and such, section so and so … My companion wriggled his feet forward and leaned back until he was lying flat on the ground and waved his cigarette in the air like a conductor's baton. The glowing tip kept time with the rise and fall of the official jargon. As I got to the heart of the matter, the baton stopped to listen.

'… therefore, as and from the above date, any convict guilty of swallowing, under any circumstances whatsoever, bed-springs, forks, spoons, nails or any other item of any shape, form and material, not removable by means other than surgical operation, shall, automatically and without exception, appeal or review, forfeit forthwith all claim to any Remission of Sentence otherwise under consideration at the time of the offence. In cases where Remission is not applicable or has already been forfeited, an additional period of six months shall, automatically and without appeal or review, be added to the sentence being served. All subsequent offences shall, each and severally, carry the same six-month penalty to be served consecutively to any previous penalties or sentences without exception.'

'Long live the Revolution!' I heard from the floor.

'Well, what about that?'

'Bollocks! The same old story. Don't understand a bloody thing, do they?'

'What do you expect? It's not their job to understand, is it? They just *make* the rules, you know, they don't have to play by them. Anyway, it's not *them* I was asking about. It was you.'

The cigarette on the floor glowed brighter for a moment.

'I'd think it over, if I was you,' I added.

'Yes, thanks a lot. But there's just one little thing they've forgotten, isn't there?'

'What?'

'The next time they cut me open, it'll be for good. Let them try to add six months to that!'

'Very clever! They'll be ever so impressed with that line of argument in the mortuary!'

'Give it a rest, mate,' sighed my companion wearily.

He nipped out his cigarette and slipped the remaining butt carefully into his top pocket. Then he got to his knees, leaned forward, waddled and wriggled backwards, until he slotted himself accurately back into his 'armchair' again. Comfortably supported on three sides once more, he stretched out his legs in front of him, leaned back his head, yawned and thought aloud into the musty darkness.

'Regulations, regulations, regulations ... Re: this, re: that, re: their dads' dicks and mums' fannies ... When will they ever learn? I can just see it! The time I'm drawing's got so

206

hard it's like concrete. Even the air hurts. I've just *got* to get through that wall. Out, out, out! That scrap of paper keeps me in. One lousy bed-spring gets me out. Work the rest out for yourself, mate – just work it out for yourself …'

# 9

# Saint John, the Illuminator

Time had tested John to the limits of destruction and beyond. Or so even the roughest tally of years seemed to show. Yet John had not cracked. Indeed, he seemed rather to have seasoned and mellowed. As he had not been crushed by the weight he carried every second of each day, John's lead in the Watching-Time-Go-By Stakes had, over the years, stretched to unchallengeable proportions.

Mind you, John was anything but a winner to look at. No matter which way you turned him, he was short, bald, wrinkled, stick-limbed, potbellied and much too long in the tooth. This last was hardly surprising since no one – neither convict nor warder – could remember the wing without him. But John was not, as far as anyone could gather, getting anywhere near getting out. More curious still, he showed no sign of minding.

In explanation, he offered different thoughts on different days. The gist of these was more or less that at some stage – too long ago by now to remember exactly when – John had lost track of the passing days and got left behind. Nothing had happened since then to convince him that the effort needed to catch up again would be worthwhile.

'In any case,' he would maintain, 'I'm very comfortable living purely in the present. It's an awful strain worrying about the past and, all in all, quite futile. Ditto the future. The former can never be brought back, no matter how fondly you remember it. The latter can neither be avoided, no matter how scared of it you may be, nor brought forward, no matter how much you might long for it.

'Apart from which,' he would sometimes offer as an afterthought, 'by now it really doesn't matter how many years have passed, nor how few might still be left. Either way is much too long for Yours Truly.'

Perhaps the main thing about the above was that the way he delivered it was so convincing. He really didn't seem to care a fig what time did with him. Even so, few newcomers could let the matter rest there. We (after a time, 'they') kept worrying away at the riddle in the hope that some clue would work its way up to the surface.

It ought to have been a simple matter to work out when John was due for release. All you needed to know was when he had come in and how long he'd got. After that, the odds on whether he would make it back out again or not depended on nothing more arcane than knowing his age. Easy enough. In theory. Such calculations did not, however, reckon with John himself.

At the merest mention of any figure relating in any way to him, the old codger would fade away like a ghost. Of course, it should have been possible to corner even a ghost in an exercise yard measuring no more than fifty metres by fifty. At least, it should not have been impossible. But cornering your ghost was not the same thing as getting it to cough up figures. Not if your ghost was John.

He was a past master at parrying questions with remarks so intriguing as to be irresistible and sidestepping enquiries with anecdotes so entertaining as to be quite beyond interruption. If you still remembered your question after either or both of these ploys, and if there was still enough time left of either morning exercise or other times-out to ask again – and if you were still single-minded enough to press on regardless – John always held in his hand one unrufflable trump card.

Anyone who became too persistent would suddenly find him either out of range or incurably deaf. As John's company was far more enjoyable than any fact or figure could ever be, everyone soon learned to leave him to his own devices.

Intake after intake reached this point. Indeed, achieving this level of equanimity came to be regarded as the first step towards maturity. It meant that a newcomer was no longer entirely lost.

It also meant that one was now ripe for serious conversation. This would sometimes begin with a reference to past concerns. To remind us that it was possible for our souls to achieve too much equanimity, perhaps. Almost as a kind of consolation for denying us the prize we had originally sought, John would venture something on the lines of: if a man was quite sure he wouldn't see his sentence out, why should he upset himself – or anyone else, for that matter – with some petty insistence on unearthing numbers which might possibly become precise, but would certainly remain meaningless.

'Is it not infinitely preferable,' he once enquired soothingly, 'to imagine oneself a medieval monk, retreating from the world and leaving all earthly cares and vanities behind? Time is not on our side. So why should one cling to its coat-tails like a frightened child?'

There and then, or so it seemed to us, he had, in some strange way, outgrown, if not outplayed, that most implacable of foes.

John was not noticeably more inconvenienced by the absence of Time's consort, Space.

'All things considered,' he would beam, 'our cells are quite roomy enough for our needs. And our population is nothing if not well regulated. Which is more than can be said of most populations outside.'

His satisfaction with the space we had at our disposal would lead him on to extol other advantages we enjoyed.

'Never forget!' he would crow, 'unlike those toiling billions out there, we don't have to lift a finger to keep this roof over our heads. No daily rat race for us! And what's more, this entire building is an uncommonly safe haven, offering far more than average protection against the inescapable excesses of Nature and the unforeseeable acts of God.

'And as for the whims of Man! Why, for us even invasion is an empty threat! Added to which – both in principle *and* in practice – no one at all is barred from the shelter of our sanctuary. Most certainly not on grounds of race, creed or colour. What other spot on Earth can really and truly boast as much?'

211

If pressed, he would concede that matters could, on occasion, take a brutish turn.

'But,' he would remind us, 'where are such things unknown? They are simply the inevitable consequence of being descended from beasts of prey. One day we'll descend far enough for us all to turn over a new leaf. By the way, who can deny that the diet we get in here encourages us in that very direction? Now, now! Don't say, "It's the screws who should be on that diet, not us!"

'Let us not forget – the staff have not been privileged to share in the benefits of the advantages we enjoy. They've only lived life from one side. You can't blame them for not understanding more than they do. It's up to us to set an example. We should be grateful for the benefits of a truly low-protein, low-fat, minimalist diet that de-energises us so we can be truly peace-loving!'

If someone still could not give up a hankering for more space, less time and better grub, John would point out our numerous other compensations.

'Our "Order", after all, is under no vows of silence,' he would warble. 'We are free to use more or less as much time as we like on perfecting the civilised art of conversation. Ancient Greeks of unparalleled wisdom and French courtiers of exquisite refinement would have envied us relentlessly for this. Furthermore, our "Order" is not, by and large, flagellant, which is more than can be said for quite a number of more orthodox religious orders.

'Why, there are many spots on this planet where everyday life is far more restricted and far more painful than in here. No, no! There's no cause to get downhearted. Indeed, when you come to think of it, losing heart is the last thing we should do.

'Just consider – if a man's character is fundamentally cheerful and full of good will towards his fellow creatures, why on earth should he behave as though it were not? And if a man is fundamentally a sourpuss, where will he come across more cheering influences than in here?

'Indeed' – John often took wing on this word – 'when you come to think of it, isn't it obvious that, irrespective of whether you're an optimist or a pessimist, the worse things get, the *less* reason there is for *not* behaving like a humane being? For in the last analysis when all is said and done, when all is lost, what else does one have, but the choice to remain humane to the end?

'Why *should* we surrender that? And where in the world can you come to understand such things more thoroughly, more certainly – and more safely – than in here? Just try a battlefield. Or a famine. You'll soon see how lucky we are!'

John's sympathy was universal and there was no apparent limit to his benevolence.

'Our warders,' he would chuckle, 'have little more control over whether they are in here or out there than we have. So why resent them? Most of the time, the poor buggers have very little say in what they do or how they'll do it. So what's the point of harbouring grudges against them? After all, the grudge you harbour hurts you too. But the smile you smile also warms *you*. Where it matters. *Inside*.'

Strangely enough, as far as their uniforms would allow, most of the warders seemed to reciprocate his feelings. This could often lead to odd situations and unexpected benefits for all. For example, whenever John was on song in the yard, the guard in charge rarely cut him short. Instead, he would stare studiously in all directions but John's, while looking sullen (if the libretto was in German) or looking solemn (if the words were Hungarian).

The sullenness at German performances was because our warders felt excluded from something that might, possibly, lead to promotion. The solemnity at Hungarian recitals was because they were pretending not to following the libretto, while, in fact, they were hanging on every word. This simultaneous concentration in opposite directions took so much effort that our warders frequently forgot all about checking their watches. The extra exercise harmed no one, while John's sermons were always well worth staying out for.

(German recitals were usually in German because something of strategic importance was on the boil. Of course, even the most Top Secret planning pow-wow would be punctuated at nicely timed intervals by suitably worded – juicy, but disinformation – snippets in Hungarian, just to keep our supervisors interested enough not to cut the exercise session short.)

Rumour had it that John had once been a spy master of no mean repute and a force to be reckoned with. Whatever the truth of this, Karl certainly viewed the old fellow with undisguised respect and was not above consulting him on points of strategy. Apparently, his comments were very shrewd and amply repaid attention. His advice, however, seemed to be available to all and sundry, quite impartially, and many of us suspected that not even the enemy would have been refused, had he ever actually asked. Not unexpectedly, John showed scant interest in how Karl's schemes actually turned out.

'Whenever you see anyone winning,' he would shrug, 'you can be quite sure someone else is losing. So, taking the Universe as a whole, nothing much is either really gained or really lost – either way. Makes winning a waste of energy, don't you think?

'Of course, Triumphal Processions can be very decorative. But they somehow lose their sparkle for me when I remember that our victory parade is someone else's funeral procession. The "where" and the "who" don't vanish into thin air for me any more just because I can't show you round the one or introduce you to the other.

'Youngsters find it easy to ignore things like that. They even manage to believe they don't exist. At my time of life, that's much more difficult. Everything I've ever come across – and much that I haven't – seems to have *some* existence as long as I can either remember it or imagine it. Even though my competitors and enemies may have lost – and may even be dead – they still haven't completely gone, as long as I'm still here to think about them.

'So what can really justify all that winning and surviving? It all seems a bit empty, unless we somehow bring about something finer and better than what would probably have come to pass if we had lost. The idea of victory – pure and simple – just gets hollower and hollower as time goes by. Far from being something to celebrate, it feels to me more and more like something for which to atone.'

Heinz had his rubber soul and Karl his iron will. But the golden tongue belonged, beyond any doubt, to John.

Obviously enough, the 'gold' in question had nothing to do with money, power or success. To us it seemed to be more a matter of shedding light. He appeared to understand practically everything and we found it very difficult to imagine anything he might not be able to forgive. Moreover, what he offered was not easy consolation for people who needed encouragement so desperately that they'd swallow anything.

Indeed, nearly everything he said, no matter how blindingly clear it seemed to us at first, became – on reflection and in other mouths – curiously ambiguous. As for solutions, he avoided them like the plague. Time and again he stated in no uncertain terms that solutions to anything were few and far between and he'd never yet heard of any effective antidote for Life.

'It's all as simple as a slap in the face,' he would chuckle. 'No matter how cleverly you all try to complicate the issue, a kick in the nose or getting cut off from everything one holds dear hurts. Just that. Nothing more, nothing less. It. Hurts. And it makes no difference to the pain whether the person feeling it is suffering for a cause, a creed, a crime, crass stupidity, plain carelessness or no good reason at all.

'Of course, these things *can* make a difference to *how* we bear the pain. The difference, then, is not in the pain – but in ourselves. And that's the one place where we *can* make a difference. But there, however, is the rub of rubs. Because that change is more difficult, more painful – not to say more downright frightening – than anything else in human experience up to now.

'Of course,' he would add, just as you'd thought you'd grasped something, 'explanations only explain. They don't

216

actually *do* anything. They absolutely don't *solve* anything. Half the time, they don't even make anything clearer, really. They just second guess. Like has-beens, wannabees and football fans. After all ...'

His eyes would cloud over and his gaze turn inwards as his voice trailed away. We could see he was on the track of a truly elusive thought. All of us would stop breathing. Hearts in mouths, we'd crowd nearer. A dropping pin would have been strangled before it hit the floor. His eyes would clear. He'd sniff. He'd blink. He was back on Earth.

'After all,' he would croak at last, 'if I could get my hands on a magic wand – don't you think the first person I'd wave it over would be me? Why, just about everything's wrong with me! To start with, the view from my apartment is truly boring. To finish with, I'm old, ugly, feeble, poor and unloved. Now, what's the cure for all that?

'The only thing that springs to my mind is an Exit, a Way Out. A very democratic one, I grant you. And absolutely free to one and all, without exception. What's more, despite the ever anxious eye they keep on us in here, it gets nearer and nearer day by day, even if I do nothing whatsoever to help it along. But even when it gets here,- it's still only a Way Out. It's still not a cure. I'm still old, ugly, feeble, poor and unloved. Only now I'm also a corpse and there's no view at all! Greta Garbo and Monte Carlo are further away than ever before.

'So what's left? What "Universal Remedy" can still be tucked away in "Ye-Olde-Cure-All-Medicine-Chest"? "Linctus of Silver Lining", perhaps? "Too old to have a future? Be thankful! You've got a very big thing less to worry

217

about." "Too feeble to compete for anything? Relax! You no longer have to deliver the goods. No more performance pressure!" "Stoney broke? Rejoice! Yours is the simple life. No more responsibilities. No more temptations. No more stress!"

'If you can swallow that kind of medicine, then take it. But to me it all sounds suspiciously like different ways of saying nothing more than, "If you can't have what you want, then want something else."

'What about those "Magic Words of Comfort" in "Them Thar Good Ole Good Books", though? "Dust to dust." "Ashes to ashes." "All flesh is grass." "The worse it gets in this life, the better it will be in the next." "See that star up there? That's Mummy." "Eternal houris of delight await thee, True Believer!" "If you're very, very good and ever so, ever so pure, then the next time round YOU TOO CAN BE A CLOUD OF ECSTASY!"

'If it makes you feel better, then believe it. But as for me, I regret to say that these days I feel more like an "Absolute Zero" than anything else. And I'm by no means sure any longer that I'm in any way a part – even an infinitesimal part – of any kind of "Inevitable Historical Process" whatsoever.

'Aaaah! But what about the PASSIONATE DEFIANCE of those Great Artists who "Speak-To-Us-In-The-Language-Of-Our-Time"? "Do not go gentle into that good night", and all that.

'Well, I must admit, that cheered me up a lot when I was young – and your passionate poet, Dylan Thomas, being Welsh and thus inheriting the accrued insights of an

218

oppressed minority, *was* a decent enough alcoholic to actually follow his own advice. And – having once heard a recording of his lovely voice – I really do bless his memory.

'But, by now, I'm a bit past that sort of "Grand Exit" myself. Also, just *look* at me! Doesn't "gentle", in fact, seem absolutely the best way for someone like me to go into that Good Night?

'"Is that it?" I hear you all say. "Aren't there any more possibilities? That can't be all?" Well, my heart bleeds for you. It really does. All right, let's give it another go. Give the bottom of the barrel one more scrape. Ah, yes, here's something ...'

Hearts leap. Throats swallow. Tongues lick lips.

'Yes – yes, indeed – billions upon billions of words and melodies and rhymes and warbling voices and fluttering tummies and flickering eyelashes – let us boil them all down and consider EL OH VEE EE! How can anyone with any spark left in them give up on the "Divine Distraction", the "Rejuvenating Rapture", the "Lustre of Life", and so on and so forth?

'Well, go to it if you can, one and all! "Make your Sun run! Gather ye rosebuds!", to borrow from your cheerful British poets once again. I'm certainly the last person in the world to breathe a word against LOVE and all that. But don't ask me to join in, not at my age and in my condition! Why, I get palpitations at the very thought of even a wet dream. Any flesh more solid than that would finish me off for sure. "A consummation devoutly to be wished!" you may well propose. No doubt, no doubt. A good exit. Even a great one if it goes well. But a cure?'

We all mull the question over in solemn silence for several more turns round the yard. Our screw looks non-committal and keeps his counsel. Eventually, John surfaces again.

'I find myself between the Devil and the Deep Blue Sea, my friends, between the Devil and the Deep, Deep Blue …'

All ears prick up.

'On one side, I see before me solutions for elderly spinsters no longer suited for anything else and desperate for any support whatsoever in their twilight days. On the other, I'm haunted by remedies for rising young bucks, eager for any excuse to forget everything but embracing life in all its sensual glory, morning, noon and night and as often as physically possible in between.

'I can't quite resign myself to the former, but I can no longer kid myself I have any business with the latter. I have to admit that my body is now more suitable for swallowing pills and kneeling before altars than anything else.

'Yet in my mind's eye, I still behold the rosy dawns of yesteryear when even I believed in endless successions of ever more exotic damsels of ever more erotic propensities, all gazing in ever more tender variations of multiple-orgasmic astonishment (tinged with undying gratitude, of course!) at nobody else – but me.'

We all grin. Our screw looks very solemn.

'Now that I'm halfway over the Waterfall, though, the drop looks awfully long – and everything else looks very far away. Well, there it is. And there's no point in complaining. Especially as complaining is usually just a way of adjusting to a problem, not of solving it.

'No. Everything is as it is and no amount of wishing and washing is going to make it anything but so. The situation is, fundamentally, not too good. So I might as well make the best of it.'

Our grins turn into question marks. The screw looks less solemn. John frowns at his feet. Tramp, tramp, tramp, tramp, tramp. Eventually, a quavering voice airs our common thought.

'Why?'

John tears himself away from his feet and turns his entire mind to the question.

'Well, if nothing else, "best" *is* usually somewhat better than "worst" when all is said and done,' quoth John, at his most slippery.

'Oh! Is that all?' quoth a disappointed someone on behalf of us all, including our warder.

'All? We-e-ell, not quite.'

'Aaah!'

'Speaking quite personally – just on my own behalf, of course – I feel I'm quite a bit happier when I'm making the best of things.'

'Happier?'

'Come off it!'

'Stop pissing us about!'

'Who are you kidding?'

'Oh dear, I'm so sorry, I seem to have disappointed you all again. But I'm quite serious. Believe me.'

'Why should we?'

John sighs. The guard smiles. We look solemn. Tramp, tramp, tramp …

'Come on, John! You owe us an explanation.'

'Yes! Come on! Cough up!'

'Happier? What do you mean, "happier"?'

'We-e-e-ell,' twinkles John, 'first of all, being so near to kicking the bucket, I'm not afraid any more. Second, the years seem to have worn my sense of guilt completely away. And third, unstinting first-hand observation and exhaustive analysis have shown conclusively that the happier I am, the better I feel – which more or less covers what I mean by, "happier".'

'But you can't just keep "feeling better" all the time, John, now can you?'

'Perhaps, not. But you *can* do your best as much of the time as possible. Try marching to a different drum. When misery lands on you, don't mirror the feeling – meet it with a smile. Enjoy even dark depressions. Wallow, really *wallow* so deep you come out the other side wearing a grin! When you get a bit of good luck, don't force the laughs. Take it easy. Remember, non-stop gaiety can cloy as much as non-stop caviar. Even if life gets totally monotonous, don't keep harping on the same thoughts all the time. Switch around. A change, as they say, is as good as a rest. Platitudes, of course. Perhaps, one would just be doing the opposite of a very basic human and animal response to external stimuli. One would be doing no more than just refusing to mirror the feelings, expressions, words, threats and so on, with which one is faced. But, then, one might bear in mind that, if we really try, we *can* do that – we really can. Animals, chimpanzees, for example, simply can't—'

'Chimpanzees! Holy shit! What on earth are you trying to prove?'

'Prove? Prove? Why, nothing, of course. Nothing at all.'

'Nothing?'

'Not a thing.'

'Oh, you're a real whore's cock, John, you really are!'

Tramp, tramp, tramp. We all frown down at our feet. The screw looks smug. John looks solemn. We all go marching on.

'Um-hwe-ell,' whiffles the elderly one, at last. 'I suppose – at a pinch – it could mean something.'

'Wha-a-at?' cries every voice as one.

'We-e-ell – that – perhaps – even – old men – still have their uses.'

'Uses? What uses?'

'Look at it this way. What do the aged have to gain from almost anything? So, who should be more free from the competitive pressures of everyday life than the thoroughly elderly? Who, therefore, should be in a better position to tell the truth? Those of us still not too senile to recognise it, of course.'

We all look solemn. The guard frowns at his feet. John smiles. Tramp, tramp, tramp, tramp, tramp …

On the face of it, John's qualifications for the post of resident sage looked distinctly promising. He certainly had the age and he had definitely passed the stage of having anything to attack or defend. Furthermore, he gave a convincing impression of impartial intelligence and disinterested wisdom.

He was also gratifyingly open-handed about speculating, calmly and impartially, on the past, present and future – and

223

he was satisfyingly generous with prophetic pronouncements of a colourful and stimulating character. There was, however, one cloud over his candidature. He steadfastly refused to take up the cross. And not just *the* cross – absolutely *any* cross.

'Heroes and Martyrs?' he would exclaim. 'Saints and Saviours? Stuff and Nonsense! Rhubarb and Rabarbara! All right and proper in Lay and Legend, Song and Story and such like and so forth. "Everyone gets to conquer Evil and outwit the Blue Meanies, but nobody gets their feet wet!" Very satisfying and enjoyable.

'But not a lot of use come Monday morning and the working week. Counterproductive, actually. Especially if the Good Guys win. Which, by definition, they can't. Heroes, Martyrs, Saints or Saviours that get to live happily ever after become the very opposite of what once they set out to be. They become the Establishment – Kings and Commissars, Bosses, Baddies and Bourgeoisies. Back to the barricades, Comrades! Back up on your crosses, Saviours! Back, back on your Mycenaean vase, Hercules!

'You see, they act as a sort of lightning rod. If there's even just one, good, solid hero around, it lets everybody else out of doing anything themselves. They can all look busy swanning around with lumps in their throats and tears in their eyes and all that.

'Enough of this and the Bad Hats don't even need cowardice, indifference, apathy, stupidity, greed, ambition, collaboration, corruption and all that any more. Lucifer will manage very well without such aids, because everyone is just too worn out emotionally through identifying with their Heroes to be able to lift a finger!

'And don't bore me with that old chestnut about a Hero owing it to his fans, to the people who've trusted him, to keep on taking on the Dragon, the Giants, the Regime, the Authorities and so forth! Very touching, I'm sure! But while our dumb Hero, egged on and on by his admiring audience, goes further and further out on a limb, his faithful followers can rarely be trusted even just to give the Villains with the Big Saw the directions to the wrong tree!

'No, no! Heroes and Martyrs are strictly for the birds. Or, to be precise, they're tailor-made for Totalitarian Regimes, Dictatorships, Tyrannies, Establishments and Juntas of every kind and colour. Indeed, if ever there was a real dearth of Heroes and Martyrs, then any regime with any intelligence (mercifully, a contradiction in terms in any but the Secret Service sense) would have to invent some.

'(Knock on wood! Just keep praying they haven't – yet!)

'Otherwise, you might just get people looking at what's actually going on instead of at the headlines. You might even start developing masses made up of individual human beings instead of numbers. No. There can be no real progress until the man-in-the-street starts thinking seriously for himself. Heroes let everyone off the hook. Heroes are for stories. Leave them where they work best!'

For all his forgiving nature, John had a decidedly cantankerous turn of mind. He delighted in stirring things up, not in nailing them down. He would happily reduce the most carefully constructed edifice of answers to a rubble of conflicting questions. Furthermore, he was only interested in Ideal Possibilities and was quite unmoved by ideas whose main claim to virtue was that they were practically possible.

The 'Art of Compromise' he regarded as a contradiction in terms no less preposterous than the notion of an 'intelligent regime'. Compromise, he maintained, was rarely more than a convenient recipe for arriving at neither one thing nor another, while wallowing in the comforting delusion of having done something – and picking up month after month of substantial pay cheques for the entire duration of this exercise.

'All a compromise ever achieves,' quoth John, 'is another compromise!'

And he was unnervingly unerring at putting his finger on just *how* those among us, who had succumbed to such temptations, had fallen between both stools. He was moved only by universal and simple truths and had not the slightest use for complex and microscopic definitions. 'Life,' he would say, 'can never be understood by reading the small print.'

While his views were nothing if not definite, he remained uncompromisingly elusive. Whenever anyone became too insistent on him defining exactly what he meant by anything, he would merely shrug and warble that he left that up to the enquirer's common sense.

This often stopped any further debate stone dead. So he was sometimes asked why he did this. After all, who on earth had more time to follow discussions through to logical conclusions than we did? Moreover, once we'd got used to an intermittent, indirect and infinite form of debate, the ups and downs of prison routine did not seriously interrupt the flow of thought. So, considering the almost ideal conditions for permanent, cooperative cogitation, was not John's refusal to entertain detailed explanation tantamount to abdicating from any meaning at all?

'By no means,' he would reply with disarming sincerity. 'Not by a long chalk. First of all, if what I'm saying is really as unclear as all that, then it's probably nonsense and it's high time I shut up anyway. Second, if whoever I'm talking to is either unwilling or unable to understand things for himself, then nothing I can say is going to improve matters. Third, if my partner in debate is really more interested in *how* we discuss than *what*, then I'm off! I don't have time for such fripperies any more. I'm much too old. I don't need hair-splitting, I need visions of Paradise – and what can be more meaningful than that?'

John's apparent lack of patience with fine details and final conclusions was not, however, the petulance of old men who can no longer keep their minds on anything for more than a skimming instant. *His* mind was far from shallow and it positively teemed with belief.

For example, about his attitude to religion, he used to say that he was not so much an A-theist as an EN-thusiast. It was not so much that he did not believe in God as that he did believe in everything else. He was not so much concerned with denying the existence of anything, but rather with affirming the potential of all existence.

If the highest form of existence was already exclusively occupied, then the possible development of all other forms was severely limited. This he quite simply did not feel inclined to accept. It was not natural. The Universe could not, by its nature, be so finite. Many Gods of numerous varieties, rising and falling, coming and going, waxing and waning – fair enough. And very much in the nature of things. Many a worse idea had had its day. One God – alone, indivisible and evermore – statistically unlikely and rather a bore!

John was convinced that intelligent life in other parts of the Universe was mathematically much more probable than that any of us would live to draw another breath. Happily for us, he was also quite insatiable when it came to speculating about what such life might be like and where it might be lurking. He gave us many a stimulating hour expanding on the possible nature of alien beings.

Nevertheless, his prime concern was life on Earth. But not sociological or political life as applicable to masses. His only use for the masses was as a huge, blunt instrument to create enough population pressure to finally force us to migrate into Outer Space and try our luck in the entire, Stellar and Galactic Universe. What interested him about Life was not quantity. It was quality. What we could – and should – do with Life. Not what Life did – or could do – with us. And here he was quite adamant. It was not up to God (nor even gods and goddesses) to get better at giving Commandments. It was up to us to get better at living life.

He was not much interested in continuity either. If we were stupid enough not to get into Outer Space, then we were too stupid to survive here on Earth. Having fallen through the bottom of social life so resoundingly himself, he was entirely unabashed at the prospect of loss or defeat or even annihilation and he felt that survival was by no means worth any price. Especially, not the horrific fee he reckoned the deal inherently cost.

'When you come right down to it,' he would sigh, 'it's not even a deal really. More like a common or garden hold-up. "Your everything or your life!" So you either give in and life isn't worth living or you don't – and then you're dead! Not too conducive to clear thinking, eh? Particularly when the hand holding the gun to your head turns out to be your own!

'Apart from which,' he would add, switching tack as the duty screw locked into orbit for optimum reception, 'there is the much neglected matter of "values". Now, I grant you, few things are worse than everybody saluting the same catch-phrase and turning into the same suffocating stereotype. But even so, we do seem to need values of some kind, some standards that we can uphold as individuals and share as a species.'

'What for?'

'Well, there's quite a selection of reasons that have proved handy enough at different times, you know. "Do unto others as you would be done by!" "For King and Country!" "For the Salvation of thy Soul!" "For the Common Good!" And so on. Many of them sound a bit antiquated by now, but most had something to recommend them in their day. Just at the moment, there's one I like best, because it seems the most basic and because it seems to work under any flag, banner or label. Or even under none at all. It's quite simply this: We must have values –'

'Yes?'

' – in order –'

'Yes, yes?'

'– to be valuable.'

'Oh, Lord!'

'Oh, Lord?'

'O Lord, make me in every way, a little better every day!'

'Yes, I see what you mean,' conceded John. 'Still, it doesn't sound *so* bad if you leave out the "O Lord" bit, does it?'

'Maybe not, but history just doesn't seem to be telling us that such a thing is feasible.'

'Did I say it was supposed to be easy?'

'It's just not practical.'

'Perhaps not. But even so, "human" values, as we insist on calling them (even though we may have no more right to them than many another being!), seem to have been around in one form or another for ages. You can be as cynical as you like, but you keep on coming across them in all sorts of unexpected places. For instance, urban life – as I remember it – is full of little rescues by random acts of kindness and generosity that keep upsetting the odds and go completely against the grain of the status quo and the survival of the fittest and all that. Furthermore, no matter how out of the blue such things may come, most people feel instinctively that there is something naturally "fair" or even "just" about such interventions. Now, that's significant, don't you think?'

'Significant?'

'Of what?'

'Of – the possibility …'

John's brow puckered in thought. Our screw tightened orbit.

'Of the distinct – probability …'

John's brow puckered into a frown. Our screw nearly trod him down.

'That such values *are* practical,' continued John, picking up the thread just in time. 'That they are not just abstract notions. That they need not be just vague phrases and empty words. That they can have concrete application and tangible results. That ...'

'Yes, yes, yes – give us an example?'

'Still with us, are you?' enquired our mentor amiably. 'Remind me to appeal against your sentence, young man. You're obviously not really suited to a place like this!'

The entire exercise yard, including the hat in charge, enjoyed a refreshing laugh for another tramp round.

'Well, now,' continued John, his eyes twinkling, 'example, you said. Let me see. Yes – among other things – values make men.'

'You don't feel that might be a bit *too* concrete, John?'

'Not if you remember that some things are most concrete when they're abstract and most abstract when they're concrete.'

'Eh? I think I just lost the plot!'

'Well, just consider education for a moment,' suggested John with every appearance of seriousness. 'That's a pretty abstract whatnot which people are always trying to pin down in concrete terms. To control it and organise it and manage it and budget it and market it – people want it as concrete as possible. So much so that education is often thought of as being *for* something. Not something in itself, but just a method of producing something else. A matter of producing people to perform functions, say. Now, I've nothing against people knowing how to do things, but with all due respect, what is really contained in *that* idea is "training" – not "education".

'The very concepts of "knowledge" and "excellence" themselves are soon devalued if you limit your idea of education to a process of training. The only "training" in any way essential to education is training in how to think for yourself. Surely, the true – perhaps, indeed, the only – function of education is the making of thinking men and women. Not the multiplication of hireable hands.

'After all, if you're seriously helping to educate someone, what you are really doing is trying to help them *grow*. To understand their best potential and see the possibility of achieving it. To be their *own* man. Not yours. Not someone else's – not a system's and certainly not a machine's. So it is at its most abstract that education is most concrete. In itself, in its application and in its results.

'There's no future any more (not even a limited nineteenth-century kind of future) in just training people to carry out specific limited tasks in specific limited situations. The tasks and the situations change. They even disappear. And more and more day by day, they change and/or disappear almost before the training that was supposed to fit people to deal with them is completed. The process is, by its very nature, too concrete to cope with change.

'You can't solve the problems of future generations for them. You can't even be sure what those problems will be. All you can really do is try to help your descendants to become capable of solving for themselves whatever problems they end up facing.

'Conversely, it is at its most concrete that education is most abstract. It is no longer itself, its application is ephemeral and its results are hardly even skin-deep. Anyone only trained in a skill, however fine that may be, is just an extension of a manufacturing process or a tool. When the usefulness of either runs out, the men left over are left with very little to fall back on. For the present, many of them can be *RE*-trained, of course. Modified to fit some other tool or process. But what happens when automation really begins to bite and no more skilled hands are needed? They'll have as little to do as we have. And even less reason for existing. At least we're here to serve sentences.'

The orbiting guard nodded vigorously.

'What,' mused John, 'will *they* be here for?'

Our satellite's eyebrows knotted in hairy perplexity.

'At the same time, there are concepts and ideals that we can value, but which do NOT seem to produce any obvious, practical benefits – concrete or otherwise.'

Relief cleared our custodian's hirsute brow and his face fell back into its customary solemnity.

'Beauty, for instance. We all like it. But it doesn't seem to actually *do* very much – if anything, at all. The Ancient Greeks, of course, said that Beauty is the one thing that doesn't *have* to do anything. It's doing what it's supposed to do by simply being what it is. Its existence IS its function.'

John paused to let us all contemplate Beauty for a suitable distance round the yard.

'Just as an afterthought, though,' he chirped when he judged we'd contemplated Beauty enough, 'it does have *one* effect that *is* quite practical.'

'Aha!'

'Hold your horses, now! It's only this: as long as Beauty is around and we retain a fairly general ability to appreciate it, it helps to remind us – to reaffirm for us – that such a thing, such Beauty, is possible.'

We all tramped on that for quite a long time.

'That may not seem like much,' continued John, reading our thoughts. 'But concepts like that are – by and large – the very values on which all the others rest. The whole system of values, in fact – if there is one. However, there *is* a rub – and here it is. In the absence of some unanimously accepted universal edict, divine or otherwise – or some obviously practical benefit that no one can ignore or deny – such values are simply a matter of choice. Preference. Desire. Will. Imagination. No more – but no less.

'How a man makes these choices shows what he prefers and respects. What he prefers and respects *is* the man. The better the ideals he holds, the better the man. Follow the better men and the way forward is clear.

'"Tricky", you may say (for any number of reasons), and you'd be right. But even among quite big ideals, some can be – and have been – considered more valuable than others.

'For example, many have considered – and some still do consider – "Truth" to be an intrinsically more valuable ideal than "Justice". Indeed, numerous thinkers – Leo Tolstoy, for instance – have felt that "Justice" depends on "Truth" and is impossible without it.

'On the other hand, whereas ideals must, in some sense at least, be universal and eternal, time and circumstance can make inroads, if not on their integrity then certainly on their practicability.

'For example, whereas it may be quite true that much of the land territory of the United States was obtained from its original owners by fraud, it might now be somewhat problematic to apply the justice that should follow from that truth. Similar situations exist in many parts of the world.

'Should our kind hosts, the Communists, one day find themselves obliged to return property appropriated in the comparatively recent past by essentially immoral – indeed, essentially criminal, though temporarily legalised – means and perhaps even to cough up compensation, how would Justice actually be done and Truth faced – right here?

'The same applies to most territorial arrangements made in Eastern and Central Europe by the victorious powers after both World Wars. Nevertheless, no matter what difficulties may arise with regard to applicability, special circumstances of time and place and so forth, there seems to be no real alternative to the proposition that the QUALITY of an ideal must, in some way, be the true basis of its value. And that if you don't somehow face the music – the *real* music – no matter how unpleasant or inconvenient that may be, you will never, ever get off your knees and bring anything worth giving to either Life or the Universe.

'Just to cloud the matter even further, the value judgement – the moral choice – a person makes must also be made without coercion or manipulation. It must spring from understanding, not indoctrination. Otherwise, it's not a choice at all. It's just a surrender in the face of superior force or the weight of prevailing opinion.

'The choice *cannot* be the result of militant or evangelical conversion. It must NOT be something grafted on from the outside, but something that grows from within. Only if it has truly grown from within as the result of individual realisation is the belief sound and the human being whole.

'The Choice and the Will must be free. Even at the risk of a rejection that results in annihilation. If a man, or Mankind for that matter, does not make the right choice, then it is actually better – distasteful though the prospect may be to some – that he, or we, do NOT survive.

'The choice we make will, in itself, merit the result it brings. We have no Divine Right to survive. The Universe can – and, quite probably, will – demonstrate that fact of life to us just as conclusively as we have demonstrated it to many of the beings – human and non-human – that have been in our power and, hence, in our care.

'It is only if we accept this and stop shitting hot bricks at the very idea, that we might, eventually, be able to think with enough clarity and reason to take decisions of real and lasting value. If we make the wrong choices, we will of course have proved, beyond the shadow of a doubt, that we were simply unfit to make the right choices.

'Apart from which, who is to say that our extinction *is* wrong? The Universe as a whole might be well rid of a troublesome and pestilential species! In any case, we will certainly not have been WORTHY of the survival we insist we prize so much, but which, in fact, we respect too little to seriously bother our heads about.

'The truth is that what we are really motivated by is not the desire to live (few of us are very constructive about WHAT we want to live FOR – or WHY), but fear of the opposite. Fear of Death. Fear of Extinction.

'However, negative motivations rarely result in anything better than the lesser of two evils. Extinction must be faced quite calmly. After all his fine words, Man should be able to accept the results of his own actions with no more fuss than the dodo kicked up about consequences that were entirely beyond *its* control.

'Once this is understood, the deadening weight of crippling and irrelevant emotions such as fear, greed, envy, can be jettisoned and our decisions can be freed from the curse of their malignant influence. If we can make the right decisions and base our characters on our noblest and most generous ideas, then our lives become worth living – and, perhaps, we become worthy of Life.

'A way of life that becomes worth living, becomes worthy of survival. This does not mean that it WILL survive. (Though it certainly improves the chances.) All it does mean is that we will be worthy of that windfall if it blows our way. The purpose of our evolving values is not to get our teeth into some Golden Carrot in the Sky. Nor to hit the Jackpot in some Celestial Lottery. It is simply to have – and live – valuable lives.'

We all trudged soberly round and round for a number of silent circles. Eventually, our guard gave up the struggle, glanced at his watch and raised an eyebrow at John. The seraphic smile that flashed back at him indicated that the old fellow was not finished yet.

'Before anyone gives way to despair,' he chuckled, 'let's just remember that, even on a purely practical and everyday level, there's a lot to be gained from serious values.

'For a start, everything works much better. On the whole, people feel better if they believe in what they are doing and are doing what they believe in. The value of wisdom, courage, goodness, kindness, intelligence, beauty, truth and so on has – more or less and off and on – been understood all over the Earth from earliest times. Their understanding has meant harmony.

'Human and other beings have been quite capable of living together in harmony – for odd moments in history, perhaps, and, albeit, in often even odder corners of the globe – and entirely irrespective of the configuration of Deities, or Undeities, that graced the skies of their nights.

'Of course, in this day and age, things are not as straight-forward as once they were because we are now so much more powerful than we have ever been before. We know so much, but have lost the support, artificial though that may have been, of all those systems of belief that depended on us knowing much less. Unfortunately, we still don't know enough to be worthy of believing in ourselves.

'The resurrection of obsolete religions cannot help us. That is simply a way of burying our heads in the sands of time. Loki and Fenrir are on the rise – and where are the Heroes of Asgard? We are no wiser, no braver, no better, no more beautiful and certainly no more truthful than we were of yore. And what's more, we are surrounded by a ring of paradoxes stronger than any ring of steel.'

The sudden ring of hobnailed boots resounding in the tunnel connecting our exercise yard with the outer compound reawakened our warder abruptly to his duties. He bellowed us over to the entrance to our wing at the double. The front third of the line was already safely inside before the heavy figures of top brass burst into view behind us.

'Take Mankind!' offered John some days later. 'The trouble is not so much that we keep using our wicked little heads to think with all the time. Far from it! The problem is that we still have too much of the old animal instinct bubbling around in one or other of our vestigial brains and *that* spills over into an incurable urge to run for the cover of Faith at the first sign of anything unfamiliar. And what, after all, are Faith and Religion but the point at which our capacity for rational thought gets overloaded and explodes into prejudice, partiality and blind belief?

'Furthermore, don't think for one moment that this is just for hallelujah-ing old ladies or weedy bachelors in dog collars! You will look far and wide before you see a finer example of a True Believer than our friend Karl, here. And which war, after all, is he still fighting?

'Now, you can get yourself to do anything if you believe strongly enough in a cause. It's much harder to commit murder if you have even an inkling of what you're really doing. Yes, humanity is still too near the beast from which it sprang, so it keeps on turning everything into Faith and reducing everything to religious equations. Just consider, for a moment, our kind hosts here – the Communists.'

At this point, our guard's ears pricked up so sharply they practically punctured his hat.

'What a good thing they had going for them when they set off!' reflected John, with no hint of insincerity. 'They were the natural heirs to every vein of progressive and humane thought that had so far flowed through our history. But they became so quickly overtaken by the fear of losing, so rapidly institutionalised and so utterly seduced by the dogma of the ends justifying the means that they have missed the boat entirely.

'Thus they have ended up fanatically religious, and as paranoid about heresy as the Inquisition. Their minds have become so preoccupied with splitting hairs and skulls that they don't even see that they have actually *become* the means they have used and have thus parted company with the ends for ever. Just as, long ago, the Christian Church turned its back on Christ. "BABY THROWN OUT WITH BATH WATER." A sad epitaph for Socialist Man.'

Socialist Man – presently on Earth in the form of our guard – sighed in sympathy. We tramped round and round in thoughtful silence.

'When you come down to it,' piped John, as we got back to where he'd left off. 'When you come right down to the nitty-gritty, almost any old system – or, indeed, no system at all – could work if you and I were only man enough and good enough. State and Church and any other superstructure you care to name can wither away to a dim memory – and life would still be worth living. But no system – not even the finest ideology in the Universe – is any use at all if we can't match up to it in our thoughts and actions and selves. That's the simple truth.'

At this point, the simple truth got overrun by the complex realities of prison life and had to postpone itself for another day. Of course, at our latitudes 'another' did not necessarily mean 'next'. Nor the day after next, for that matter. In fact, no one could be at all certain when our meditations would continue or, indeed, that when they did continue, they would go on from where they had left off. This, however, never seemed to incommode anyone unduly and everyone got pretty thoroughly acclimatised to thinking up and down and backwards and sideways and around and through, instead of only straight forward.

'Paradox and Contradiction!' chirped John one bright morning. 'Paradox and Contradiction! Consider, for a moment (if you can spare the time) the following random selection of slaps in the face of the innocent and pure-of-heart!

'ONE: the qualities needed to *gain* wealth or power are, almost always, diametrically the opposite of those necessary for the exercise of either to any purpose of any value.

'TWO: everybody keeps harping on and on about "peace", while at one and the same time committing the bulk of available capital – both in money and in minds – to the development and production of engines of war.

'THREE: in those parts of the world that most pride themselves on their democratic traditions, the race for votes has entirely replaced responsible government. (As for creative leadership for the benefit of all – forget it!)

'FOUR: modern medicine has eliminated most of the epidemic diseases that used to decimate Mankind, only to replace them with a single and uncontrollably accelerating plague – Mankind!

'FIVE: fortunes are spent on persuading populations to consume, not according to their needs but according to the needs of vast factories, which aim above all and at any cost to stay in production. And, moreover, in production of more and more of the same thing. What all this production seems, in the end, to produce is essentially holes and garbage. Even these, alas, are not always so coordinated as to leave the one filling the other.

'SIX: nothing was done at the right times to prevent the horrors of unemployment that resulted from unbridled Capitalism. By now – in reaction to this – the idea of full employment has, in certain countries, become such a fetish that hordes of people are employed in activities producing nothing but employment. Movement is inextricably confused with action. Eventually, of course, the bill will arrive and then who – or what – will pay for all that unproductive movement? And how will the Powers That Be – whoever they turn out to be by then – cope with the super-unemployment that will follow when their cheques bounce?

'SEVEN: not so long ago, Education was the privilege of the chosen few. The rest lived in outer darkness and utter illiteracy. So now the watchword is, "Education for All!" Wonderful! Only the slice of bread that now has to be buttered is immeasurably larger than any ever buttered before. And it's supposed to get buttered *without* dramatic changes in the priorities of National Budgets. As if that wasn't problem enough, Education must now concern itself more with avoiding denting self-esteem than with pursuing excellence. Not even the dullest intelligence must get the slightest hint that it may not be the equal of Einstein. (Just in case Mummy and Daddy switch their vote!) As a result, Education has been spread so thin and packaged so conveniently for instant absorption by even the most impervious brain that it has been reduced to the level of the most unenduring consumer perishable.

'EIGHT: for centuries the world has been riddled with Dogma, Fanaticism and Superstition. Progress, however, has by now led many of us to such a peak of enlightenment that we no longer believe in anything at all. This seems to have left us surrounded by boredom on an international scale and an increasing inability to sustain the momentum of life even over the traditional three score years and ten. How, then, shall we manage when – instead of being confined to one small planet – we have to start living the much more extended life-spans needed for inhabiting the infinite Universe? (Unless, of course, we are to assume that Contradiction Number Two was deliberately designed to ensure that we should never have to face this problem at all.)

'NINE: on both sides of the Iron Curtain, the people with the most leverage for getting things done are still those with the most money and power. Obviously, however, such people have no shortage of pleasurable potterings about with which to fill their daily round. This, unfortunately, means that those with the most means to influence events are also those with the most events to influence them against making any changes.

'So the poor and the downtrodden, the unfortunate and the unsuccessful are still necessary because they are the last Custodians of Truth. For they have so few distractions to divert their attention from essentials and so little power to alter the parameters of everyday existence to suit personal whims, that it is only among such wretches that one may still hope to find the odd pair of eyes unclouded by excess

– or the occasional character still uncorrupted by any interest irretrievably vested in the Status Quo.

'The Paradox is that those whose lives are simple enough to see the truth are usually too poor to do much about it, while those who are rich enough and powerful enough to do anything about it are far too far from the truth and much too busy with other things even to spare it a glance.'

John could go on and on in such veins indefinitely. However, the one thing furthest from his mind was actually convincing anyone about his ideas. His speculations, he maintained, were in the best traditions of the Philosophers of Classical Antiquity. They were simply a way of exercising the intellect and passing the time. Beyond this most humdrum and practical of applications, they had, he insisted, no value whatsoever.

For those of us hoping to build up enough spiritual armour to protect us from our all too human condition, John's lack of seriousness was a continual source of frustration. We never developed any way of telling when the golden tongue was in his cheek and when it wasn't. John played with words and ideas like a porpoise gambolling among waves. His predilection for paradox was as permanent as a dolphin's grin and just as difficult to decipher.

What John had was something whose validity he steadfastly refused to admit, but which – in an unguarded moment of over-exuberance – he had once referred to as, 'The Doctrine of Logical Oppositivism'.

'It's nothing at all,' he squeaked, catching the gleam in our eyes. 'Even on a good day, it's no more than an insubstantial curlicue connecting concentric paradoxes! The first puff of trained intelligence will blow it all apart. It's not worth another thought!'

Paradox Number One was that the Doctrine was propounded in an obscure prison in a nothing town in a backwater country where only nobodies could possibly hear it.

Paradox Number Two was that this was just fine by John. Indeed, according to him, this was absolutely essential for preserving the integrity of the Doctrine (if it had any) and preventing it (if it existed at all) from fermenting into a Militant Creed, an Ecclesiastical Institution, a Political Party, an Economic Policy, a National Anthem, a Banner of Liberation, a Revolutionary Manifesto, an Example to Posterity, an Ultimate Amendment or any of a hundred other intoxicants guaranteed to bring a tear to the eye, a lump to the throat, a gun to the hand and reason to its knees. If it were ever overtaken by either of the above fates, the Truth of the Doctrine (if any) would be utterly undermined and the faith of its adherents (if any) utterly invalidated.

So we arrived at the Third Paradox, which might well have been a corollary of the Second (if it was not, in fact, an extension of the First). To wit, the elements most indispensable to the Doctrine retaining any semblance of Vitality (assuming it had any in the first place) were for its Word to remain Unheard and its Message to remain unpreached.

'Either that *is* true,' warbled John once, when pressed, 'in which case it will still – and probably – only remain true if no one hears it. Or it is *not* true, in which case the fewer that hear it, the better!'

Regarding Converts, the ideal number was none. ZERO. People ought, in John's estimation, to discover the truth for themselves. They ought to arrive at faith (if that was what they wanted) without outside influence, intervention or pressure of any kind. Especially from the Doctrine itself! (Of course!) For only in this way might anyone understand deeply enough to realise that life, limb, livelihood, God, Harry, Fatherland and Mother Country are all just shackles of lead by comparison.

Paradox piled upon Paradox, extending, evolving, correlating – into, out of, over, under, around and through each other. Quite often, at one and the same time. We all lost our bearings, but never, our hope. The LAST PARADOX (at the Number of which, none of us could even make a guess) was that only at the moment that we were absolutely prepared for Death would any of us be fit for Life.

'Just remember!' John would chuckle. 'Such a Doctrine can never be any use to you. It might – at a pinch – just be a way of deserving life. But it will never be a way of earning a living. At the first disciple, it will vanish into bricks and mortar, print and proverbs, robes and ritual, and you will be left where you all are anyway – in the dark, on your own, clutching at straws.'

Every few weeks, some newcomer would get so exasperated they'd ask John if his goddamn Doctrine was so bloody fragile then what the hell was he doing revealing it to a bunch of convicts who couldn't be trusted not to shop their own mothers let alone to keep their traps shut about a Doctrine of Universal Life?

246

Quite unabashed, John would usually laugh. Then he'd say something along the lines of, 'Why, men like you are the perfect audience for ideas like these. I'm absolutely certain that every last one of you will have forgotten every word I've said by the time you get out. And if not, any memories still lingering on will certainly be washed away by the floods of relief released by release. But if you don't find my idle speculations amusing, why let's say no more about them and just call it a day.'

At which, the entire yard including the duty guard would look daggers at the unfortunate wretch who had been the cause of John suggesting we abandon this life-giving game.

'However,' John once added after we'd tramped a silent round of the yard after a similar incident, 'if by some mischance any of you *do* recall anything when you get out, I hope you will – for old times' sake – recount anything you think you remember only in the most fragmentary and paradoxical of terms.' Then he chuckled to himself and shook his head. 'Ah, do what you like! It won't matter anyway. After all, no one outside will be able to make head or tail of anything said in here. Why, this is the last sanctuary of Perfect Freedom of Speech.

'This is the one place on the whole planet where a person like me can say anything he likes without having to worry about the consequences. That's why I never even dream of leaving and why I feel so sorry for all of you who are fated to go, sooner or later, back outside.'

We called him 'Saint' John, not because we thought he was particularly pious – nor, even, because we thought he might have something saintly to teach us, if only we could overcome his obstinate conviction that he did not.

He got his nickname from some irreverent wag observing once, that John's head, even if it had just been severed from its neck and was being served up on a silver platter for the titillation of his murderers, would, even then, come up with an ingenious, optimistic and uplifting interpretation of the situation.

It was a pity that John had not been born in the Middle Ages. In that era, his inexhaustible patience and endless inventiveness might have left a mark. An illuminated manuscript or two, perhaps, that might have survived the centuries to please the eye and excite the wonder of posterity.

As it was, he remained entirely unknown and devoted his declining years to illuminating the hours of any odds, sods and sinners who happened to cross his path and whose need he deemed to be greater than his own. Since his needs appeared to be less than minimal – that included just about everyone.

# 10

# Hot Showers and Good Intentions

Flooding down in torrents, the hot water washed away weeks and months and years of dusty floorboards and chill stone walls. It poured new blood into veins and fresh marrow into bones. The steady drum of the showers damped out all sound. Cocooned in steam, we were hot and wet and happy.

After a good, long time, I poked my head out of the stream of water and looked around. We were in a huge box canyon of a room. Bare concrete and iron pipes. But surprisingly few cracks, little rust and not much limescale. Long, wooden benches along the walls. Handy for changing. In a place where almost nothing was handy for anything. The far wall sported a door. Shut. No sign of a warder. In the row of showers to my left, a cluster of colleagues was hard at work making the most of this moment. No one moved a muscle or said a word.

We'd been rounded up after lunch and marched off with the usual detailed explanations. Up to now, I had not even suspected the existence of this building. Nor, as far as I could judge, had anyone else. Showers had not been part of our daily routine. Hot ones had been the stuff of dreams.

A face poked itself out of a column of warmth, surveyed the room, met my eyes and split into a broiled grin. It was Robert, our resident Canadian.

'What d'you make of this?'

'As much as possible!'

'But what's with this sudden pampering?'

'Don't ask! Just wallow!'

'Where's our duty screw?'

'Who cares?'

'Could he be disguised as a bench?'

'If he is, let's go and fart on him!'

Robert laughed and pulled his face back inside his shower. The water showed no sign of running out or cooling off and the room still seemed to have no one in it but us. Everyone carried on soaking up lovely luxury. The water drummed steadily on, interrupted only by the odd sigh, gurgle or splash. Eventually, the gravitational pull of unsupervised conversation reasserted itself even against the counter-pull of unlimited hot water. One by one, heads popped out of showers all along the line. Grins shone, eyes twinkled, faces beamed as bright as boiled crabs.

'Hey, Canada!'

'Hi, Rostock!'

'Getting out soon, aren't you?'

'Not soon enough!'

'When's that?'

'If everything goes according to schedule – three months, two weeks and three days.'

'Just keep your head down, Robert!'

'Straight home when you get out?'

'Bet your life! First plane out!'

'What you going to do when you get there?'

'Everything!'

'Every what thing?'

'Everything I been doing nothing of in here!'

'Make up for lost time, huh?'

'And then some!'

'No chance! Lost time is lost for ever, even in the Free West!'

'But what you going to do first, Robert? What's the very first thing you'll do when you reach Canada?'

'Stop drooling, bird-brain! Before he even lands, he'll have forgotten all about all of this! And everyone of us!'

The flurry of cheerful chit-chat faded. Faces straightened quietly and eyes clouded over. Blissful water drummed down undiminished and everyone retreated into its comforting embrace once more. Bodies basked. Minds pondered.

'Well,' spluttered Robert, surfacing again, 'it's not over yet, you know. Still got to haul butt through every second of every hour of every day. No way round that!'

'Yes, but you can see the hands on the clock closing in on zero hour now. So nothing gets to you any more.'

'That's right! They kick you in the crotch, you just grin and bear it. Cos your mind's not on your balls at all. It's on the *be-yu-tiful* feeling that by the time the pain's gone, you got one foot through the front door.'

251

'Know what you mean,' said Robert, trying not to sound smug. 'But all the same, I'm not going to forget all this till the day I die.'

'Pull the other leg!'

'Pull your own! This kind of thing doesn't just roll off a man like water off a duck's back, you know.'

'Oh no? What about all those "Habituals" who come back time after time? What didn't roll off their back? Or, if we look at the bigger picture, what about all those "Old Soldiers" and "Family Patriarchs" and such who still get tears in their eyes recalling the good old days in the front lines and all that?'

'That's different. That was their finest hour and so on. Golden youth in a good cause, defending civilisation and so forth. I can understand that, can't you?'

'Oh, sure. They survived. They've got to tell some tale. But d'you really believe war looks that heroic? At the time and close up? Any war?'

'Probably not. But there's one difference between their situation and ours that nobody, not even you, can argue away.'

'Oh? What's that?'

'In war you've got no time to think of anything but saving your skin. In here, you've got all the time in the world, but it's too late to save anything. Not even your skin, if you're not careful.'

'You got a point. But so what?'

'So with everything lost anyway, you got no need to waste your brain worrying about unnecessary things. So you can really stop the clock and work out what's been happening to you and why and what you really want out of life and where you went wrong and—'

'Now this I just don't believe!'

'You don't believe what?'

'I just don't believe what I'm hearing!'

'Listen to the nut! He's already operating a Package Tour – INSIDE HOLIDAYS – WHERE TIME STANDS STILL AND WAITS FOR YOU TO FIND YOUR TRUE SELF!'

'FREEHANDCUFFS!'

'DISCOUNT LEG-IRONS!'

'FIRST-CLASS BARS!'

'TRANSCENDENTAL REVELATIONS GUARANTEED!'

'SPECIAL RATES FOR LONG STAYS!'

'AFTER ONLY ONE YEAR YOU WILL KNOW THE MEANING OF LIFE! AFTER ONLY TWO YOU WILL DISCOVER GOD! AFTER A MERE THREE THE SECRET OF THE UNIVERSE IS YOURS!'

General merriment drowned the mock commercials. Everybody made the most of their best laugh in weeks. Then the hot showers drowned the last guffaw and we wallowed in steam, heat and wordless wetness once more. After a nice, long while, a head poked out of a shower again.

'Hey, Canada!'

'Hello, Königsberg!'

'You're not really swallowing all that crap, are you?'

'What crap is that?'

'About "reforming your character" and "mending your ways" and all that.'

'That is certainly crap in the way our Lords and Masters mean it—'

'*Gott sei Dank!* I thought you might have flipped your lid just when you was about to get out!'

'But in other ways, maybe it's not such crap.'

'Oh, *Gott in Himmel!*'

'You mean there's degrees of crap?'

'You better have an explanation for this!'

'Well …'

'Ye-e-es?'

'Lemme think a minute.'

'Think all you like – you got three months, two weeks and three days!'

'More could be available if you need it!'

'You don't say? Maybe I don't need to think so much, after all. Maybe I better just gut react. So listen, ah, the way I see it – it's like this. Outside. After you grow up. Say, two or three years after you stop being a kid—'

'Say four or five, but get on with it!'

'Well, you kind of settle down into a fixed pattern—'

'A fixed pattern?'

'Habits, attitudes, relationships, people, places, jobs, dos, don'ts. You know what I mean, don't you?'

'Do *you?*'

'Shut up! Let the man speak.'

'Well, after a time it's easier to just carry on with the pattern than to try to change it.'

'Right. He's right about that.'

'And after a bit more time it gets difficult even just to *do* something – anything – anything that isn't exactly the same

254

as what you were doing before. You know, you get frightened, impatient, irritated by anything that is not familiar. Anything that is not pretty much exactly the same as what you've already got used to. You don't think things out from the bottom up any more. You don't even really *see* things any more. You just recognise a vague shape or face or phrase or whatever and you just react – exactly the same way you always have before. And you take everything for granted.'

'Such as?'

'Such as, for instance, clothes, money, jobs. Because of these, you assume that certain people are more important or more powerful than you, while certain others are less. So you find yourself a pigeonhole and you roost in it for the rest of your life. After a bit, it's no longer a matter of not being *able* to change, you get to a point where you don't even *want* to change!'

'So who wants to change all the time, anyway?'

'All your options can't stay open all the time, you know! The second you head north, you kiss goodbye to south, east and west.'

'Maybe so. But still. Everyday life is still too much being stuck in ruts. And you can't get out of them. You end up far too soon not even *wanting* to do anything or get anywhere. You know, just snoring and noshing and shitting your life away.'

'So everyone should come in here and *stop* snoring and noshing and shitting their life away?'

'Well, at least in here you can't pretend it's *not* happening. If nothing else it squeezes the bullshit out of you – and that's a start!'

'It hasn't squeezed the bullshit out of you, Canada! Go back to boiling your head!'

The showers showed no sign of slackening. Still there was no sign of a warder. A few bright pink bodies got out of their columns of water and paraded up and down, steaming like puddings and wondering how long this could go on. As soon as their pinkness dulled down, everybody decided it was not, after all, possible to have too much of a good thing. Especially when there was no guarantee of ever getting any more. So everybody got back into their showers again.

'I don't think you're right, you know.'

'Right about what?'

'About forgetting all this as soon as you get outside.'

'So how do *you* see it?'

'Well, look at it this way. If you're a professional criminal or a spy – or something like that – you can't forget about this, because it doesn't let you. You've done so much time, there's nothing else you can do. So you have to go back to your old game. Unless you let go altogether, of course, and become a dosser or something. But even then you don't forget.'

'And if you're an amateur? If you just caught your wife having it away with some bum and were dumb enough to choke her or something – what then?'

'Same difference. You still can't just wash it out of your hair! Because there's still a bloody, great big hole between when you went in and when you come out.'

'Yes. And there's still no *improvement*, is there? There's no *progress*. You didn't *learn* anything, did you? All that happens is they take the iron ball off your ankle and open the cage.

Then you just go back to being the same old set of conditioned reflexes and fixed ideas that you always were.'

'I don't buy that. It's not for me. I've been rotting in here much too long to just go back to being the same old knee-jerk. When I get out, things are going to be different!'

'Oh yeah! How?'

'Well, for a start, one thing I'm not going to waste any more is *time*. For instance, if I meet a chick I fancy, I'm going to come straight out with it. First time. No more mooning around for weeks, worrying about how to meet her just by chance and what she's going to think and how terrible it will be if she says "No" and all that. No, sir! Straight to the point. If she says "No" then she says "No". That's just fine. No harm's done and lots of time and creative energy has been saved. We both move on. Every day's big with human opportunity. Every bus queue is a social gold mine.'

'Not every prick had problems pulling fanny before they ended up in here, Canada. But all right. Let's allow that one. Let's say that's an improvement. Just for the sake of argument. So what's next? Or is "Instant Flesh" the Holy Grail of years of spiritual development?'

'Of course it's not! What about making real use of the one life you ever get? What about doing what you really want? All those bright ideas that nobody does anything about?'

'Well, what about them?'

'Well, that's not for me. Not any more. Next time I get a bright idea – or someone offers me one – I'm going to sit right down and work on it. I'm going to write it up and cost it and research it. I'm going to work out all the angles. Get any advice I need. Find out who I have to see. Call them. Write if necessary. See the man—'

'You'll never get anywhere like that! They'll never let you past the front door! You try that, you really will be wasting your time with a capital T!'

'Wasting my what? How can I possibly be doing that after seven years in here? Even if they slam every door in my face all day long, it'll feel like Tender Loving Care compared to being in here! Even if—'

'I give you two weeks! Fourteen days! Including the weekend!'

'Never! I'm never going back to the same old rut. Not after what I know now.'

'The first week you get out, you'll be walking on air. By the end of week two, the pavements will start sanding your legs down to sticky stumps and you'll soon be no taller than any other sodding dwarf again!'

The argument flowed back and forth for what seemed a wonderfully long time. Had the Powers That Be forgotten us completely? If so, how were we going to get anything to eat? And what would we sleep on? And what about the hot water? Was it endless? From what any of us could remember, we'd already had more hot water in here today than the whole of Budapest put together! Unless, of course, the Promised Land of 'True Communism' had finally been built out there, while we were all doing our time in here.

A few more rounds of idle chatter and we'd had so much hot water that a few of our thinner skins had actually had enough. They were standing about puffing and blowing and drying themselves off. Whether it was the rejuvenating effect of the showers, or the sobering influence of prison had finally made us see the light, the prevailing mood among us was heady optimism. For the moment, at least, many of us really believed that we wouldn't totally blow it if we ever got a second chance.

Our chief pessimist, however, was as obstinate as a mule and refused to let the matter rest. The debate dragged on until it was reduced to little more than foul-mouthed reiterations of opposing opinions. Eventually, a big lobster, tiring of the clash and clank of locked claws, sidled out of his shower and boomed, 'Hey, John! What do you think? Are you going to be a new man when you get out of here?'

No sooner had the words left his lips than the lobster's face collapsed into a grin more sheepish than crustacean. He needed no telling how thoughtless and down-right stupid his question had been.

'Ha! Ha! Ha-a-a!' growled a voice from somewhere further along the line of showers, not without a touch of menace. The water drummed steadily down through the embarrassment. John was sitting on one of the wooden benches ranged against the further wall. He seemed to be melting in the heat. His short, round body was still red and dripping. His matchstick legs seemed hardly equal to propping up his elbows, while his forearms appeared much too scrawny to support the glistening globe of his bald head. His face was flushed and puffy and he seemed very old.

The cloddish lobster was the first to shake off the silence. 'Sorry, John. No offence. But now the cat is out of the bag, so to speak, what's the point in pussyfooting around? So tell us, old feller, what do you think, eh?'

John glanced up uncertainly and mumbled, 'Not a thing. Not a thing. I can hardly even breathe, never mind think.'

Our mutton-head was not, however, to be put off so easily.

'But is it thumbs up or thumbs down?' he rumbled. 'Surely you can tell us how you figure the odds, old friend?'

With some difficulty, John gathered himself together and focused on his boiled inquisitor. Only an utter numbskull could have failed to see that the eyes that had teased us so merrily through so many long days were dull and watery and very weary indeed.

'Can losers ever be winners?' John sighed weakly. 'Or are we all – for ever – damned?'

'Well,' burbled the boiled one, still quite unabashed, 'since you put it like that, which do you reckon?'

John mopped his face for a moment and then draped the damp towel over his steaming skull. All around, the hot water drummed steadily down for more long moments. Not a sigh, not a gurgle, not a splash punctuated the soundtrack. One after the other, bodies pink and steaming sloped out of the showers and slid bare bums on to the nearest empty spaces on the benches. When, at last, John looked up again, he had a hushed and expectant audience, but there seemed to be only the faintest spark of life left in his eyes.

'Life, Life, Life,' he wheezed, 'dirty, filthy, old Dog's Life, eh? Double-dealing, back-stabbing, *two*-faced, *two*-timing, *un*-scrupulous, *ca*-pricious, *dis*-gusting, *frus*-trating, *ex*-asperating and endlessly disappointing … Life, life, oh, careless life! If ours were not the only life any of us ever got, who would not trade you in for practically anything else? The only thing about Life you can depend on is that you can never depend on anything. Ever. At all. Dependability is strictly and only nothing but a fairy tale ...'

'All right, all right!' conceded Lobster-Kopf magnanimously. 'Forget it. Just forget Life. Who needs it?'

John's glumness began evaporating – whether at the possibility of relinquishing unrequired life or in relief at the prospect of not being bothered any more, who could say?

'Stuff the Philosophy!' came a sudden squawk from the end of the furthest bench. 'Tell us one of your dependable fairy tales instead!'

John's eyes retreated almost into the back of his skull. He wilted visibly.

'Oh, stop playing the Dying Prune, John!' demanded a hoarse voice from the other end of the same bench. 'This Canadian prick is getting out so quick it's a ruddy piss-take. Just give us your views on the argument – one way or the other – or, anything in between. Come on, just to cheer us up!'

'No, no,' cried a kindly voice, leaping to the old man's defence. 'Can't you see he's absolutely done in? This is a good day – a very good day – let's not spoil it.'

'Too right!' bellowed another voice. 'Let's not spoil it with silly arguments! But why not top it off with something good for the soul? Why, John, you know yourself how much better you feel after you've spun a really pretty yarn. So, please, why don't you do us all a bit of good? Make our day – a little mouth music is meat and drink to a mind like yours? Come on, John old boy, nothing heavy, something light. Screw that

261

old nut of yours and just round the day off for us with a warm and witty, big-city short story. What d'you say?'

John swayed. Somehow he stopped himself falling off his bench. Gradually, his swaying slowed and he sat there, steady and steaming. His eyes uncreased a crack. His gaze alighted on our armour-clad crustacean. They looked at each other – the one with clumsy hope, the other with sincere distaste.

'Just to round off the day,' wheedled the scarlet carapace, blithely ignoring both the old man's disapproval and his own uncouthness. 'Before anybody gets here and turns us off, eh? A funny story – doesn't have to be long – even an anecdote will do …'

John closed his eyes again and mopped his brow sadly. Nobody breathed. The showers drummed down. The steam thickened. John's towel stopped moving in mid mop. The jets from the showers seemed to congeal into solid strands of water. Even the steam stood still.

'We-e-ll,' warbled John just when we all thought he must have passed away, 'this might not be quite what you had in mind – but, you see, nothing – really nothing at all – comes into my head right now …'

Everyone stared at him, grinning in steamy anticipation. He swayed and seemed to doze off again. A couple of faces fell. After a few moments and without opening his eyes, he cleared his throat with a splutter and a wheeze and muttered, 'I'm not even sure I can remember it properly, so you'll have to excuse me if it gets a bit disjointed at times – or if I repeat myself – or—'

'Sure thing, John,' rumbled an encouraging voice. 'No sweat. We'll excuse you – you just kick off, huh?'

'Uh-oh,' sighed the old fellow with his eyes still shut, 'this really is nothing very much – and probably not really appropriate—'

'Appropriate?' echoed Robert, with a rich chuckle. 'Who the hell around here cares about appropriate?'

'A-ah,' sighed John again and carefully stretched his neck, as if warding off the urge to nod off once more. 'What I mean is that this might not really be appropriate for grown men like you – you see, it's just a little bedtime story, really, a sort of ballad with lullabies. My grandmother used to sing and recite this for me – at bedtimes – long ago – when I was just a little child. I can't sing for you – not now – I can't remember the songs and, anyway, whatever voice I once had has gone. So you'll just have to do without the lullabies and I'll just have to render the rest as well as I can in words – just plain words – no songs – and you'll have to imagine whatever melodies you can ...'

We all smiled and squirmed our bums more comfortable on the wet benches. Suddenly, John let out a last, long sigh and his eyes sprang wide open – and they were young again and sparkling.

# 11

# Words Without Songs

*A long, long time ago* – long before there were any human settlements in the great, circular valley that we now call the Carpathian Basin – by a long lake of turquoise water, there lived a Princess. Lovely as the dawn she was, her skin as fresh as dew, her eyes dark and soft and her glance more melting than a lakeside summer night.

Few human beings passed through the valley then and none had found the lake. So the Princess lived quite alone, her only friends the wild creatures of the valley and her only courtiers a faithful flock of goats. But her days were happy for her companions were very special goats, unique to the lake. Like her, they were small and delicate. Like her, they were kind and gentle. Like her, they were astonishingly light on their feet. But, unlike her, they were mute.

Nevertheless, they were always gay and friendly, with smiling faces and twinkling amber eyes. Tossing their fine heads with their short, neat horns and curling beards, they gambolled around her as she strolled the shores of the lake.

Best of all, however, they liked to gather about her and sit on their haunches, listening intently while she sang. For although she had many wonderful qualities, her greatest gift was her voice.

Her songs were loved by every living thing around the lake and no creature knew any moment of contentment deeper than those evenings when she sang. There she would sit on a handy tussock or convenient rock, surrounded by her faithful flock gazing up at her with amber eyes, while every branch and twig bent under the weight of innumerable birds and small climbers, every stalk and blade of grass crawled with insects of all descriptions and every clearing and glade was packed with animals too large to perch on anything less solid than the good earth itself.

On such nights, her voice outshone the starlight and her songs were more soothing than even the most refreshing of those gentle breezes that relieved the heat of the long, dog days of high summer. On such nights, no hunter hunted, no prey fled, fear was banished and every living thing knew that its soul truly was immortal. On such nights, the sun itself lingered in wait just beneath the dark horizon in hopes of delaying the stilling of her voice for one more song. On such nights, the only greeting that eventually met the dawn was adoring silence.

So seasons passed and all living things were happy with their lot. The dawns were as tranquil as the loving sun could make them. The lake had grown more limpid and more beautiful than ever. Only the Princess herself began to feel unease.

So small were the beginnings of this feeling and so lacking in any reason or cause known to her, that at first the Princess did not really notice that anything was amiss. Furthermore, her loving courtiers were so sensitive to her every mood and feeling that they instinctively redoubled their attentions, amusing her with gymnastic jests, showering her with tender glances and little acts of solicitude and affection, all serving to divert her attention from her self.

So before she realised what was happening, the perfect tranquillity of her heart was disturbed. Even when she came to admit this to herself, however, she could not guess at any reason for her disquiet. Nor could the amber eyes of her courtiers, gazing upon her with so much sympathy and so much love, discern the slightest flaw in their existence.

Yet the heart of the Princess grew heavy. Sometimes she ignored the best efforts of her faithful friends and sat staring dreamily out over the lake and sighing for no reason that anyone could fathom. At such times she thought she could imagine a feeling she had never felt. Of course, since she had never felt that feeling, she could not know what it was. Still she felt that something was not there. That her world was no longer perfect. Yet though she sighed, she could not say what this something that was not there could be. She grew sadder and sadder and gradually something new crept into her songs. A sense of longing. For what or why, she could not say. Yet there was no denying the longing.

When she finished such a song, her heart felt lighter for a while. Her next song would be brighter and more playful than any yet, and her listeners appreciated the marvellous extension of her repertoire and were happier than ever. The gay songs cheered them up no end, while the sad songs plucked at their heartstrings in ways none ever had before.

It was the latter that first came – passed lovingly from breeze to breeze one starlit summer night to the ears of a stranger.

The Prince of the Horse People had ridden fast and far that day, leaving even the proudest of his warriors further behind than eyes could see or even their swift steeds could run from sunrise to sunset. His wind-swift mare was exhausted. More than a match she was for any stallion in all the seas of grass that stretched beyond the sunrise. Yet it had only been the fiery spirit of the Prince that had kept her going for so long. Now she was no more than a shadow lying on the dewy grass. Her sides heaved and her legs ached. She could hardly stretch out her tongue to lick up the dew that she knew would surely refresh her.

Though he loved her more than any living thing, the Prince did not stretch out his hand to comfort her. Still unwearied, he sat on his heels with his back against a tall tree and stared up at the stars. His frown was troubled. Thoughts crowded his mind, chasing each other in and out without rhyme or reason.

For several moons now, his spirit had been in turmoil. He knew no other life than following the horses over the endless plains and had always gloried in his freedom. Nothing had ever given him greater joy than mastering a wild stallion at full gallop, with the wind streaming through his hair. Ever since he could remember, the whole world and everything in it had been his. All he had ever had to do was reach out his hand and grasp.

Yet for many a mile now, he had felt there was something that was not there. That his world was no longer perfect. Though he frowned and ground his teeth and rode harder than ever before, he could not say what this something that was not there could be. So he had grown silent and gradually something new had crept into his moods. A sense of longing.

Now he was glad of the silence. Glad to have lost the others at last. Glad to be free of raucous warriors and milling herds. Glad to be alone with his thoughts even if they raced round and round in his head and gave him no rest.

It was when the breathing of his mare grew calmer that the first notes of the song reached his ears. At first, he assumed they were thoughts in his head, even though they were sadder and more beautiful than any he had ever known before. Gradually, he realised that they came from somewhere outside his mind and began to listen. He cocked his head and concentrated. Gradually, he heard the song more clearly and, still without understanding what it was, he was astonished at how perfectly it reflected the feelings in his soul. Rising with the effortless grace of the panther, he stalked across the clearing on soundless feet, following the song.

At times, a pause in the melody or a shift of the breeze would throw him off the track for a moment. He would freeze in mid stride like a hunting cat, straining with every sense to pick up any sign of his quarry. Then his ears would catch that sweet, sad sound again and he would be off once more. So he crept from phrase to phrase, from note to note, getting nearer and nearer. So engrossed was he that he forgot the turmoil of his soul and his mare beyond price and all his former life and everything else but the marvellous song that led him on and on.

Indeed, so engrossed was he that he never once looked down at the ground. Had he done so, even once, his keen hunter's eyes would immediately have spotted innumerable prints of hoof and paw all leading in the same direction. Thus he would have arrived at his goal much more quickly. But not with such intense and inexpressible longing. Not in such a state of heart and mind that he could hardly breathe when he first beheld the singer of that song.

Never had he seen anyone more different from his own people. Where they were dark and hard and rough, she was pale and soft and smooth. Where they were quick and fierce and proud, she was languid and calm and humble. Where they were coarse and full of force, she was delicate and kind. Without a thought in his head, he stepped forward into the starlit clearing.

When she first saw him, the Princess had never seen any other human being at all. She was swept almost off her feet by the strength standing in the starlight and pierced to the heart by the glance that leaped towards her over the horned heads of her quiet courtiers. On the last note of her song, her longing flowed forward to meet his.

So began the season of joy. Prince and Princess could not have enough of each other. Each word was a revelation. Each step together, a voyage into a world unknown. Each touch, the spark of life itself.

She – who had never been less delicate than the most gentle of breezes – grew robust enough to keep pace with his most vigorous stride. He – who had never been less forceful than the most ferocious of steeds – grew tender enough to cradle her in his arms.

The season was one of joy for all. The creatures of the lake, being no less loving than their mistress, were happy because she was happy. They bathed in the sunlight of her smiles even though her smiles were no longer meant for them.

Her courtiers welcomed the Prince with open hearts. The amber-eyed goats found his exhausted mare and befriended her. They took her to the freshest pools and lushest grazing and gambolled around her like mischievous imps. So taken, indeed, was the wind-swift mare by her new friends and the charm of her surroundings (not to mention the benefits of her extended rest) that she was hardly aware of her master's present indifference to her – who had once been the apple of his eye.

In time, the warriors and the great herd caught up with the Prince. The warriors did not know whom they found most astonishing – the Princess or the new man that had been their Prince. Riding and fighting and breaking in horses and men were of no interest to him now. The Princess was everything to him.

Since their Prince was hardly aware of their existence and, since they too were charmed by their new surroundings, the warriors quartered themselves around the lake and settled down to enjoying a life they had never known before.

The horses, too, were somewhat astonished by the change that came over their masters. But, since they didn't really feel the affairs of men were their concern and since they had never tasted pasture as delicious as that around the lake, they just put their heads down to the grass.

The creatures of the lakeside, for their part, thoroughly enjoyed their new guests. The beetles found a whole new source of nourishment and the flies found a whole new source of amusement. Birds and squirrels and foxes and badgers and rabbits and stoats and goats and all and sundry had a wonderful time perching upon and riding around on the backs of the tall horses, and chasing each other round and round between their long legs.

The most wonderful times of all, however, were still those nights when the Princess sang. On those nights, each glade and dell was more crowded than ever. The stars shone even more brightly than before. Yet her voice outshone them all. Her songs were mainly gay and playful now and everybody loved them. None more than the calloused warriors who swore they had never known such gladness – nor such beauty – in their lives before.

The Prince, however, never forgot that first sweet, sad song, that had led him to the singer by the lakeside and, from time to time, would ask for it again. Then, with a sparkle in her eye, the Princess would oblige, adding a stanza here or a note there. She and the Prince would gaze at each other, smiling in fond remembrance of the longing that had brought them together and sharing their secret knowledge that the pain was now no more than a melody to be sung.

Even the warriors agreed that this song was the best of all and, though more than a few could not hold the tears from their eyes and buried their heads in the flanks of their horses, they never tired of hearing it again.

So the season passed and the great herd grew fat and multiplied and the riders were no longer lean and iron hard. From dawn to dusk the lazy sun warmed the lake with his smiles. The nights were like velvet and lit by fireflies. Neither man nor beast had ever known such ease. This season of joy, it seemed, would never end.

Those were the days when happiness was long. Yet even then, no joy could last for ever. The great herd grew and multiplied many times over. The pastures around the lake, however, did not. They were never, in truth, made for such numbers of large beasts and gradually the grass grew sparse. The horsemen (for by now they were warriors no more) watched the first of their steeds waste away and die and knew that the days of their joy were numbered.

Still the Prince and the Princess had eyes only for each other. Still he marvelled at her loveliness and still she sang her songs. Her amber-eyed courtiers saw all things and were wise beyond their years. But they could not tell her that the flame of human love – though it burned never so bright – cannot last for ever. For they had not seen such a flame before. And they had always loved her. And they were mute.

At last, the grazing gave out. Horses and men had grown lean and hard again. The great herd must move on or starve. The men became warriors again and grew impatient. If all their horses died, they would be no more than walking peasants, bound to the earth once more. Horses and men were filled with longing for new pastures. They *must* go on!

At last, the warriors were desperate enough to tell the Prince what must be done. At first he did not believe them. Then his mare carried him around the lake and he saw for himself the bare earth where lush grass had been and what was left of the starving herd. Still he could not bring himself to leave the lake, to part from the Princess of his heart, to hear her songs no more.

His men were warriors, but not hearts of stone. They too had listened to her songs and loved the lake.

'Let her come with us,' they begged their Prince. 'The great plains are vast. Riders are small. The more the merrier. Only let us go before all our horses die.'

Though she loved the lake and had never been far from its kindly shores, the Princess was not afraid of the endless plains. But she knew her courtiers could never keep up with the swift steeds and that without their lake they would be lost. They understood and their amber eyes begged the Princess to leave them. But the more they begged, the more she saw how much they loved her and the less she could bring herself to go.

So the Princess stayed. And the Prince stayed. And the men stayed. And horses died and nights were no longer made for singing. One day, the wind turned cold and lashed the waters of the lake until the waves leaped and the horses sniffed the scent the wind brought them and caught the smell of distant grass. They were strong, rather than wise. Swift of foot, rather than self-denying. So they sniffed the scent on the wind, tossed their manes, turned their tails towards the foam-flecked lake and ran.

Soon horse after horse joined in until the whole herd was moving. The men saw what was happening and knew that if they did not ride with the herd, they would be left behind and lose everything their fathers and forefathers had bred and cherished over countless generations. So they mounted up and rode off.

Still the Prince tarried, torn between his great herd and his love. At last, his wind-swift mare could wait no more.

'Come,' she whinnied. 'You cannot let your men roam the plains and brave the many dangers there without your strong hand to guide them! When the herd grows fat and the grass grows green again around this lake, we shall come back and her songs will be yours again. But come! For soon they will have gone so far that even I will never catch them.'

So the Prince leaped upon her back, promised the Princess to return and galloped away swifter than the wind after his horses and his men. The Princess and her courtiers watched until his cloud of dust was gone and the lands around the lake were quiet once again.

So began the season of sorrow. At first, the Prince could feel her touch upon his skin and hear her voice in his ears and her song upon the wind. At the same time, the Princess felt his glance upon her face and heard him striding through the reeds and saw his footprints in the sand. Perched upon that convenient rock in their favourite spot, she gazed eagerly across the waters of the lake, anxious to miss no moment of his return as he galloped round the shore to meet her.

But the great herd moved very fast and nowhere was there enough grass for the horses to remain. Always the wind brought the scent of distant pastures to their nostrils from somewhere far away towards the sunrise. The Prince rode as hard as he could, but even his wind-swift mare took many long days to come upon the track of the herd.

When finally they came up with the men and horses, it was to find that other eyes had seen them too. Other men marvelled at the greatness of the herd and other hearts burned with the desire to possess the bounty his forefathers had left him. So it was a time for warriors once more, for many long moons, until many men and horses would never ride again and blood had flowed and the herd had wandered so far into the sunrise that few could still remember that season of joy beside the lake.

Slowly, the day came when the Prince could no longer feel her touch upon his skin, nor hear her voice in his ears, nor her song upon the wind. He had become the greatest of warriors, scarred and hard, and the hairs in his beard had grown grey. His enemies feared him, but their numbers swelled. His friends were few and dwindling. His wind-swift mare was long-since dead. Only the memory of a song was left to cheer him. Sung once upon a time, by a Princess he had known in youth. Then slowly, he forgot the colour of her silken hair.

One last, sweet, sad song she sang and all the creatures of the lakeside knew that their season of joy would never return. Sadly, she gazed upon her courtiers. Sadly their amber eyes gazed back. The sun did his best to cheer her. But his smiles only burned her skin.

Slowly, she bid farewell to every living thing. Slowly, she turned from her friends. And slowly – she walked into the waters of the lake, singing the last of her sweet, sad song.

When they saw that she was leaving, her courtiers rose lightly to their feet and followed her every one. As they reached the water's edge, each goat stepped neatly out of its dainty hooves and tiptoed into the lake in the wake of their mistress. At last, the song faded and all were gone.

Now her songs are no more. Only the lake sings brief, half-remembered snatches from time to time when the crowds are gone and the wind blows from the right quarter and ears attuned to hear are listening. The Horse People did come back to the lake – many hundreds of years ago – but that was even longer after they had left, so those who still remembered anything about that lovely singer were few and far between. The Horse People settled in the region, forsaking their former life of wandering the great grasslands with their herds. However, to this very day, their descendants love sad songs above all others and cherish many curious memories and strange beliefs.

As for the goats with their amber eyes and smiling faces, why all that remains of them is their hooves. People take these to be little cloven shells, but no one has ever seen a mollusc in them. They still lie where their owners left them – in the sand and mud and reed-beds – along the shores of the lake that is now known to us as the Balaton.

And the Princess? Yes, I see in your eyes that you are all wondering about her. Has there never been any sign of her during all these long years? Has there never been anyone like her again? Well, not – I am sorry to say – as far as I know. She has never – to my knowledge, at least – come back. Neither as a ghost nor as a girl reborn. Though many lovely women have lived around the lake. And some of them could certainly sing very well indeed. Now, only a dwindling number of ageing crones and fools like me – here and there, and from time to time – occasionally tell her story to old lags still silly enough, and children still innocent enough, to love her.

# Afterword

Notes for anyone who may wish to know how Hungarian names and words encountered above are pronounced. This is not necessary for understanding the stories – the unfolding of incidents is the same, irrespective of language or pronunciation. However, the atmosphere of place and period may come across with a little more colour if the reader is not impeded by uncertainties of pronunciation or meaning.

'á': pronounced 'ah' as in 'park', 'start', 'gasp'.

'ály': 'igh' as in 'high', 'eye', 'fly'.

'c': 'ts' or 'ce' as in 'quince', 'mince' or 'pincer'.

The Hungarian 'cs' sounds the same as the English 'ch' – so 'Csepel' is pronounced 'Chepel'. Csepel is a district of the capital city, Budapest. It is an island in the River Danube and was a proletarian, industrial enclave, much favoured by the ruling Communist Party during the period of Soviet domination. A Comrade (Party Member) originating from or representing this district would have been quite a top dog at that time.

'csajka': pronounced 'chuykuh' with short vowels. This is a cheap, all-purpose, aluminium bowl useful for containing anything liquid, solid or powder – edible or not. It was basic equipment in Iron Curtain prisons and armies and among the more underprivileged classes of the classless masses.

'csávó': in Romany, the language of most Hungarian Gipsies, this means 'boy', 'lad', 'young man'.

'cz': also pronounced 'ts' or 'ce' as in 'quince', 'mince', 'pincer' in English. 'Rákóczi', the name of a great, Magyar noble family, of which two members were famous leaders of ill-fated movements of national independence, is pronounced 'Rah-coe-tsy' in English.

'é': 'ay' as in 'hay', 'weigh', 'grey'.

'í': 'ee' as in 'clean', 'seen', 'mean'.

'Karesz': pronounced 'Koress'. This is one of the two basic diminutives of Károly (pronounced 'Car-roy'), the Hungarian equivalent of 'Charles'. The other basic diminutive is 'Karcsi'.

'na': pronounced as a very short English 'nuh' and often repeated, as in 'na, na'. These are not really words, but rather sounds of punctuation. They are used similarly to the usage in English of 'well' or 'well, well' or even 'now, now'.

'ó': 'oh' as in 'Ko-ala', 'go', 'Glencoe'.

's', sometimes 'ss': 'sh' as in 'shoe', 'shop', 'push' – so 'Pista' is pronounced 'Pishtuh'. Pista is the basic, usually affectionate, diminutive of István, the Hungarian for Stephen/Steven, and equates to Steve/Stevie.

'Schmasser': my own Anglicisation of a term from Germano-Hungarian slang. The word is simply used in Hungarian as a slang term for a prison warder or guard. It is analogous with the English old lag's term 'screw'.

'sz': English 's' (sibilant) – so 'Tisza', the name of the country's second largest river, is pronounced 'Tissa' in English.

'Zoli': the basic diminutive of 'Zoltán', a fairly common, masculine given name among Hungarians.

List of place names on page 152: 'Ungvár, Munkács, Beregszász, Szolyva, Ilosva, Huszt, Tecsó, Rahó, Késmark, Lőcse, Kassa, Pozsony, Újvidék, Temesvár, Arad, Kolozsvár, Nagyvárad'. These are all ancient Hungarian towns and cities not found within the borders of present-day Hungary. All the syllables and sounds within these names have already been clarified, apart from the following:

'a' as in 'Arad': 'o' as in 'god', 'bog', 'lot'.

'e' as in 'Temesvár': 'e' as in 'egg', 'pen', 'neck'.

'gy': 'dy' as in 'd'you', 'due', 'duke'. NB: This consonant is somewhat more difficult to pronounce for speakers for whom English is their mother tongue when it occurs in the middle or at the end of a word – as it often does in Hungarian! For example, 'nagy' meaning 'big' or 'large' or, as here in the name of the city, 'Nagyvárad', where it means 'great'. However, with a little concentration and practice, it is by no means impossible for non-Magyars to pronounce this quintessentially 'Magyar' consonant quite perfectly.

'ő': the 'o' in 'no' enunciated with an extreme Sloane Ranger accent, or an 'o' with an umlaut (the German 'ö') but lengthened.

'u' as in 'Ungvár': 'oo' as in 'moo', 'rude', 'brood'.

'új': 'ooy' as in 'ooyer rotter!', enunciated with a heavy Mancunian accent.

'zs': the 's' before 'u' in 'treasure', 'pleasure' or 'leisure'.

All remaining Hungarian names or words used in this book are compounds of those given above and are pronounced accordingly.